DU

DU 07/13

03. AUG 13.   − 5 OCT 2016

                    2 0 OCT 2016

19. OCT 13.   2 8 MAR 2018

06. JAN   26/5/22

31.   1 1 JAN 2024

31.   − 2 JUL 2024

05 MAY

FEB

48 MAR 18

Donation

I was
Baby's
I didn't
scenario

ago
ied

he

1

A Secret Kept

Copyright © P. A, Ramsay 2009
Published by Pamela Aitken Ramsay
ISBN 978-0-9574889-1-5

Grateful acknowledgement to Calum Kennedy for his translations to
Gaelic for the authenticity of the story.

For Lauren, Blair and Darren

A Secret Kept

Prologue

Aluinn sat on the farthest rock, surrounded by waves unfolding in a rhythmic path to the shore. The sky was clear, the sun warmed her mind and body. Fear had slipped away.

From the rock she looked back at the Island she called home. Her place. When the time came she hoped to die there amongst its hills and rocks, and be returned to the land she loved.

Fearless of the distance or the water's strength, she had swum out alone as she often did, just to fill herself with the sight of it. She swam well, natural ability strengthened by her temperament. *Rag* her mother called her, stubborn. Undaunted by the journey back, she surveyed the shoreline, and then her eyes swept up to the hills beyond. Seeing them she was filled with longing. Basking on the rock with the grey seals pleased her. But there was a stronger desire in her, a need to lose herself on those heather clad hillsides. She closed her eyes. In winter, up there, the waterfalls became so cold they froze into solidified shafts, huge, icicled shards. Eerily enchanting they glistened like finest crystal in sunshine not yet strong enough to release them from their frozen prison.

When would she be freed?

Chapter One

Spun late at night, often in drink, the strange tales we called *sgeulachd* had always held me spellbound. Especially when the Elders grew unmindful of younger ears listening in.So as I think back down the years I am unable to recall a time I didn't know about the secret. Yet I could not have foreseen how it would twist itself around my life, how my days would be cursed by it.

For now, I simply want to tell the story as it occurred, nothing more, nothing less. A simple task, surely, resurrecting the past?

I'll begin not at the beginning, but the day Sarah arrived.

*

Behind the rise of another wave, the skyline blurred. Standing in the bow, facing the horizon, Sarah struggled to stay upright against the harsh winds flailing her bones. She loosened her grip on the ship's rail, reaching to tighten her collar, knowing the gesture was futile. Other passengers had relented and passed her by, some with hands clasped over mouths. But she stood fast.

She had expected a small fishing boat to take her to the Island. Finding the ferry's ungainly structure waiting in the harbour, she'd been disappointed. But now, seeing the way the sea rebelled at their intrusion, she was glad of its strength. Down below the sodden lower decks, the waters made their journey, first one way, then the other, no pattern to their frantic motion. She tried to focus on what should have been the horizon, refusing to give in to the unbearable motion. Vision hampered by the rain, hair streaming across her eyes, she looked again. Her hand tightened on the rail as a land mass appeared suddenly, faintly, out of the mist.

She had imagined it many times, yet nothing could have prepared her for her first sight of the Island. At its northern end black, volcanic mountains rose up out of the seabed, high and daunting. In the dying light, they looked just what they were – primeval, untouched and unalterable.

Sarah said a silent prayer that her new home would seem less threatening with the daylight upon it. Her quiet petition didn't bring the calm she'd hoped for. How she longed to feel the earth beneath her feet again. But even as the thought formed the sea became more menacing, the grey sky more foreboding. As they drew slowly closer, the foreshore lay in darkness. No welcoming lights, then, no joy at her coming.

Doubts assailed her. Once the ferry had departed, she would be alone. For a brief instant she thought to face the horrors of the return journey, to go back to all she knew.

The Island, at least the idea of it, had seemed like a haven. At twenty eight, running a school single-handedly had offered a challenge. But that was not why she had come. She had wanted to give her broken heart a place to heal. After years of waiting for him to loose himself of his bonds, he had finally made his decision. It seemed he did not want her after all. All those years, watching her hope change into fear, her longings into childlessness…In comparison to the pain she had been through, making a new life in this tiny island community had seemed easy.

Still the sea showed no sign of relenting. Sarah shuddered, fighting back bile and bitter memories. Seagulls flew low overhead, a sign they had almost reached the shore.

For now this was her home.

Slowly, the Island revealed itself. Had there ever been a place so forlorn? Irregular sea cliffs, a hundred feet high and sheer, dropped to deep waters. At their feet boulders ten feet across lay scarred by the movement of the sea. From her vantage point Sarah could understand for the first time just how isolated the place was. She picked out a dozen low built crofts, scanty, dwarfed against the dark hills. There was one larger house, built on the highest point. That would be the Manse. The other, hidden sides of the Island would be no different, tiny smallholdings scattered amidst the birch hazel scrub, which held the peaty earth of the Island together.

How had it avoided the fate of all the other islands on the west coast, those tourist meccas? The Islanders, fearing the loss of their traditions, had held out resolutely against the 'tartan invasion'. Visitors received a cool reception. Sarah squared her thin shoulders. Why listen to idle talk? She would make up her own mind in time.

So the Islanders protected their isolation. Wasn't that the very reason she had accepted the post?

She only hoped they would accept her. The Islanders had fought tooth and nail to have their children taught at home, as they always had been. But the law had won. A school was to be established, and she, Sarah was determined to make it work.

As she readied herself to disembark, she scoured the quay. There was still no welcoming committee. Left alone with her luggage she cursed silently at her dejection. When a voice spoke behind her she almost jumped out of her skin.

"Y*h*ull b*he* the sc*h*ultech*ter*, ay*he*?"

Sarah recoiled at the sight of the old man. His spine curved at the strangest angle, as if defying gravity. She felt the urge to pull him upright, to straighten out his deformity, but realised it was too late. The man would only get worse in whatever time he had left.

"Hi, yes, I'm she. My name's Sarah Tomminey."

He ignored her greeting.

"Y*h*ull b*he* w*h*antin' Pastor McGregor."

Sarah was taken aback. Why would she want to see a man of the cloth? These days people where she came from made their own rules. Religion played little part in life. Clearly, her expression betrayed her surprise.

"N*ho* doot it's strange to y*he*, meetin' wi a pastor, but y*h*ull find things different here."

"I understood there wasn't a Kirk on the Island," Sarah replied, irritated at his patronising tone.

The crooked little man became defensive in his turn. "Nae Kirk! W*he*'ve our own ways." He scrutinised her, seeming to find her wanting. "Well, thurs the new schullhoose up there, top o' the brow. Ah'll get y*her* bags, shall ah?"

The man repulsed her. Not his deformity, his manner. "I've managed them this far, I'm sure I can manage the rest myself. Thank you."

He muttered something. Sarah neither made it out nor wished to as he scuttled off, as though chased by a flame.

Hardly five minutes off the boat and she'd made an enemy already. She could hear her mother's voice echoing round her head; '*Leaving your perfectly good job for uncertain reward'.* Her mother's nagging had helped make up her mind, truth be told. If it didn't work out she could always go back. But not before she had proved her point. She could and would go it alone. Standing on that dismal hillside, looking at what she could scarcely believe would be her home, a little voice in Sarah's stubborn head wondered just how long that would take.

She shook off her doubts. Her own pigheadedness had brought her there. No doubt it would see her through what was to come. Pulling in her raincoat tightly, she shifted her bag across her body, ignoring the ache that instantly formed in her neck, and hoisted her case. Hoping no one was watching, she headed up the hill in her less than sensible footwear.

The road wound upwards, a tortuous mix of pebbles, gravel, and uneven ground. Five minutes later, she was cursing her own stubbornness and the little man who had sneered at her. If only he had been less suspicious or she less thrawn. At least this way she owed him nothing, not even a smile when their paths crossed.

Weary and footsore she finally reached the cottage door, to find a key nailed firmly to its wooden frame.

She stared at it. *What would it feel like, that kind of trust?* Perhaps things would not be so bad when she had settled. Gratefully she dropped her suitcase, taking in the shabby décor of the tiny hall passage. Rubbing her hands to warm them, she jumped as a Wagnerian knock shook the door. Her nerves were shot – she had almost shouted her fear. Opening the door, she was amazed to find a handsome man smiling at her from the threshold. Sarah smiled back.

"You must be Sarah! I'm Pastor McGregor. I do apologise. I had meant to meet you off the ferry, but I was delayed."

So *this* was Pastor McGregor? Though his name had been on the interview panel, he had been called away when the meeting took place. Far from being the old man she had expected, McGregor was in his early forties and *very* striking. And he seemed genuinely pleased to see her. Sarah felt her heart warming. Pastor or not, he was not the least bit intimidating. Actually he was quite charismatic.

Despite his educated accent he was dressed in shabby dungarees, paint stained and ripped in rather sensitive areas.

He saw her take him in. "As you can tell by my attire, I've been working."

Sarah smiled her best smile, self-consciously brushing her untidy hair out of her face. "Please excuse me; it's been a long day."

"I've brought you a few provisions," he said, handing her the box of essentials he was carrying.

"Heavens. Thank you. I hadn't really planned this far ahead. I was just concentrating on getting here safely."

He smiled at her gratitude, looking better with every passing minute. There was a slightly uncomfortable pause. Embarrassment made her blurt out, "You're not what I expected. I was imagining more fire and brimstone, if you know what I mean. By your accent, you're not a local?"

He looked rather pleased. "Not technically. My family have lived on the Island for generations, but we seem to be the only ones who venture further afield. I was educated on the mainland, Edinburgh. But I came back when my father died. He was Pastor here before me. Someone has to keep the traditions going, and it fell to me, as I always knew it would."

"Well, I'm very glad to meet you. Hearing an accent from home, the Island doesn't seem quite so daunting anymore."

They stood in silence for a moment, smiling at each other. His friendliness gave her comfort, enough to face the night ahead so far from home.

"Old Archie told me you two had gotten off on the wrong foot. It's nothing personal, I assure you – he's a funny old chap. Can I give you a word of warning, Sarah?" His eyes were kind. "The Islanders are very suspicious of what they call 'incomers'. We don't have any here as a rule. You'll find your way, but don't expect miracles to begin with. There was a lot of… ill feeling about the new school. I would ask that you respect their fears. The Islanders want the old ways upheld. Give the children the standard of education required by law and that should keep everyone happy."

She would do better than that. Sarah meant to allow these children to flourish, and almost said so, but thought better of it. Pastor McGregor might be the only friend she would find on the Island. As he began to walk away he called out. "You can reach me at the cottage by the church. Though I own the Manse, I don't live there – too big and draughty. I'll call in again tomorrow to see how you've settled. I'd like to keep in touch, to monitor the children's progress. Oh, and one more thing, Sarah…" He had closed the gate, forming a barrier between them. Turning round to face her, he smiled reassuringly. "We meet as a community sometimes, up at the Manse, to discuss Island business. Nothing of great interest. It's best you stay away until you're invited by the Islanders to join us. No point in upsetting anyone. You do understand?" He softened his tone. "I'm telling you now so you don't feel excluded when the time comes. If you're aware of our ways from the beginning, it'll be easier to accept them in the long run. Change takes time, especially here."

"I'll remember, thank you, but I've no ambition to get involved in Island politics. I really just want to help the children achieve what they can."

The Pastor laughed. "Oh, I wouldn't worry too much about academia, Sarah. We're a tight community; no one ever wants to leave. The children you teach will spend their lives here, farming and raising families on the Island, just as their parents did."

Surely he was exaggerating? There must be some children who would travel to the mainland to further themselves? She said nothing, smiling once more to hide her confusion.

"Anyway, Sarah, I'll go and let you settle. If you need anything let me know."

"I will."

As he walked away, Sarah pondered the draw of a place, which would bring such a man back to it. He could have the world at his feet, yet had chosen this tiny Island. McGregor appealed to her. She acknowledged the fact to herself, feeling strangely low at his departure.

The box had grown heavy. She disappeared inside to deposit it onto the small kitchen table. The room was clean, well aired and cosy. She suspected the Pastor had placed a few small comforts here and there and thanked him again silently.

There was no television on the Island, but she'd had the foresight to bring her radio. She'd manage. Sarah opened the back door to the garden. As the night air touched her face she saw for the first time the sea view that would be hers for as long as she chose to stay. It was breathtaking. Immediately it calmed her. If nothing else here measured up to her expectations, the scenery exceeded them. She breathed in her aloneness, realising it was easier to bear than she had imagined. The front of the cottage faced the harbour, but all around were open fields and hills. Eager to explore she decided to use what was left of the weekend to discover what she could about the place. When school began on Monday, she would be too busy for anything else.

The following morning she ventured early to the small harbour area, to the only shop on the island. No more than the front room of someone's home, she'd been told she'd find basic provisions there. The Islanders survived on what they produced themselves. Like the other women she would need to bake her own bread, but she hoped to buy milk and other necessities. It was only as she came nearer that she realised her mistake. The mainland might have relaxed its opening hours, but here the Sabbath was still sacrosanct. The tiny shop was closed.

She smiled at two women standing in the recess of its front door waiting for them to acknowledge her. But it was clear they had no intention of cutting short their conversation – which, if she was any judge of character, was about her. The dialect sounded harsh and unwelcoming. Her face reddened at their disrespect. She stood there, waiting. Finally, they had to recognize her presence.

"I'm Sarah, the new teacher. Can you tell me when the shop opens tomorrow?" Her pleasant tone belied her anger, but she was determined not to let them see how their unfriendliness had hurt her.

"Door's open. Just take w*hit* y*he* need Pastor says. "

"Oh, so do I tell him what I owe or do you?" Sarah asked.

"M*h*aks n*h*ae difference, he'll know by whit's missin'." The woman turned her back, dismissing her.

"Fine so." It was said more to herself than them. She looked around the scant shelves, picking out items, aware of the women's eyes on her from the doorway. She was damned if she'd rush off. Their whispered conversation grew more heated. Though she'd learned some Gaelic in preparation for her new position, they used words and sounds Sarah had never heard. The dialect must be some obsolete language shift unique to the island she realised. Well, she'd soon learn it. She was a quick study. They would soon regret the day they had belittled her.

As she walked past them, one of the women drew her skirts aside, as though afraid of contamination. Furious, Sarah turned to chide the woman for her ignorance when something caught her eye. Hiding a short distance away behind some creels was a small child.

A girl. There was a wildness to her, as if she were *feral* almost, vibrant, almost defiantly alive against the greys of the harbour wall. Yet at the same time she was the picture of innocence, her exquisite skin like porcelain. Her face was beautiful, alluring, yet it faded into nothingness beside her mane of hair. Tangles of curls in a red so rich they looked almost as if they were ablaze. It shone in the sunlight, falling around her thin body, forming a shimmering blanket around the child's small frame. As the breeze moved through it, it seemed almost alive. For a moment the child was all Sarah could see.

As their eyes met, they exchanged a hesitant greeting, though the child's expression barely changed. Sarah moved towards her, saw fear appear on the child's face. Perplexed, Sarah turned her gaze, to see what had caused the child such distress. Both women had made a sign with their hands, a sign Sarah had never seen before. But she understood the viciousness of it.

They had given the child *an Droch shuil,* the evil eye.

Knowing Sarah had seen it, they hurled out a curse. The words, spat so cruelly, fell like venomous drops on the child's form. She shrank back, afraid. Sarah turned back to the women. In that instant the child disappeared, as though she had been swallowed up. Her torturers too walked away, leaving Sarah confused and angry.

Why would anyone treat a child so cruelly? Why would they try to wound one of their own like that?

As she made her way back to the cottage, the incident played and replayed in her head. The child had seemed... miraculous... *otherworldly* almost. And, Sarah realized, the women had seemed almost afraid of her.

Sarah felt thrown by the incident. Intellectually she knew the two women would have treated any stranger the same way, with the same fear and suspicion. But their bigotry was still incomprehensible to her. For all she knew, she could be teaching their children tomorrow. Maybe the adults here required educating, not their offspring. As for the mysterious child, presumably she would meet her too. As she headed back to the cottage, her thoughts were full of her wildness and beauty.

There was something terribly wrong with a community that treated a child that way. If they ostracised a defenceless bairn like that, what welcome could she, a stranger, expect? What if she couldn't break through their defences? For the first time, she realised the immensity of the task she had taken on. Their bigotry would have already poisoned the children.

Once inside the front door of her cottage, hot tears rose to the surface of her emotions and burst through in a torrent. Sarah howled, sad, angry, homesick tears, unable to control the hurt. Dropping her burden in the small kitchen she wept unrestrainedly, full of self-pity and despair at her own stubbornness and pride. *What if her mother was right after all? What if this was no place for her to heal?* She sat at the kitchen table, head on her arms, weeping more quietly now. It was several minutes before she heard a faint noise behind her. She turned in alarm. There, stooping in the small door frame, stood the Pastor, anxious to explain himself. "Your door was ajar. I didn't mean to startle you. I see you've already been upset by something else."

Sarah struggled to regain her composure. She had no wish to have him see her so troubled. "I'm just glad it's you."

He understood it seemed. "You've met some of the Islanders then." He began picking up her groceries strewn across the badly tiled floor. "A cup of tea and it won't seem so bad." He smiled sympathetically. Moving towards the chipped enamel sink he turned on the huge, unwieldy tap, till the water burst through loud enough noise to waken the dead.

"I'll have this looked at for you, Sarah. My handy man Stuart will come and fix it."

"Thanks," she sniffed, wiping away tears. "I should be the one offering you tea," she smiled, picking up the last of the strewn items.

McGregor seemed unperturbed, whistling tunelessly as he waited for the kettle to boil on the ring. Sarah couldn't help but smile, despite her unhappiness. She watched him gratefully as he prepared two cups.

How ridiculous to be so upset. He had *warned* her how it would be. Suddenly she giggled.

"I've been told before that my whistling has a certain entertainment value."

"Sorry no, it just dawned on me how stupid I've been. I let them get to me. I can't believe I crumbled so easily."

They laughed together at the truth of it. The laughing, more than her tears, made Sarah determined never to be so weak again. The Pastor smiled at her.

"It will take time, Sarah," he said, sipping the scalding brew Sarah was resisting for fear of burning her mouth. "On an island like this, life is lived at a different pace. It can be frustrating, but it has its compensations too. There's no fast lane here; the rat race has never been heard of. They're simple folk, with few needs and wants. Just to live and breathe and stay here on the Island is enough for them."

Sarah held her cup to her, drawing warmth from the heat within. "There's no call for such rudeness, Pastor. You above all people should agree a basic moral structure is required."

"Moral structure? That they have." The Pastor pulled the only other chair out from the table, checking first it was safe to sit on. "But it may be different from any you'd recognise, Sarah. Here on the Island, just being a teacher doesn't automatically earn you respect."

There was a ragged hole in the sleeve of his navy fisherman's jumper. *If he had a wife, it would be darned surely?* Sarah reddened at the unbidden thought, more acutely aware of his strength than ever. "One of them moved her skirts from me! How can they despise someone they don't even know?" She watched every movement of his facial muscles as he spoke. He fascinated her, with his dark eyes in his weathered face, not strictly handsome but so powerful in its masculinity.

"That's where we differ most from the mainland. There people give you the benefit of the doubt. Declare yourself as a member of a community and that's that. Here it's not so simple. The Islanders have to *let you in*, and that takes time. There's a deep-rooted heritage which has to be respected. I told you last night, it's nothing personal, Sarah. It's just how it is."

She couldn't contain her indignation. "But it's so…unnecessary, Pastor. Surely you agree?"

He shrugged his shoulders. "Whether I agree or not makes little difference. These people spend their entire lives here. They don't care how things work away from the Island. It's that simple. I, for one, wouldn't like to see their ways changed. There is a way of life here that needs to be protected at all costs." His striking face was resolute.

She wouldn't be silenced. "What about the children? The world is changing, Pastor. Surely they'll need help integrating within larger communities away from island life, if that's what they want?"

Was it her own inner anxiety or did he seem agitated? His voice was calm. "You're racing way ahead of yourself, Sarah. Think for a moment. Could not your attitude be perceived as arrogance? This is only your second day here, yet already you're trying to change things that have been in place for hundreds of years. If you take things a little more slowly, you might make friends more easily."

Sarah was indignant. "I have many friends, Pastor, but if those women this morning were an indication of the bias I'm up against, I doubt I will find many here - no matter how long I stay. They had made up their minds about me. That 'tunnel vision' is part of the reason I've been sent to the Island in the first place. It's too inward looking, unhealthy."

McGregor looked suddenly far more serious. "The Islanders will not take kindly to you placing notions in their children's heads of the wonderful world waiting out there. The world is *not* a safe place for anyone Sarah, let alone young people starting out their lives. Are you going to glorify drugs and prostitution now? We have no need of such things here."

"Please, Pastor, you're twisting my words." She was genuinely shocked, but before she could defend herself further, he soothed her.

"I ask you Sarah, give this place time. Appreciate more fully life on an island, far from the dangers of the mainland." Standing abruptly, he drained the last dregs from his cup, before adding smugly, "It would be easy for innocents to end up confused by conflicting messages. I'm sure you as a teacher would at least agree with me on that."

Sarah could hardly believe that an educated man could be so short-sighted, yet she feared his disapproval should she continue. "Ok, let's call it a truce for today. All I want to do is teach, Pastor, that's all."

"Then do that, Sarah," he said, and then added seriously, "but only that. It will more than suffice."

A warning sounded in her head. She had the strangest feeling that the Pastor had just warned her off. Had she imagined the underlying threat in his voice? This had been more than a heated discussion between two adults. Her own views had not even registered, never mind been tolerated.

Yet still she wanted to like him, her only confidant so far from home.

*

It was not the mix of ages, but the sullenness on the children's faces that took her aback. It was clear her new charges would rather be anywhere than within the confines of the school walls. *What kind of children were they? Where was their openness, their willingness to explore the new?*

Right at the back sat the child Sarah had seen the day before. Her beauty was even more evident in the light of day, breathtaking in its rareness. Was it because of her looks that she sat apart from the others? Sarah's heart went out to the child, sensing her loneliness. Sarah worked her way gradually through the register, memorising each child's name quickly, though there was only one she was curious to discover. It came as no surprise that the child had a name as unique as herself - Aluinn, pronounced Alin. As the day went on it became clear that the little flame-haired child didn't have a single friend among the other children.

Demoralising. That was the word screaming inside Sarah's head all the first week. By the end of it, she could at least tell them apart, though they were so similar.There were the McGregors, a dozen children from two families, neither directly related to the Pastor. Birth control was not high on the agenda or else sex was the only entertainment the parents had. The children were stepping stones, barely separated by months. Then came the McKenzies, sixteen children scattered through five families. Finally, the sickly-looking McDonalds, with a miserly four children between three families. She had learned their names, knew who were the leaders were and who were happy to be led.

One or two were more difficult than others. Morag McGregor was already proving to be a thorn in her side. Pity she wasn't a relative to the Pastor. If she had been, she would have liked to discuss the girl's attitude. Morag held within her a bitter resentment Sarah could not fathom. Not resentment at herself, as she had originally thought. It was directed at all she represented, at the world, at all the things they neither needed nor wanted. Her pasty faced sidekick was Rory McKenzie, a bully boy if ever there was one. Those two she doubted if she could change at all.

Only Aluinn, the red-haired child, had the curiosity, the eagerness Sarah had come to expect in the young. There was something about her, a way she had that astonished Sarah. Perhaps that was why the others were so venomous towards her. Their loathing of her was complete.

Sarah had tried to draw the child out all week with little success, wanting to understand her better. Frankly, despite her firm resolve to do her best by them, she cared little for the others. They were an unremarkable lot, not even very likable, as far as Sarah could see. Usually she loved all children, even the boisterous or naughty ones, but these bairns were…different. Or rather the *same*. It was as if they were determined to become clones of one another, to the detriment of the entire group.

It had only taken a week for Sarah to understand her real purpose in coming to the Island. When she first seen the red weal's on the Aluinn's pale skin they had angered her deeply. She had no idea whether they came from the other children, or if they had been inflicted at home. How could anyone abuse a child so fragile?

After three weeks, Sarah was ready to complain to the Pastor, when she realised she had no evidence to back up her claims. She almost wished that Aluinn's abusers, whoever they were, would go just a little too far, so that she could intervene. But they were cunning.

As for Aluinn, she maintained a silent dignity, which surely infuriated them even more. Sarah realised that was how she retained control over her persecutors.

The Islanders were as cold to her as ever. She noted everyday kindnesses amongst them, barters made of one produce for another, though none came her way other than by the Pastor's hand. She saw them talking together and laughing, heard shouted greetings as they went about their day. But she remained a non-person to them. It was as if they had decided she didn't exist.

She used her free time to walk off her frustrations, planning lessons in her head as she got to know the Island's walks and pathways, tramping across the damp heather moors. As she passed the farmlands scattered over the area, she had to admit a grudging respect for the Islanders. Each holding was a thriving cottage industry, worked along traditional lines. She couldn't put laziness at their door. The Island survived alone. She should have been captivated, enchanted by people who busied themselves by the land, and kept their homes in such good order. But how, when her cheery hellos were met with stony silence?

She had to remind herself constantly of the Pastor's words. Tradition dies hard, and these folk were diehard traditionalists. Determined to be accepted, she threw herself into her work. It was soul-destroying, the response she got from the children. Without Aluinn, who daily seemed to her more captivating, she would have despaired. The child soaked up the lessons Sarah set like a sponge. No one could fail to see the potential in her quick mind, all the more intriguing for her fey-like quality. She would grow up to be a real beauty.

The weeks passed quickly enough. Sarah was encouraged, even if her little school wasn't the miracle of progressive education she had hoped for. That afternoon brilliant sunshine had lifted her mood. She had decided to stay on late, preparing a topic she hoped would capture the children's attention. Through the classroom window, she saw Aluinn walking over the small courtyard. Sarah loved to gaze at the child. On days like these, the sun lit up her hair, like a halo on a madonna.

She was unsurprised when Aluinn approached the other children. The child tried constantly to belong. But without warning, Morag

McGregor lunged forward and knocked the smaller child off balance. Aluinn sprawled face down in the dirt, the stony surface cutting into her skin.

Face twisted with his own self-importance, Morag's sidekick Rory McKenzie sneered "Get up, g*h*irl!" Others had gathered and formed a circle. Aluinn struggled to her feet. Sarah stood watching from the window, determined not to intervene. No matter how much she liked the child, she had to learn to survive on her own. It would do her no good to be known as the teacher's pet. But as Rory advanced on Aluinn, her fear for the child had her banging on the glass.

The children scattered. Sarah called Aluinn indoors. Why did no parent arrive to demand justice for this child? Where was the moral structure the Pastor was adamant the Islanders possessed? Aluinn had so many gifts. She was bright, inquisitive, and beautiful. But she lacked the basic support system any child required to thrive.

She could see to Aluinn's emotional needs as well as her schooling. The thought was almost unconscious at first but grew rapidly. The child needed nurturing and Sarah had love to give. No one else was remotely interested in what she was trying to achieve here. Why should she not put her efforts into the one child who could make something of herself, rather than being stuck on that God-forsaken isle forever?

When Aluinn came into the classroom and saw the compassion on her teacher's face it was too much to take. She burst into tears.

"Oh child, come here," said Sarah gently.

Aluinn ran into her arms, crying hard now. Eventually, when her tears had subsided, Sarah said, "It can't be that bad, surely?"

"No, you're right Miss, …it's worse thun that."

"What's wrong, Aluinn? What's going on here?"

Aluinn slumped down into her seat. "Ah wish ah knew Miss, honest ah dae. They aw hate me. They make fun o' me aw the time, though a*h*v done nothin' ti deserve it. An' when ah go home, yu'd think ah'd be safe, but ah'm noh."

Tears fell as Aluinn spoke through her bewilderment. "Ah jist dinnae belong anihwhur. Why dis naebody like me, Miss? A*h*m ah bad?"

Sarah held her close, hoping the child would draw strength from her. "Listen to me. You're a lovely, caring girl. The fault lies with them, not with you."

"Ah' d bettur go a*h*fore a*h*m missed.A*h*v chores ti dae a*h*fore m*h*a tea."

What was she so afraid of? "I've got a good mind to go and see your mother, to find out how things are at home. There's something you're not telling me."

Aluinn struggled free of her, her panic evident. "P*h*lease Miss, no! It w*h*ud be worse f*h*ir me when y*h*e left. J*h*ist leave it how it is. D*h*innae m*h*ake it w*h*urse, ah c'*h*ouldnae stand it!"

Sarah calmed her. "There's no need to get upset. If you say no, then I won't. But listen to me, Aluinn, I'm here whenever you feel you need somebody to talk to, anytime, day or night."

Aluinn reached forward unexpectedly and took Sarah's hand."But ah'm g*h*lad we're friends, Miss, really ah ahm."

"Things will turn out alright, Aluinn. I'm here for you, remember that. It's a promise." Sarah stroked the child's hair. Its texture was of finest silk, yet it was wild and free, just like Aluinn herself. "Come and talk to me whenever you feel low, or if they're getting you down too much. You can say you're helping me. You can study here too, anytime you wish. Peace and quiet, Aluinn. Whatever you need to keep you safe..."

"Y*h*es, miss." There was gratitude in the child's eyes, a dawning comprehension that maybe, just maybe, things would be better from now on. It tore at Sarah's heart, because seeing that spark of hope she finally understood the misery the child had endured. The words were out before she could stop them. "I want you to know I'm not going anywhere until you're grown, that's a pledge."

What would become of the child, if she didn't stay? There were tears in Sarah's own eyes as the child hugged her. Aluinn was coming up for fourteen, though she had seemed so much younger when Sarah had seen her first, so fragile and small. A year or two, to protect her protégé, how bad could it be? It would be worth it, to see the child flourish as she deserved.

*

The weeks turned to months. Sarah grew used to the Islanders' strange ways but was always glad to return to the mainland at weekends. The Pastor arranged passage with a larger fishing boat, for there were no regular ferry drops at the Island. Sarah was grateful. Gradually, as her fondness for Aluinn grew, her trips home became less frequent. Sometimes she would feel the pull of home, but then she would remember Aluinn. She was the reason Sarah always returned, a draw from which she refused to unbind herself.

She hadn't known how stubborn she was. There was her refusal to give in to the apathy of the Islanders, a contrariness that made her demand their attention for their children. It insisted she invite them to discuss the children's progress and her plans for the forthcoming term. The Pastor had offered to place her handwritten posters around the Island, so that even if the children forgot, they would still know about it. Sarah wanted no excuses.

Finally, parents' night arrived. Sarah had requested wine from Pastor McGregor and prepared sandwiches to welcome the families. As she sat in the small classroom, its desks rearranged to make room for her guests, she felt content. She waited, dressed in her Sunday best, hair immaculate, make up carefully applied, watching nervously as the clock hands approached the time of the first appointment. No one came. Sarah paced nervously, looking repeatedly out of the windows, hoping. The clock hands moved slowly, until Sarah had sat a full hour. Still she was alone. Her eyes stung with realisation. No one was coming.

It was a turning point. She sat there a long time, hurt but increasingly angry. Silently she vowed it would be the last time she would try to involve them. If they had any complaints, let them see her themselves. She would not waste her energy.

Pastor McGregor never mentioned the fiasco, and neither did Sarah. She wondered if he had known all along that no one would come. Had he meant her to be embarrassed? The Islanders seemed to take his word as law in every respect. Had he not asked the parents to come along? Her need for at least one ally on the Island kept her from delving too deeply into such thoughts. But the suspected betrayal was at the forefront of her mind every time they met.

In other ways, he had been more than kind, so different from all the other men on the Island, with their strange ways. Not that she had much contact with them. They would see her approach and take off as if the devil were at their heels. As the weeks passed, she took their behaviour less personally, though it certainly rocked her perception of herself. She had always considered herself a confident woman, a woman of character. The Island seemed to bring out the worst in her.

Her reliance on the Pastor suffered another blow. He came himself to discuss the children's progress. All had done well enough, obviously told by their parents to work hard so that Sarah might have no complaints. But when she emphasized Aluinn's gifts, the Pastor had grown agitated. "I'd advise you not to treat that child any differently from the others, Sarah. She has problems enough fitting in with the others. She's different and they know it. Don't make the situation worse for her." Sarah's protests of dismay met with tight-lipped disapproval. He excused himself minutes later, leaving her angry and frustrated.

*

She had thought he was angry with her, so she was genuinely pleased the following day when she saw him walking towards her. "Pastor, I had no idea you liked walking up here in the hills."

"Normally I have more pressing duties, Sarah," he said, smiling warmly. "But when I saw you leave your cottage I thought, perhaps presumptuously, you might like some company?"

" I'd very much like company."

"Good, I'm glad my instinct was right." His eyes looked at her searchingly. "I know you must be lonely here, Sarah. I get lonely too. The Islanders are fine people, but they don't have the intellectual curiosity I need. That's what makes me seek you out."

"I'm flattered, Pastor, that you rate me so highly." Sarah was touched and amused.

His bright smile flashed, flooding her with gratitude that they had made their peace. "Let's walk together and discuss what bemuses and irks you about this place!"

They walked together for miles over the sweet grasses, past thick carpets of azaleas native to the Island, and on through the heather, past the crowberries and flushes of pasture, then down towards the windswept shoulders and ridges of the cliff tops. Sarah stopped from time to time to pick a wild flower. From time to time McGregor pointed out a variety she had missed. Once their hands reached out at the same instant for a colourful blossom, their fingers touching. She had never noticed the eruptions on his skin before, the blisters on his hands, wet and painful looking. Without meaning to, she shrank back.

He had seen her response. "I don't usually expose myself to vast amounts of sunshine. A glorious day, but it doesn't entirely agree with me." He rolled up one sleeve to reveal a patch of inflamed broken skin, hardening and tightening. It looked aged and rough, unsightly. "It gives me a nasty reaction, wouldn't you say?"

"Do you want to turn back?" Sarah was genuinely concerned. She couldn't enjoy the day at his expense. Now she thought of it, he covered his skin at all times.

"The discomfort is bearable when the company is so rewarding."

Sarah blushed slightly, flattered but shaken by the comment. She had been attracted to him initially, but thought they had settled into a platonic friendship.

Following their rugged course, they walked on, often in silence, lost in the beauty and tranquillity of the Island. Neither hurried, enjoying the quiet companionship and the spiritual uplift their route gave them. The Island was like no where else she had ever been. "What a pity," Sarah found herself offering, "that we can suspend judgement on nature, but can't do the same for our fellow man."

He looked at her curiously. "What do you mean?"

"We don't look at a view and say, 'That tree is too small, or that cloud could be a bit wispier'. So why do we criticise our fellows that way?"

McGregor laughed. "There's a sermon in that thought, Sarah. Thank you."

His smile beguiled her. But there it was again, the nagging voice in her head that urged her to be careful. She felt herself drawn to him almost against her will. He was such a contradiction. Though his Island mentality appalled her, in other ways he was a great man, a towering intellect. She could not shut her heart off to him or the strange pull he had on her. When they were together, he gave so much of himself. He made life bearable. The admission was a hard one to make, but easier because of the part of herself she held back. She could not, would not, lose her heart to him.

They had just reached a shady spot and stopped to admire the view. She felt almost frightened when he moved towards her, too close, too quickly. Before she knew it he was kissing her, forcefully. Shocked, she was unsure what to do, unsure of what she felt. But the growing pressure from his mouth became as unwelcome as the strong hand rising to her breast. She pushed him away with an abruptness that must have hurt his pride.

He looked at her stonily, wiping his mouth, as she straightened her blouse that had become undone. She felt a scorching humiliation as his eyes followed her fingers.

"My apologies, Sarah. I thought you wanted that to happen. Why have we spent all this time together otherwise?" His eyes were cold now. "I sensed a need in you."

Sarah stood tall, her composure recovered. "I'm sorry, Pastor. I like you, and I'm sorry if I gave you the wrong impression. What you sensed was loneliness, nothing more."

His expression was remote. "Again, my apologies. I'll take my leave of you now, and not waste any more of your time."

Sarah was perplexed. "I hope we can still be friends, as before?"

"No, Sarah, we can never be friends now. You've seen to that."

Stunned, she watched as McGregor marched past her, down the sloping path. She wanted to say something, anything, to undo the moment and lessen his pain. Part of her craved him, just to ease her own loneliness. If they were known to be together surely then she'd fit in with these damned people? But she knew it wouldn't be right.

She followed him downhill with a heavy heart, knowing that for the first time on the Island she was truly alone. Worst of all, she had no one with whom she could share what had happened, not even Aluinn. The child had an intense fear of the Pastor she wouldn't explain.

Chapter Two

Aluinn devoured everything Sarah taught her. Best of all she loved to listen to talk about life away from the island. As she listened, Aluinn's eyes lit up in wonder, kindling her desperation to escape. At Sarah's prompting, she wrote her thoughts down. All her uncertainties, all her feelings for the Island were poured into that book. Shyly she showed Sarah a poem she had written. It had touched Sarah deeply, she said, her poem for a homeland Aluinn loved and feared with equal measure. A place she yearned for, yet yearned to leave.

Separation
I walked for miles, you never changed
You called to me, you spoke my name
Whispered slowly, cried, then roared
Filled first my heart and then my soul
Till I became, at your behest,
A creature who would know no rest

Farewell your waters rippling by
And breezes soft as butterflies
Farewell to hills of green and gold
Farewell your mountains' shielding hold
For other places call to me
I hear them beckon 'cross the sea

I cannot rest, though fear's grip chills
Oh Island, say you need me still
Lest one day soon, I bid farewell
To these fair shores I love so well
And curse your weeping evermore
As mourning echoes at my core

When Aluinn read it out in class, they had laughed. It was only after school she had felt their anger. They'd surrounded her on all sides, all the faces that had scorned her ever since she could remember.

Hemmed her in till there was no way past them. Panic had risen in her, but she'd said nothing till a hand thumped her back, making her cry out. As she'd turned, her hair was tugged violently from behind. Tears formed in her eyes as anger rose.

"L*h*eave me be, all o' y*he*, y*he* hear!"

"Oh, l*h*ady Aluinn wants us tae l*h*eave her alone. Why should w*he*?"

"L*h*eave me if y*he* know what's good fur y*he*, or a*h*'ll curse y*he* aw!"

They had looked at each other, less brave now. They had no wish to be cursed; Aluinn was strange enough to be able to do just that.

"Dinnae talk daft, y*he* cannae curse us!" Rory McPherson had shouted.

"Oh can't ah? Well j*h*ist y*he* keep it up, an a*h*l show aw y*he* whit ah kin dae."

"We're no feart i y*he*, Aluinn."

"An a*h*m no feart i o*h*nih o y*he*, so be gone fih me, for a*h*m angry now!"

They had opened the circle and let her through. Her legs almost betrayed her, but she had bluffed well. They were too superstitious to bring harm their own way.

Turning towards the now silent crowd, she had stood proudly. "Mark m*h*a words, there will be ah great storm the night. It is only because a*h*m ventin' ma rage out towards the sea instead of at y*h*ur homes. So be careful a*h*fore y*he* goad me again."

Just as Aluinn had predicted, that night a fearful storm battered and ravaged the beaches. Yet strangely, no harm befell anyone, or their property. It was a wonder to everyone, except the children who had taunted her. After that the bullying stopped. Instead, they had ostracised her entirely. But from that day on she had no longer hesitated to use her gifts to protect herself.

Combing her fingers through her hair, she watched it catch the light. She lived in fear that they would cut it off. She knew it was wrong to be vain of it, but it was more a comfort than a vanity. It hung so low she could sit within it. Often, like now, it kept her body warm, like a giant shawl, comforting her when no other would. She knew its colour set her apart from all the rest of them. It wasn't light, like the McKenzies', but the very deepest red, an auburn that shone like the leaves up by the Broch in the autumn time, just before winter began.

It gave her strength. It was the only thing she was proud of.

That, and being part of the Island. All her life she had run wild, instinctively seeking out its secret places, its highest peaks and deepest recesses where the others were afraid to go. For a while, work at the dam had kept even her away from her favourite haunts. All the Island children had heard the tales of the great beasts that lived beneath its workings, deep below the earth. In her bed at night, Aluinn replayed the legends in her head, limited by nothing save her imagination. But Aluinn feared her imagination, knew what it was capable of. That was why she had gone to see for herself.

The Island had been divided over the dam for generations. The Pastor's grandfather had begun the excavation work, sharing his dream of harnessing the power of water, of advancing the Island beyond its limitations. But his great vision had come to naught. Back then the rocky ground had proven too difficult to conquer.

Years later his son, the Pastor's father, had taken up the task. After a few weeks, work had stopped abruptly. There was tremendous disappointment as this second generation of men refused to continue the work too. Just as their forefathers had, they said the hardness of the earth had beaten them back.

Aluinn had been only six when the old Pastor died, a bairn. But even at that age she had sensed his protection of her. No harm had come her way when he lived; he had halted even whispered conversations about her. It was only when his son returned that her problems had begun.

The young Pastor had been educated on the mainland, his youth full of privileges denied the rest. There had been rumours about him. Many felt the city had enticed him far longer than was necessary. It was whispered he had enjoyed all the pleasures of the flesh, had used others to his advantage. But it seemed he had studied hard too. When he had come home he brought with him knowledge, enough to convince others to restart work at the dam.

The older men were dead set against it. His own father, already ailing, had refused his blessing. It had caused bitter arguments between them.

The old man's death had been a tragedy. They'd found him at the bottom of the quarry, a fall of over a hundred feet. His brutal passing weighted the whole Island with sorrow. Aluinn remembered even her own mother's face contorted with grief. A report of heart failure had been passed. There were some who believed it was not the whole truth. There were those who wondered what a sick old man had been doing up there all alone.

Having lost his father to the dam, no one could refuse McGregor the right to tame it. In the weeks that followed men, experts they were told, had come to the Island from the mainland, working under McGregor's supervision. A few Island men were handpicked to join them. Work progressed. The men refused to be drawn into discussion about what went on at the site. It was as though they had been sworn to secrecy. McGregor must have been paying them well too, for the work was hard. It seemed that for this generation too the earth refused to surrender its secrets. But McGregor was undaunted. The men wearied, becoming more exhausted by the day. Unexplained accidents began to occur, but still the work continued. One by one the men left the works, swearing never to return. Wild rumours began to circulate about what they had seen up there in the dark earth.

The womenfolk said their men had changed, become fearful since the work had restarted. Some nights on coming home they were overcome, shot through with a deep sadness, ominous thoughts, turbulent emotions. Little by little the whole atmosphere on the Island had changed. It was like a sickening almost. Disagreements which would have been raised at Elder Council or else tactfully avoided became full blown arguments. Minor problems became dilemmas. Men taunted each other. Women fought like men. Anger overpowered and possessed even the smallest of the children, adding to the misery their parents already reaped upon themselves. The fear and anger gathered momentum, but on the day the dam reached completion and the water was released, it all stopped.

No one could explain the peculiar venting of emotions that had swept the Island. It was never spoken of again, resting, on the very edge of reality, of all that was, and was not.

What was it that had made the Islanders turn against each other in that way? That question had been playing on Aluinn's mind the day she had made her way to the quarry, taking great care not to be seen.

McGregor had caught her anyway.

She had been standing at the edge of the huge crater dug far deeper into the earth's surface than she had ever imagined. Reaching down, she found the soil peaty and soft to the touch, and wondered to herself. It was the rustling that told her she was not alone as she had intended. When his figure appeared through a break in the bushes, her instinct was to run.

"What's your name, child?"

She spun around, terrified. He towered above her. "Aluinn."

"Do you know who I am, Aluinn?"

"Y*he*'re the new Pastor."

"That I am. But why are you up here all by yourself? Won't your mother worry?"

"Ah go where ah want." She had spoken defiantly. Something inside told her to be brave around him.

"Ah," he smiled. "Now I know whose child you are. You've spirit for one so young," he said, then stretched out his arm towards her and rested it on her head. He began gently stroking her hair. His fingers ran through its length, till his weighted palm lay against the curvature of her fragile spine. Then he retraced its path, following the shape of her head back towards her crown. Young as she was, she understood the invasion of her privacy. She stood rigid as he spoke again."So beautiful…tantalising really. Such a waste here." He put out his powerful hand for her to take. The image of it would haunt her ever after.

She rose slowly to obey his command, appearing submissive. But at the last second, she slipped by him, scurrying away, as only a child who is used to aggressors can do. As she ran, she heard his laughter behind her. Afterwards she had been unable to put her fears into words, knowing only that if she had stayed alone with him some ill would have befallen her. Some innocence would have been lost, never to return.

She had sat the following day at the rocks at the base of a waterfall. Its silvery cascade had become another hiding place. Watching the water, its flow fastest in the narrows, she gathered some of its strength to herself. She would never know why they singled her out. It mattered little. She had other things to give her joy. She *sensed* things, in a way others could not. As an infant, she had tried to share it, but soon understood this was something one hid. Sometimes her gift scared her, especially when she foresaw things – saw Islanders die before it came to pass. *Darna Sealladh* they called it, the second sight. It no longer frightened her, as it had done. Just as she was no longer afraid to see the *bean-nighe* as she was known, the spirit of death. They had grown familiar to each other over the years.

Several times of late they had been forced together, she and the *taibhse* that foretold a passing. Aluinn kept silent about what she saw, knowing instinctively that she mustn't share it, or tell anyone, especially her mother. Sometimes it felt too powerful a secret for her to keep to herself, but as she matured she became stronger. Besides, she could only imagine their reaction. She had no wish to listen to their taunts, nor have her body hurt once more.

She had had the dream again. She knew it was not just the sleepy workings of her mind, a way of calming the terrors that haunted her by day. She had never had thoughts like these, thoughts that terrorised her. But on waking they were so weakened, so fractured, that she struggled to pull them back to her consciousness. In her dream the ground before her was closed, but she sensed all was not as it had been before. The two figures either side of the earthen fissure were so close she could have reached out a hand to touch them. But she did not, for fear they would drag her to the ravine she knew was there, down to their domain. As her heartbeat quickened, Aluinn shrank to conceal herself. Their faces blurred and contorted, but she could still make out their shapes. One, the younger, taller creature was darker, his blackness tinged with crimson. The older creature, still powerful, was leathery and mottled. The dream was always the same, first the ritual, then the attack. As she watched them, they fought for survival, neither giving way, neither prepared to pay the ultimate price of their encounter. They held their blades high, fighting with cruelty and courage. Their battle raged, exhausting both creatures, until ultimately the death blow was struck and only the darker one remained. Even in her dream Aluinn wept for the Island's loss.

Disturbed, she had gone to her most secret place, to feel its power and restore herself. As she threw stones into the watery calmness that pooled some way down from the waterfall, Aluinn looked down and saw the outline of a boy take shape in the unsettled water. Gradually the shape darkened and emerged, almost like in a dream, in the reflection of the blue ripples directly behind her shadow. As the form grew larger the stillness of the water slowly returned, until he was standing there behind her on the water bank, tall and beautiful, his dark hair cascading to his shoulders. She didn't turn immediately. Instead, she sat gazing at his reflection. When he smiled at her, Aluinn couldn't help but smile back, feeling that at last she had found a friend.

"Who are y*he*?" Aluinn asked him, still without turning around.

"Ah a*h*m the Connall. Ah want tae be y*h*ur friend, if y/hu'll let me." His smile in the reflection was full of mirth, and it spread to a grin that matched her own.

"Will y*he* disappear if ah turn round, C'*h*onnall? Are y*he* ah water imp?"

"Y*he* can turn, a*h*l still be here. Ah share y*h*er g*h*ift, ah huv the sight, and ah see the *bean-nighe* tae. Only y*he* must never tell of me, fur onlih y*he* can see me. "

"Ah dinnae care. Ah want tae be y*h*ur friend Connall. Will yhe come a*h*n find me whenever a*h*m alone?"

"A*h*lwiehs, Aluinn, least ways till y*h*ur grown."

She stood and faced him. To Aluinn he was as real as she was. She sensed he was a *taibhse* too, but a guardian, sent to safeguard her. She sensed his goodness, knew he would protect her from that day forward. Aluinn understood that, was awed by it as she stood admiring his beauty. He was slightly taller than she, his dark hair a stark contrast to her own, adding to the beauty of the Island itself. His eyes were the deepest, darkest green, the colour of the moss on the rocks around the pool. When he smiled, it lit up his face. Aluinn loved him, that very instant, for he understood her. As they shook hands, solemnly, they bonded souls, then laughed like the children they were.

"Y*he* used that storm comin' tae scare them good, Aluinn," laughed the Connall.

"They d*h*eserved it. If it gives me peace, then so be it."

"Y*h*ur special Aluinn.That's w*hiy* a*hv* come tae protect y*he*." The Connall gently touched her hair, admiring its beauty with his fingers.

"Y*he* like mah hair, Connall?" Aluinn asked.

"Tis beautiful, Aluinn. Don't evur change it. Bet y*he* cannae get tae the b*h*roch a*h*fore me!" he shouted, already running ahead of her.

"Wait for me, Connall!" called Aluinn, as she hurried behind him, a small child alone, a child of unusual spirit.

Chapter Three

Morag did not fear Aluinn, for all her strange gifts. She *hated* her, hated her for who she was, for the awe she inspired in the others. What must it be like, to be able to instil dread that way? Morag dreamt of being able to terrify like that, with a mere look, or a gesture. But as long as Aluinn walked these shores, there was little chance of that happening.

She seized every chance to goad and torment her nemesis. It was her calmness she hated most of all. But Aluinn's defence was always the same, implacable, accepting. The calmer she remained, the more demented Morag became. As she grew older her cunning grew with her determination to bring Aluinn down in everyone's eyes. Until she discovered just how powerful Aluinn really was.

Aluinn rose early at weekends so she could escape to the hills after her chores. Everyone knew the wild one's ways - she spent every waking hour up there, lost in a world of her own making. That morning Morag had persuaded Rory and a few others to follow her up as far as the Old Broch, trailing their target without her knowing. They had watched from a distance as Aluinn claimed the tower-like stone turret as her own.

The ancient tower had always been part of the Island. Their tales, the *sgeulachd*, were filled with stories in which the Broch played a role. It must have been one of several at one time. Ruined stone rings were the only footprints left of ancient megaliths that had thrust their dark granite skywards. Even now the place was known as *Magh Turieadh*, the Plain of Towers.

The Old Broch stood alone now, sole survivor of centuries of wind and war and weeping. Aluinn had come there since she was a young child, understood the secrets it kept within its walls. It was one place she could go to be alone.

That morning her spirits were high. Sarah had heard from the mainland. Her poem had won a prize! Not first prize, but to Aluinn that made no difference. She had never felt more…alive. How could recognition come from so far away, from beyond the only shores she had ever known, when she had never known praise from those around her? And why did it make such a *difference* to the way she felt?

Aluinn sat within the tower boundary, her fingers spread across the soft, damp grass. Raising her head upwards to take in the sun's rays, she closed her eyes. She knew she must be patient. He only came when she was still. She turned her head and looked out through a narrow slit in the round stone wall. Beyond it, ancient crofts lay neglected, shells long since forgotten, except in the memories of those whose ancestors had left them for other places, where life was not so hard.

Those ruins held their own stories, their own legends, known to those who kept them. Aluinn closed her mind to such thoughts. Not now. No intrusions. It was only a matter of time before the *Connall* would appear, to talk with her, to play their games, to stop her losing her mind. Negative thoughts kept him away. To be alone had been bad enough. To be alone now and deprived of his friendship…

"Aluinn… Aluinn…"

There it was, the gentle whispering she loved, echoing through the stones of the enclosed tower.

"Connall, ah thought y*hu*'d furgotten about me."

"Never, Aluinn. Ah protect y*he* a*h*waihs."

"A*h*m glad y*he*'ve cum. Let's g*ho* runnin, be wild. A*h*m happy Connall, truly happy fur the first time in ma life. A*h*'ve succeeded a*ht* somethin'. Now ah know ah can dae what ah set ma mind tae."

The *Connall* looked at her sadly, his aura tinged indigo. Today was a milestone. He had nurtured this child when no one else had cared. He already understood her success marked the start of the change. "An' y*he* wull, more than y*he* can understand yet Aluinn. Y*hur* no longur the bairn ah came tae, weepin', aue thae years ago. Y*huv* g*h*rown strongur. Soon y*hull* no longer need me. Ah cannae stay much past the summer." The Connall looked sad, as though he knew he had come to care too deeply for this beautiful child in his care. "Y*hull* forget me, they aw dae."

Aluinn's happiness evaporated at the thought of losing him. "D*h*innae say that. Ah'l need y*he* ah'waihs. Is there no way r*h*oond it?"

"Others call tae mih ahready. Ah hear thir need b*h*ut m*h*ah time whih yeh isnae done yet. A*h*n *w*heill awewies be bondit. If yeh shud call tae m*h*e, if y*h*er life whis threaten'd…"

"Ah d*h*innae *w*hant things tae change, Connall. Ah *w*hantae stieh here *w*hih yeh."

He reassured her gently. "One day y*h*ull simplih stop b*h*elievin' a*h*n' ah'll move o*h*n tae a*h*nuther who needs mih as y*h*e once did."

Aluinn looked at the *taibhse* sadly. "But fir now we'll carri on as a*h*fore?"

"Aye, ah'll keep y*h*e safe, till y*h*e fulfil yer destiny."

"Mah destiny?" Aluinn asked, puzzled.

"Patience, lass. Aw whill b*h*e revealed in time."

She would have to make do with that, for now. For now it was enough to know that if she called him again, she still had the power to make him come to her. There was so much… wickedness. And it didn't always manifest itself in wild and frightening ways. She thought of the cold, calculating determination of the Pastor, of his cultured, insensitive spirit. A handsome man, yet she had seen the evil in him, seen it grow and convulse…

She must not fret, or show her fear. They had so little time left.

In Aluinn's mind, she left the confines of the tower, side by side with the *Connall*. Morag McGregor and her sidekicks, hidden amongst the birch trees, watching her in bewilderment, seeing her lips move in her animated face. The boys sniggered.

"Shh, y*h*e twa! If Aluinn gets wind o' us a*h*fore ah want her tae, ther'll be trouble!"

Rory, perhaps more stupid or less afraid than Morag, snorted. "Ach, she c'annae hear us fih there!"

"Wheesht! Ah want tae hear whit she's sayin'!"

They watched as Aluinn left the tower to sit down beside the burn, which ran alongside the Broch, deep in conversation with the *Connall* all the while.

"Whereull we go then?"

The *Connall* replied, for her ears alone. "Wherever y*h*e wish."

"Ah wanna see the high cliffs. Or we could go tae the cove. Aniwhere wih y*h*e, Connall, is fine wi' me."

Morag watched in fascination as Aluinn poured her heart out to the four winds. Convinced she had lost her mind, the boys laughed again, till Morag silenced them sternly.

Rory turned on her. "If we're no wanted here weul be off!"

"Go then, ah dinnae care!" hissed Morag, as the boys upped and ran away towards the bay.

Morag turned her attention back towards Aluinn, who sat staring into nothing, a strange look of contentment on her face.

All the while, the *Connall* held Aluinn's hand and spoke softly to the child. He tried to hide the pain in his own heart, to understand her need to belong to someone that was not him. Had she even noticed how different he had become in the years since they had met? How he had changed, was no longer the young boy she had first seen, how he had become stronger, become her protector? He had tried to make the transformation as gradual as possible, so as not to frighten her. And he still had so much to teach her.

"Y*h*ur days fur runnin' wild are a*h*most ower. Fur awe its faults y*h*ur very much ah part oh thih real world, Aluinn. Soon y*h*ul noh need me."

Aluinn stood up in her anger and frustration. "Ah'll nevur stop believin' in ye…"

The desperate note in her voice pained him. Before the *Connall* could reply, Morag McGregor stood up and moved towards them through the trees. In that instant, the *Connall* faded away.

The scorn on Morag's face only added to Aluinn's fury.

"Whae are y*h*e talkin' tae, y*h*e daft eejit!"

"Go away, Morag. This is mah place a*h*n ah'll noh b*h*e sharin' it wih y*h*e!"

"Y*h*oor place! Whae dae y*h*e think y*h*e are, M*h*iss High 'n' M*h*ightih!" She started running towards Aluinn. "Y*h*eh micht scare othurs wi y*h*er strange ways, but no me…"

On the verge of retaliating, Aluinn stopped short, taken aback by the vision she saw over Morag's shoulder. It was of Morag, not much older than she was now. She was swimming out in the bay, the sun shining on her freckled shoulders.

Morag stopped abruptly, frightened by Aluinn's expression, not knowing that the *'bean nighe'* had appeared behind her, the sign

Aluinn accepted as loss of life. Simultaneously, in her mind's eye, Aluinn saw Morag, frightened now and alone, the sun still shining on her pale skin, screaming her death dread as she was dragged beneath the waves.

Immediately Aluinn's anger subsided. She had seen the mark of death on her. It was a certainty. Aluinn pitied Morag then. The girl's torment would be seen in the light of compassion from now on.

"Is it any wonder, Morag, if ah talk tae masell? Ah've had n*h*aebodih else awh these years tae play whih, since ye're ah sae feart oh me."

Morag spat into Aluinn's face, a shining globule of loathing. "A*h*m no f*h*eart i y*h*eh Aluinn, ah jist hate y*h*eh, that's awe!"

Aluinn shook her head sadly. "A*h* cannae d*h*ae ani*h*thin' a*h*boot it, can ah?"

For the first time Morag felt real fear. Something had changed in Aluinn, something in her *presence*. She had some undisclosed knowledge that made Morag want to flee. She tried to sound braver than she felt. "Am no stieyin' here, list'nin tae y*h*eh haver. A*h*m goin' hame!"

Aluinn watched her go, feeling the same sadness she always felt when the future had shown itself to her. All those foreshadowing's over the years, stored up inside her like the wrecks of the fishing boats and trawlers she saw lost at sea. Was this part of her destiny, or would it go too when the *Connall* left her?

At first, when it happened. She had tried to warn them, but she had only made them fearful, made them fear *her*. It was that gift, her second sight, which had set her apart all those years ago. Even her own mother had tried to silence her, had almost broken her spirit in doing so. But in putting her down she had forced Aluinn to lose her fear.

At some level, she understood that it signalled the end of her childhood, this understanding of pain and death. Some day, soon, she would leave the Island behind and start again.

If she stayed within its boundaries, she would be destroyed.

Sarah noticed small changes in Aluinn's behaviour at first. The girl had a new confidence she had never possessed before. The other children seemed aware of it too. Winning that prize had clearly lifted her out of herself.

They had become closer than ever as the months passed.

Watching Aluinn grow made Sarah want to walk through her own fears. It was that desire to be true to herself that had prompted her to share Aluinn's good news with the girl's mother. She shivered at the memory.

Aluinn was so brilliant, so light in her being, Sarah had not expected the mother to be such a daunting presence. Physically the two could not have been more dissimilar. Though both were tall, the mother was a cumbersome woman with coarse, dark hair and brows set in a permanent scowl. She understood immediately why Aluinn was afraid of her. Sarah's first instinct was to retreat. Her heart went out to the child, her own fear replaced by anger.

"Hello, I'm Miss Tomminey, but I suppose you already know that." Sarah wished she could sound more like the authorities she represented. Part of her still hoped for a kindly response from this woman. "I've come about Aluinn."

At the woman's stony expression, Sarah felt her words rush out in a torrent, as an indefinable panic rose in her. "Aluinn's won a prize in a competition for her poetry. I'm so delighted for her..."

The woman's strong voice cut her off abruptly, "It has tae end. Y*her givin'* her ideas, w*hastin'* y*her* time, a*hn* hers."

"That's hardly true. Aluinn beat thousands of other entries, surely that must impress you?"

"W*hastin* her time w*hih* b*hooks!*" The woman scowled. As she moved her menacing face closer, Sarah's only thought was to get Aluinn away from that brute of a woman as quickly as possible. "Stop tryin' tae change her, or there'll bih hell tae paih!"

The woman moved ever closer, her huge features set for maximum effect.Her tone was softer now, but somehow more threatening. "Y*hou'*d best bih careful how y*he* go about on thi' Island. It kin be ah dangerous place."

"Is that a...a threat?" Saran was bewildered.

"Y'*heh* kin take it howe'er y*he* wish. Ah've said m'*hah* piece."

"I just wanted to show you Aluinn's work," Sarah said, placing the poem she had framed on the stone step. Perhaps the gift might pierce the woman's conscience when she was gone. As Sarah turned to leave, she couldn't help herself. "She's such a gifted girl. You should be proud of her."

The only response was the slam of the door.

No wonder Aluinn dreaded going home. And what of the other children? What went on behind their closed doors? Whatever it was they seemed to accept it, despite all their whispering and secrecy...

Aluinn was different. Sarah sensed it instinctively. Or was she simply transferring her own emotions onto the child? She had struggled for acceptance, sad that the Islanders still treated her as the 'outsider'. The women still pulled back their skirts wherever she went. No one smiled or spoke a kind word. She had grown used to the stares as they muttered about her. The dialect was so distorted, Sarah could still barely make out every tenth word. It confused and irritated her that she had not become more fluent. Perhaps that would have helped to ease her isolation. But she doubted it. There was something fundamentally warped about the mindset of the Island, some secret its people shared that she couldn't get to the bottom of. As soon as Aluinn was safely away, she would follow her.

Back home on the mainland she changed the subject when her mother asked how things were going. She hid her troubles, knowing any other teacher would have given up long ago. Meantime, she concentrated on her work, filling all her spare time with assignments no one took care over. All except Aluinn, who excelled consistently. It was enough. There had never been any complaints about her work. Ironically, it was because Sarah lacked any diversion that she had achieved so much.

She had taught her unwilling pupils all they needed to know for life there. Moreover, it seemed that there would be no more children in this generation. She could leave in good conscience. What she had achieved would have to be reward enough.

Feeling peaceful having made her decision, that peace seemed to spread to her charges. But one autumn morning a fight broke out before the school day had even begun. Most likely some petty argument from the weekend being continued on her territory.

It was no surprise to see big Morag McGregor ladling into a

smaller child. But when she realized who that child was, she took to her heels and made straight for the girls. It looked as if Morag was out to murder Aluinn this time for sure.

Sarah literally ripped their bodies apart, her anger at its limit.

"Morag McGregor, you should be ashamed of yourself. Look at the mess her face is in!" she shouted, dragging Aluinn behind her back to protect her.

Morag had no fear of Sarah now. Her true nature, the twisted side she normally disguised, was on show for all to see. "She deserved it. Ah hate her!"

"Right, that's it you two, inside, now! Everyone else go back to playing the way children are supposed to…NICELY!"

Sarah frogmarched both girls into the classroom. She forced herself to look as though she were equally disappointed in both girls. Less would have given away her own feelings.

"So which of you would like to start?"

"Aluinn said shi saw mih dead!"

Sarah stared at Morag who looked less upset now than satisfied.

"Is this true, Aluinn?"

Aluinn raised her head. Noting the child's swollen eye and bloodied nose, Sarah's stomach knotted.

"Ah didnae mean it tae come oot like that. Ah jist couldnae stand it any longur; M*h*orag, wis bein' cr*h*uel. Thi a*w*e whur!"

Morag was standing waiting for Aluinn's punishment.

"Morag, I want you to go back outside. Put what she said at the back of your mind. Words cannot physically harm you, remember we've spoken about that. I'll deal with Aluinn."

Morag looked disappointed. "Aw, Miss, bit…"

Sarah used her authority. "No *buts* Morag, you shouldn't have hit her. On you go. "Morag left sullenly. Sarah's eyes never left her until she had closed the door.

Aluinn never uttered a word, until she saw Morag had rejoined the others outside. "Aah shoudnae uv told her. It wisnae f*h*air."

Sarah stared at Aluinn in disbelief. "Are you telling me, Aluinn, that you really believe Morag is going to die?"

"Miss, ah know it."

The sadness in her voice told Sarah not to doubt the child. As she studied Aluinn's injured face, she wondered how the child could be so battered and bruised, yet still no amount of injury could detract from her beauty. Looking into her eyes, Sarah understood everything then, why Aluinn was such an outsider. She was gifted with instincts others lacked. Morag should be grateful. Surely now she had a chance to change her fate?

"It can be avoided Aluinn? If she stays away from whatever it was you saw?"

"It wid onli happen wurse if she did."

"So how long have you 'known' about these things, Aluinn?"

"Aue mah life, Mhiss. Ah used tae thell them, uhntil... thi tellt mi tae stop. Now ah jist keep it tae masel."

"I'm sorry, Aluinn."

Sarah rose and filled a bowl with warm water, taking a cloth from the sink to bathe Aluinn's inflamed face, "Is there more you haven't told me?"

The child shook her head, but Sarah sensed she wasn't able to tell her any more.

"You shouldn't have to put up with this, Aluinn. It's nothing short of barbaric."

Aluinn grimaced, as the cloth touched her swollen cheekbone, "Please, Mhiss, dinnae dae ahnythin' tae pit yhursel' in danger."

"Maybe I should have a word with Pastor McGregor?" *And that would give her another chance to straighten things out with him.* "At least he's been on the mainland. He'll understand."

Aluinn's answer rose till it was shrill in her ears. "Nah miss, no him, please dinnae tell him!"

Sarah realised there was real terror there. "It's alright, Aluinn, I won't. Sit still, you've got water everywhere. If I have to stay quiet, you must confide in me. What makes you so afraid?"

Sarah gently wiped the child's bruised face. A silence fell between them as Sarah allowed Aluinn to digest her words.

Finally, much to Sarah's surprise, Aluinn spoke.

"Huv yhe heard thi dark tales o' thi Island, mhiss?...thur mheant tae tell o' times lhong gone, bhut thur nho... thur sthill happenin' here."

"What do you mean, Aluinn?"

"Thi Island's curse. It began long ago, when thi veri first settlers braved superstition an' laid doon roots here. Thih didni knowh othurs hud bin thur afore thim. It seem't as thoh thi island lai deserted, bit that wis ah lie. Thur wis somethin' hid'en deep wi'hin its veri darkness." Aluinn smiled at her, drawing her into the story, weaving its words. "Aw' wis well fur a time, long e'nough fur those weari travellers tae settle, tae spend thur laughter an' joy at findin' such a place fur it please't thum greatli. Thih spread oot, claim't it as thur rite. But thur laughter hud drawn thi hidden tae thi surfice. Thi wisht tae bei hon'urd, wur'shipd. They showed thur strength, demandin' festivals an' ceremonies, reverence fur thur kind. Great fear replaced thi laughter. Thi demanded women. Thi men were unwillin' tae gi'e o' thur ain kin, so thi travell'd furth'ir afield an' brou't back young lassies tae satis'fi thum, an' win thi right tae co-existence. It's still here, thi dark force…"

The child paused as though afraid to repeat all she knew. Sarah prompted her gently. Fanciful as the story was, it represented a breakthrough.

"Tell me Aluinn, I'm listening."

"Thurs a newer tale, no' so old or forgotten. It goes back three generations tae thi Pastor's grandfather. He wis up bi' thi Broch w*haur* thi dirt road dips tae thi side a*hn* disappears intae thi sea. He had stopp'd one night tae g*haze* at thi stars in thi m*hoonlikt*. A*h*tween y*he* a*hn* m*he*, miss, ah i*h*magine i*ht* tae b*he* like he had twah much b*heer* in his b*hellih*, confused as tae thuh wie hame!"

Sarah laughed at the child's clumsy effort to lighten the mood between them. Her heart reached out to the child again, glad that they could share these moments at least.

"So there's thi Pastor catchin' his breath. Mi*h*bee i's b*hin* r*hunnin*', m*hiss*. Awe a*ht* once he sees thi g*hroond* a*h*fore 'im openin' up."

Aluinn's face was alive as she retold the ancient folklore, so convincingly Sarah could picture him.

"Well *he*'s scare't, m*hiss*, so *he* crouches low amongst thi roowin trees." Aluinn stopped, looking round to make sure no one had entered the class before she continued. "It's then *he* sees it, ah creature unlike anythin' *he*'s ev'ir seen a*h*fore or ev'in heard a*h*bout. Awe o' ah sudden thur it wis, ah… *dealradh* " Clearly there was no word in English that corresponded exactly to what she wanted to convey. Aluinn's eyes were shining, as she pictured it before her. "It means, ah great brite'ness, M*h*iss." Aluinn focused her thoughts more clearly. "It blinded his path, so thit *he* covered his face wi' his hands. When thi dirt settl'd an' thi brite'ness left, *he* gazed through thi nite an' saw thi mighti form. It stood nae maire thun ah man's length a*h*waih." Aluinn's eyes grew wider, as though she too saw the beast."Thoh he wis a Pastor he wis terrified, fur *hc* believed in the *deamhan taibhsean,* the evil spirits who li*v*e amongst us. "The teacher in Sarah realised the child was resorting to her mother tongue in her agitation. Or perhaps it was that the words she knew in English could not fully explain what she was seeing? "Its veri frame grew wider." Aluinn stood up and threw open her arms, "Huge wings spanned thi openness. I*h*t st*h*ood ten feet tall, towerin' above him, fillin' thi night sky against thi m*h*oonlikt."

Aluinn retook her seat, as though suddenly weary. Her voice was lower as she continued. "Eeh w*h*as petrified, thinkin' such ah cr*h*eature whid surely devour 'im. But i*h*nstead it lifted off thih g*h*round, a*h*n fl*h*ew as ah d*h*arkened shadow again'st thih moon."

Sarah sat transfixed. The child was a born storyteller. The legend had come alive in her hands, as she wove it through the silence and Sarah's mind. Suddenly she understood another of the child's gifts. Aluinn was a word weaver. She had heard of them, of course, should have known from her poem. But the child had gone on. "Thih Pastor coodneh take his eyes off thih a*h*pparition. But as he was tremblin' wi' wonderment a*h*n enchantment, thih great b*h*east fl*h*ew down in one fell sw*h*oop a*h*n, carried him d*h*ownwards, into thi split in thi earth and thi ground cl*h*osed behind thim wi' a thunderclap. Ground that shood 'av lain u*h*ndisturbed."

Aluinn paused, as though unsure whether she should continue. Sarah prompted her gently."Go on Aluinn, I want to hear the rest. "

"This is thi bit whur thi legend reallih begins M*h*iss…Thi Pastor w*h*usnae seen fir sum time. F*h*eart deed, lost it sea or w*h*urse. B*h*it, one day he jist r*h*eappeart…. o*h*nly 'eeh whisnae thih s'*h*ame. Set a*h*boot tackin' over thih r*h*unnin' o' thih I*h*sland, changin' everythin'." With a storyteller's instinct, she lowered her voice. "I*h*t whis s'ade thit e*h*very y*h*ear *h*e went back tae thi spot, wantin' tae bi taken back doon. An' when *h*e had ah bellyful o' *poteen, he becames'h*omethin' tae b*h*e f*h*ear'd." Aluinn stopped and took a deep breath as though she shared a great taboo. "*H*e t*h*elt thum awe he'd seen below thi earth - n*h*aebodi e*h*ver questioned awynithin he did fae then on. He was the Pastor that began the new laws..."

*

At home that night Sarah went over everything Aluinn had said. The story telling had been a diversionary tactic, or a way for the child to give her back something for her help. There was something badly wrong that a child should relate such tales so matter of factly. It was as if she had convinced herself the stories were true.

What bothered Sarah still was the child's reaction to Pastor McGregor. Aluinn had been petrified at the very thought of his being told of the other children's cruelty. Sarah had long been aware of the strangeness between himself and the child. He seemed to make a point of purposely drawing Aluinn to him, though he could tell it irritated her. He would place his hand on her head, or reach out and touch her hair as she passed. Not in an obvious way, but now Sarah's awareness was heightened, it was…devious…somehow. And it clearly distressed the child.

McGregor was a powerful man on the Island. He had the ability to control circumstances to suit his own ends. His position as owner meant no one queried him.

Was something amiss between him and the child?

Since their friendship had been spoiled, she had seen little of him. There were so many things here she didn't understand. She'd give a lot to know what happened up at the Manse. She had taken to sitting on the back steps of her cottage in the evenings, looking out over the sea. Three or four times she had seen processions of torches weave their way around the bay and up towards the big house, alongside many more boats in the harbour. At the time, they had seemed faintly ludicrous. Why all the secrecy? Why were their festivals not out in the open, reasons for celebration? In the light of the folktales Aluinn had shared, which the Islanders took as their truth, their traditions and oral history seemed darker, somehow fearful. The thought struck her - *was* there something more sinister happening here? McGregor had taken pains to tell her to stay away from their gatherings, from the first.

Speculation could be very dangerous, especially in such a close-knit community. She would keep her thoughts to herself for the moment. And keep her eyes open.

She longed to walk and discover more of the hidden beauty of the Island, but after her row with McGregor, she was afraid to bump into him alone. Yet the next day when school was over, the sun was shining. She found herself starting along the dirt track to pick the blood red flowers, which grew along the edges of the rough road. She had no name for them, though she felt sure the Pastor had told her several times already.But she had grown to love the sweet scent with which they filled her cottage.

It was then Sarah first noticed Stuart McDonald, watching her. She hadn't seen much of him since the Pastor sent him to fix the kitchen tap. McDonald was a lone wolf, an underhand operative if ever she had seen one. A man Sarah would instinctively avoid at all costs. And yet, he was the Pastor's errand boy. When he saw her notice him, he turned away and walked back down towards the harbour. She didn't give him another thought.

Later that night, she lay curled up on the small, uncomfortable couch she had long since grown used to. The children's papers were scattered around. She had just finished marking an assignment. As usual, no one had shown any interest in the work she had set. Except Aluinn, whose effort shone.

Being alone so much, Sarah was especially aware of any sounds outside. It was not unusual for small rodents to scurry about at night. She had become used to them. But the sound she had noticed had been louder. Perhaps a stray sheep had wandered down from the hills, become separated from the rest. Curious, Sarah went to the window and drew the curtains back abruptly.

What was McDonald doing, prowling around outside her cottage at night? Heart beating erratically, Sarah marched to the front door and pulled it open. It took her eyes a few seconds to accustom to the darkness. By then Sarah could no longer see him. But she sensed him still. And then she *knew*. He was her 'minder', as surely as she breathed. If Sarah left the confines of her cottage at night, the Pastor would know about it.

Shutting the door as quietly as she could manage, she crept upstairs to bed. Had McDonald been watching her since her arrival? Readying herself for bed, she determined to make sense of whatever madness lay behind the Island's apathetic façade. There was something sinister afoot. Thoughts scudded around her mind, fitting together to form a disturbing image. Sarah knew enough about life to know when it had turned sour. Aluinn was the only person on the Island who ever really gave her eye contact. Only she ever looked directly into Sarah's eyes with honesty and innocence.

Lying between the cool sheets, the moon shining through the thin cotton of her bedroom curtains, Sarah was afraid. With the exams almost over, she had arranged job interviews for Aluinn on the mainland. The child was approaching her sixteenth birthday; officially, she would be an adult. She had made arrangements, secret arrangements, to take Aluinn off the Island. She had told no one her plans, not even Aluinn, for fear the child would betray them both. If her mother found out, there would indeed be 'hell to pay'. But Sarah had never backed down from anything in her life. This was the right thing to do. Aluinn had to be free to grow into the woman of promise she deserved to be.

She was sick of teaching children who didn't want to be taught, with no support from their care-givers. With Aluinn free, she would be able to leave herself. Knowing that the Islanders were so afraid of her that she had been given her own "minder" helped her decide once and for all. She would tell Aluinn tomorrow.

"Are y*he* no comin' wi me, Sarah?"

"No, sweetheart. I have to stay another few weeks until the term finishes, then I'll follow. Don't look so afraid. You'll love Edinburgh. It's such an exciting city. My mother will adore you and you'll adjust easily. You are so beautiful, Aluinn, you've no idea how beautiful. Everyone will fall in love with you. My mother and her sisters will want to give you a makeover, dress you up in the latest fashions. *Please* don't let them change you too much before I get back." Sarah felt her heart swell as she looked at Aluinn's sad face, still so striking despite her distress. Determined to stay upbeat, she added softly, "Aunt Maud will most likely descend on you first. She's a bit eccentric and loud but don't be scared, it's just her way. Don't take any fashion advice from her. Though I doubt even she could make you look bad. You are so blessed Aluinn, despite all you've suffered. You're a survivor. You just remember - there is no pain and no suffering you can't outlast." Sarah held back tears as she pulled Aluinn into an embrace. "This is a new beginning for both of us. I'm sure it won't be anything like you expect, but it has to be better than what you've known till now."

"Can't ah just wait fur y*he* then?"

"No, Aluinn it's safer this way. I'll know without doubt that you're safely in Edinburgh."

She hadn't expected Aluinn to balk at the first hurdle – it took a lot of persuading to make her promise to leave first as arranged. Fear of the unknown, she supposed. It was a daunting experience to leave her Island home and travel so far alone. But Sarah stood her ground, determined it was for the best. Besides, she still had a duty of care to the other children, and this way there would be no connection between Aluinn's disappearance and her influence.

"So it's agreed. You'll be fine on the ferry, and my mum will be there to meet you, I promise."

"Am no worried a*h*bout me, Sarah. Ah'll worry a*h*bout y*he*, fur they'll no be happy when ahm gone. No one ever leaves here. They'll suspect you of helping me. Y*hou*'ll be the reason fur their upset. Y*he*'ll no be safe."

"Oh Aluinn, please, superstitious nonsense and the very reason I need to get you away. They wouldn't dare hurt me. The authorities would be up in arms if they assaulted a member of staff. You don't need to worry about them anymore or their strange ways. "

" Sarah, you're no listenin'."

"Yes, I am, Aluinn. And that's exactly why I must stay, to prove to you that you have nothing to fear any longer. They won't dare hurt me, and I'll be with you before you know it. Once I come back home to Edinburgh things will be so different. You'll blossom there. "

Sarah was stubborn, but the real reason she was staying behind was clear. Part of her, the part of her that had been hurt and rejected by the Islanders, was determined to be there when Aluinn left. She wanted her revenge, to enjoy her victory over them when they realised she had beaten them. She went back to work, satisfied. Aluinn silently acknowledged the *bean nighe* as she appeared by Sarah's side. She looked strangely sad, as though weary of her task. Or was it always hard for her to take one as noble as Sarah?

Aluinn's tears fell silently. Her gift had become her curse.

*

It was first light. Her excitement had roused her too soon. Sarah lay in bed under the coombed ceiling of her attic room, reliving her dream. It always began the same way, the dream, first her happiness at Aluinn's departure, then the fierce arguments, long and drawn out, with the Pastor until Sarah felt all the energy drained from her body. And then the image of Aluinn, always the same pleading expression. In her dream Sarah won, just as she had done in reality.

The day of her departure, far from being a celebration, had been so painful. Aluinn was distressed, begging Sarah to leave with her on that ferry.

She had had to steel herself, promising the child everything would be okay, that she would be with her soon. She had lived and relived that moment countless times in her dreams since. Lying there, Sarah tried to recapture the look in Aluinn's eyes, but no matter how she tried the image was gone.

Suddenly Aluinn, it seemed to Sarah's mind, stood directly beside her. "Sarah, why did y*he* noh listen? A*h*m too late fur y*he*."

Sarah reached out towards her, tried to touch Aluinn's beautiful face, but she found herself alone, bereft, her arm lifted upwards, clutching at empty space.

What a horrible way to begin the day her life would be reclaimed as her own. Her duty to the school was done. Aluinn was free. She had beaten them all.

Now it was her turn to leave. Let them all stay together, as they belonged, with whatever it was that they kept so secret. Fear and pride had kept her away from those covert gatherings, as much as Stuart McDonald's watchful presence. The Pastor was right – why try to change their ways? Throwing back the bedcovers, she rolled her neck, trying to work out the kinks, forcing herself to relax. Apprehension, that was all she was feeling – she had better hurry if she didn't want to be late for the ferry.

She smiled grateful her ordeal would soon be over.

She had really missed Aluinn the last few weeks. It wasn't until the child was gone that she realised how all her energies had been focussed on that one small, shining light. Yet it had been worth it. Aluinn was special. She would go on to achieve great things, Sarah was sure of it. She was so proud to have been able to help her.

Hopefully, a few weeks away from the Island would already have given Aluinn some perspective on the place. With any luck, she would be able to laugh at the powers she had once credited its inhabitants and realised how unfounded her fears had been.

As she made her final preparations, Sarah was perplexed by her own emotions. Worry kept rising to the surface, fear that there would be some kind of scene before she left. She finished packing, trying to play down her anxiety, knowing that what she felt was only a fraction of the deep-rooted fear Aluinn had suffered. And they had been unable to break *her* spirit, her joy in life.

Her own bitterness no longer surprised her. Their jealousy of Aluinn had turned them into souls unworthy of pity. Sarah despised them. They lived by their own code – now she understood what the Pastor had meant by 'their own moral structure'. They were small minded, dour and resentful. After she left, she would never look back. Sarah longed for Edinburgh once more, knowing she was truly free. She was exhilarated by the very thought of a stranger smiling at her. Of being surrounded by people who passed the time of day, enquiring after her, giving freely without restraint. How she missed the everyday courtesies she had taken for granted.

Sarah smiled a wry smile to herself. She had made no recommendation for another teacher to take over. As far as she was aware, her position had been unsuccessfully advertised for the second time. She was relieved to leave it far behind. It gladdened her heart to think of Aluinn happy. She couldn't wait to show Aluinn all the treasures of her home town, the museums and art galleries. It would be a joy to tour them with someone so hungry for knowledge, to see the awe on her beautiful face. Had the past few weeks made any changes in her? Would she be more aware of the fey beauty she possessed? That same beauty would have been wasted on another child. In Aluinn, it merely served to capture some inner light. Men would adore her. Yet there was no vanity in her.

Carrying her much-battered suitcase, Sarah approached the harbour, remembering the night she had arrived two years ago. Back then, there had been no welcoming committee, but it seemed there were many more than willing to see her off the Island for good. Even from a hundred yards away, she was acutely aware of the group of men gathered at the water's edge. Absurd to be so afraid. She was leaving.

Even if they shouted abuse at her, ridiculed her, it wouldn't matter. Aluinn was settled on the mainland. She had a job, and until she found her feet, a home. She was out of harm's way.

The panic receded. She had done her duty and more besides. She had nothing to recriminate herself with, certainly not removing a child from danger.

Up ahead several women had huddled by the corner wall built before the slow turn onto the narrow cobbled road, which led down towards the harbour. Her case weighed heavy, but she held her head high, refusing to show discomfort. As she passed them, they jeered at her. One woman spat vulgarly. The saliva briefly met Sarah's cheek. She turned her head, sickened. Wiping the excess away with her forearm, without releasing her case, she walked on. She had no intention of rising to their bait. All she had to do was reach the ferry. Then she could put this sad and sorry chapter of her life behind her.

As she turned the corner, more Islanders were standing waiting for her in a long line, a gauntlet winding all along the stretch to the quayside ferry approach. The boat was late. Sarah shivered, acutely aware of how alone she was, how vulnerable. They heckled as she made her way slowly forward, closing in on her until she had to come to a stop, their heated jibes and hissing unbearable.

It was then she saw him. McGregor stood slightly apart from the crowd. Even then, she looked to him for a reassuring smile. The look on his face was bitter. He glowered at her, his hatred clear for all to see. And then she understood. He was their leader.

Her instinct was to turn and run, but there was nowhere to go, even if she could have broken through the barriers of bodies. The whole harbour had drawn inwards on her it seemed. There was nothing else for her to do, but stand and accept their ridicule, at least until the ferry arrived.

It was their Island.

The men stood behind the women. The children, those same children who had come to her school every day, and sat in her class, had lined up with their parents to jeer and taunt her. As she looked at their faces, at this vast sea of hate, she knew they were giving vent to the feelings they had felt for her all along.

"So Sarah, you'd leave us today?" McGregor threw his arms out theatrically, as though he were centre stage at some West End play.

Sarah's bravery had departed. Her throat dried. "Yes". The half-hearted effort died in her mouth. He stood staring at her, and she knew he was enjoying this sick charade. Their eyes bore into her. Their whisperings were more than she could stand. She prayed it would be over soon.

"There's been bad news, I'm afraid. The ferry's been postponed."

Sarah's spirit sank. "But why…? I didn't know."

His tone was pure venom. "How could you know?" And then she heard the triumph in his voice. "Wasn't I the one who postponed it?"

The crowd drew inwards again, and suddenly there was a feeling that anything, anything was possible. Sarah imagined herself being crushed to death there on the cobbled street, suffocating, compressed by the human mass until the last breath left her body. Her whole being shook. They forced in on all sides, until she was held fast by the mob, cocooned within their hatred. Then, just as suddenly, they withdrew.

Sarah was thrown into confusion. Had they finished their game? Or was there more to come?

Pastor McGregor spoke again, his tone far calmer now as he

approached. The crowd parted for him. "Don't worry, Sarah, you'll be leaving today as you'd hoped. Though perhaps not as you had intended."

Sarah relaxed. They had merely wished to remind her of their strength one last time before she left for good. They were as keen to get rid of her, as she was to leave. Most likely, they had arranged a small fishing boat. Sarah tried to look McGregor straight in the face, but was forced to turn away from the anger of his dented pride. She had done that. Warily she formed the question. "What do you mean? If there's no ferry…?"

He smiled for the briefest moment, and for a second Sarah recalled their very first meeting, the sweetness of it. "Follow me, Sarah, I'll show you."

There was something about his eagerness. She held back, pulling herself up to her full height. "No. I'll just go back to the cottage and wait till tomorrow."

Sarah realised her instinct had been right. What else could explain his low, meaningful tone?

"Sorry, Sarah but it's much too late for that."

Sarah cried out, oblivious to the watching eyes. "I won't go with you. You can't make me!"

He drew closer, grabbing her roughly by the arm. No matter how she fought, there would be no release. "Don't you see? You've already spoiled our plans for Aluinn for a while. We're not prepared to let you go as easily. On an Island like ours accidents, can and often do happen. Look at poor Morag last week, such a tragedy, a young girl drowning like that. But completely unavoidable, as I'm sure Aluinn told you."

He pulled her so close she had no choice but to look directly into his eyes, "Think about it, Sarah. Why do you think Aluinn wept so bitterly when she left? Why do you think she begged you to go with her?"

The Pastor's face twisted in shocking delight, as he taunted her. "How painful for her to see this day and know there was nothing she could do to prevent it. I hope any happiness she has found away from this place is marred by the guilt she feels…"

Sarah recalled her dream, understood Aluinn's' warning. But it was too late.

She must make him see sense. "Please, I just want to go home. They'll come looking for me if I don't get back."

"I agree, Sarah, they will, since it'll be such a 'tragic accident'."

Her body fought for the strength to resist the inevitable as he went on. "They can't argue with fate, can they? And who'll be able to say differently, when we're all together on it?"

Sarah screamed and with an almost superhuman strength broke free from his grip. She ran this way then that, looking for some way to escape. She heard their twisted laughter, saw their wide mouthed joy at her fear, and heard her own terrified screams as they lifted her body high in the air, suspended above the crowd.

They carried her, flailing wildly, her own terror almost drowned out by their excitement, to the very edge of the highest cliff, overlooking the harbour wall. Now she knew what her destiny was to be. That image in her dream became clear, Aluinn's face, pleading with her.

She would never see the child again. Sarah closed her eyes, shutting off the fear and the sights around her and pictured Aluinn's beautiful face. She felt a strange peace in her soul. It had been worth it.

Chapter Four

The small cemetery was tucked neatly away behind busy Edinburgh streets. Folk went about their business unaware of the mourning going on behind its ancient walls.

In return for the stories I had shared, Sarah had shared her own stories with me. So I knew many of the people standing by her grave. All around me, her people were weeping, bereft, still reeling from the shock of losing her. Sarah's mother, with great dignity in honour of her daughter, stood surrounded by her sisters, Sarah's aunts.

They held me responsible. I sensed their bitterness, felt how they shrank from me, as though I might cause some other calamity to befall them. There had been no anger, at least not openly. But the atmosphere was familiar like the sullen hostility I had endured for so long. I knew Sarah would not have wished her people to blame me. But their instincts hadn't deceived them. I *was* responsible. Unable to cry, I stood apart, my feelings of guilt bottomless. I wanted to scream, that I had loved her, that she had been my only friend.

The minister droned on, empty words that echoed on the damp air. I hoped the others found some solace in the ritual. My only comfort was that Sarah had accomplished what she had set out to do. I was free. She couldn't have known that I would carry the burden of her death for the rest of my life. No matter what the inquest said, her death had been no accident. Even after all I had suffered at their hands, I couldn't fathom that they had taken Sarah's life, just because I had gone.

Even in death she had taught me - I would never be safe amongst them. I could never return.

I wanted only to escape, but knew how disrespectful they would think me. Reluctantly I followed on to the wake. I'd just arrived at the small hotel when my fears were confirmed.

"Ally!"

In my grief, it took several seconds to register that she was talking to me. Wanting to forge a new identity I had shortened my name. I had liked it, sensing the freedom it gave me. The distance it gave me from the Island.

"Ally, I need to talk to you, dear."

Although we had never been introduced, Sarah's descriptions of her aunt Maud left me in no doubt that was who she was. The woman's brashness gave her away. Sarah had told me several stories of Maud's embarrassing and thoughtless antics. As she looked at me, I could see what Sarah had meant. Maud would be sure to *'do the right thing'*, regardless of the damage she inflicted.

Taking my arm, she pulled me none too gently to the side. "Nobody else will say it, Ally, so if falls to me. I know Sarah cared a great deal for you, but you must appreciate that things have changed now." You could almost smell her glee in being the bearer of unwelcome tidings.

I wanted to laugh aloud. Out of respect for Sarah's memory, I let her go on, sure that whatever she had to say, it would hurt. I had expected some thoughtless comment, not this eager, soul-destroying cruelty.

"Did you hear me, dear?" Obviously, my silence meant I hadn't been listening. "Let me put it bluntly, Ally, shall I?" The veneer fell away, revealing her true viper's colours.

"You can't stay on at Sarah's dear; it's just too painful for her mother. Every time she looks at you she remembers all she has lost. "I nodded. I had been expecting it, though I had hoped for a few days' grace. There was no thought of returning. I would stay in Edinburgh. Much as I missed the Island, its greenness, Sarah had lost her life there, for my sake. I would never let her down.

Maud smiled a smile she imagined to be friendly. She grabbed my arm roughly, so that her podgy fingers nipped my bones. "You do understand what I'm saying, don't you, dear? Best for all concerned if you make yourself disappear?" As I turned to walk away, I looked for Sarah's mother. We had shared almost two months together. I had watched her growing excitement at Sarah's impending return, first with confusion and then with understanding. So this was how mothers' felt about their daughters…

Across the room, our eyes met and held. I attempted a half smile, for I had grown to love her too. Sarah's mother looked away. Maud had enjoyed her meddling, but she was right for all that. It would be better if I left.

If only I could tell her how my *sight*, normally so clear, was blurred around those I loved. Ever since the appearance of the *bean-nighe* at Sarah's shoulder, I had been terrified of what would happen to her, allowing myself to hope that somehow her very goodness would save her, or that somehow I had been wrong. Besides, whatever happened, I was powerless to prevent it.

What good was there in adding my pain to the pain she already felt? The numbness overpowered me. I passed quickly through the room, the mourners a sea of dark shapes. Tears threatened. My mind's eye held the image of Sarah's face. Her words echoed in my head. "*You'll see, my family will love you just as much as I do. You'll never be alone there. As long as I live, you'll be safe.*"

I ran from the hotel, and along the cobbled streets, Maud's words thundering through my head. The rain fell relentlessly, the bitter north winds hammering the city. My mind felt battered too. There was no release from the hurt. I had lost Sarah, and that loss had opened up a whole world of pain. Instinctively I made my way to Arthur's Seat, ascending the long, winding route around the volcanic mass, half-blinded by tears as the denial I had been sheltering in gave way. She was gone, and it was my fault. Passers-by turned to look at me, a young girl, wide-eyed and tearful, traumatised by some dilemma or other. I longed to shut my brain down, scream, anything rather than face the pain so intense, the guilt so profound that I was afraid I was losing my mind.

Beyond hope, I found myself standing at the cliff face, looking out over the city, which filled the horizon. I looked out at Holyrood Palace, with the castle in the distance, all the landmarks I had grown to love.

New worlds to conquer, Sarah had said. Perhaps the grief and pain caused a blow out or a short fuse in my mind. For a brief moment, I was able to escape from my despair. Still standing on the red edge of the Seat, in my mind I escaped to the Island. Hovering somewhere over the pain, I stood on the sheer cliff, looking into the sea which now seemed to stretch far below, watching the kelpies in the spray. Mischievous, horse-like *taibhsean*, they rose on the waves, swayed violently by cold north winds, rising to the crest, their pleasure increasing with the violence of the water. When the wave broke they turned back, waiting for another tumult, never tiring of their game. As I looked down at the seabed, they called me to join them, to jump off the cliff into the water, where they were waiting for me. They lulled me as I watched them, increasing my longing to be gone, to be free of the pain forever.

Why did I hesitate, when no one cared whether I lived or died? I fought the turbulent emotions, my life force ebbing. But as the pull to join them grew greater, the *Connall* appeared at my side, breaking their spell.

"Mach A Seo!" he bellowed. "Be gone!"

They turned away at the sound of his voice, his anger resounding over the surface of the waves.

When I turned to thank him, he was gone.

*

Four years had passed. I had carved out a good life for myself, one the shy, scared girl who had left the Island would have been proud of. Every morning on rising I whispered a prayer that strengthened me, gave me hope. *"You kept your promise to me Sarah and I'll keep mine. I'll make you proud of me. Whatever the future holds, I won't be broken."*

I had few friends, was still afraid, perhaps, to give of myself. But I had been drawn to Lorna from the beginning. On my first day at the huge, complex insurance building, amongst the others in our intake, she had stood out. Physically, of course, but in other ways too. Tall and slender, she could easily have been a model. But Lorna would never have allowed herself to join a cattle market full of 'photogenic bimbos'. Like I said, she stood out.

Just to look at her people knew that Lorna went after what she wanted and got it. She had everything, with her near perfect body, her long limbs. But her real appeal wasn't in her clear skin or glossy hair.

She fooled everyone with her act, except me.

With that sixth sense that binds the vulnerable, I sensed the unhappiness behind the mask. Life had dealt her some blows. She longed, as we all do, for someone to love her, for acceptance. Perhaps she sensed a germ of that in me too; from the beginning she took me under her wing. Thanks to her rough kindness, we became mismatched friends, her brashness a foil for my shyness, my good sense a brake to her determination. We shared ambitions, clothes and secrets. She never made fun of me, not of my hair untouched by scissors, or the way I dressed, or of my painful naiveté. Gradually, imperceptibly, she moulded me until I passed as a city girl. I learned from Lorna, from her mistakes as well as her successes. Too well perhaps, till we were almost indistinguishable from each other. But in one particular we remained unalike. Lorna favoured careful promiscuity. I remained a virgin.

After Sarah's funeral it was Lorna I turned to. I knew she wouldn't turn me away. Sensing my despair, she took me in hand. Now she was more determined than ever to 'educate' me, or at least to stop me being hurt again. I became her project, as it were. She left no stone unturned in her quest to make me more 'sophisticated'. With the enthusiasm I had come to love in her, she shared what she knew with me, from shortcuts through the city centre, to fashion faux-pas and the foibles of the opposite sex. She gave her time to me and her wisdom.

Four years on, I still missed the Island, missed its calmness, that feeling of belonging to it. I found myself craving green, like a physical longing, a need to be out in the glory of it. Edinburgh's parks held little joy, hemmed in by the city skyline. Illusions of tranquillity might be all that the mainland folk required. For me it would never be enough. Those green spaces had little merit even as a momentary retreat. Could no one hear the traffic and the chaos roaring endlessly by?

I missed the quietness of the Island, its solitude. But I was aware too how dangerous my longing was. I had become someone who couldn't look back. So life moved on; neither one thing nor the other, a curious hybrid of city and sadness, I lived in a world between worlds.

My old life before was proving surprisingly difficult to leave behind. I had thought it would be easy, that a new beginning would be all it took. But the longer I was away from the Island, the more I realised it was a part of me – I had brought it with me. The values I found in the city, the anonymity of it…Sometimes it was all I could do to accept that people would chose to live that way. And so I lived in a kind of self- imposed limbo, disconnected from those around me, dislocated from my home.

It hadn't taken long to realise that the Island was not all that had come with me. My gift of sight was as active here as at home. At times I could barely differentiate between what was real, and what existed only in *Darna Sealladh.*. My friend Connall I had not seen since the day of Sarah's funeral, when he had saved me. But I saw other *taibhsean* . It amazed me that those around me could be so blinkered to their existence.

Many were spirits which had never passed – ancient spirits some of them, often from the tribe whose home the city had once been. Others more recent, but all alienated from those they wanted to be with. Some days, when I kept myself busy and got myself out of myself, I was only vaguely aware of them. On other days my line of vision was so blurred almost all I could see were those beings.

*

Lorna saved my sanity. I owed her so much, trusted her. With her I felt able *almost* to be fully me. So much so that sometimes I would let my guard down. Then I would feel her look at me strangely. But Lorna knew what it was to keep a secret and let me keep mine. We settled into a pattern, working hard weekdays, partying hard at weekends. Lorna always found ways to entertain herself. She said she saw her life afresh through my curious eyes, relishing my delight at the simplest pleasures life in a city offered, my wonder at what each day would bring.

Some things Lorna preferred to know in advance. Sitting crossed legged on the floor, wine glass filled as far as the laws of physics would allow, she shuffled a pack of tarot cards, inexpertly but with her usual enthusiasm. Having completed her own spread to her satisfaction – she should be wary of a tall, dark, handsome stranger - she had begun reading mine. That was one of the things I loved most about her – her openness, her eagerness for all things possible.

The wine must have already been loosening my tongue as she laid the cards out on the dirty carpet. Normally I went along with everything she said, but the drink made me brave.

"Leave it be, Lorna. You know I don't believe in this stuff…"

"What do you believe in then, Ally? Everyone has to believe in *something*. I was sure when I met you you'd be all Wee Free church. But it's not a church thing with you – pathetic virgin though you are."

I heard her laughing in…bemusement? Was that the word I was looking for? Sometimes my English failed me, even now. Not a church thing, no…but behind the safety of my closed eyelids I could see the Broch in the sunshine, light pouring through it in golden shafts, creating a cathedral effect.

"One card, Ally, just one – to see whether I can't get a better handle on you. You're such a closed book sometimes."

What was the harm? Feeling like a magician's assistant, I sucked some of the red wine between my teeth and drew a card from the spread laid out at random.

Turning it over, I stared at the upside down image of the Tower, trying to fathom it.

Lorna, delighted I'd given in to her, was thumbing through her book to find the explanation. "Got it! 'Throughout our lives'," she read seriously, 'we strive to find our sense of self. We attract people, places and things to us that help us to maintain and project what we believe that identity to be. Piece by piece, brick by brick, we build our ego, represented here by the Tower.'

I turned the image round to face me. It was strangely disturbing. Something terrible had happened to the Tower - a sudden, shattering bolt of lighting had broken it in two, making it fall. Two figures, one male, one female, were being thrown from it. I had a sense of them dying in the air. "The two figures are symbolic of our dual nature," Lorna explained, taking a generous swig from her greasy glass, and grinning at me. "The Tower is often drawn when something bad has happened to the querant. It symbolises loss, when someone has deliberately set out to damage or destroy something we hold dear. It is the card of deep trauma."

I could feel tears forming in my eyes. Try as I might, I couldn't take my eyes from the female figure on the card, freefalling through the air, fiery red hair tumbling around her body. Hair like mine. Her face was curiously impassive, as though she was willing herself not to feel the fear. Like me. My world too had fallen apart. I knew exactly what she was feeling, how it felt to be so rejected, to lose everything you loved, to plummet powerlessly through the days.

For the first time I understood my sense of isolation. In leaving the Island, I had lost my identity.

Lorna was still wittering on, oblivious to the pain coursing through me. "When the Tower card is reversed in a reading it symbolizes the querant's refusal to crack under strain, pressure or shock. Very often it depicts someone who has armour plated themselves in order to survive a situation."

For the first time she looked at me instead of her book, head to one side, looking at me strangely. "That sounds like you alright, Ally. You've bricked yourself in emotionally."

It wasn't meant cruelly. Amazing. I had gone all those years, locking the pain away, my psyche cleverly shielding me from the worst of it, allowing me to function. And one stupid card was enough to breach the dam. But now it was breached, all the pain came flooding out.

In between the tears and sobbing explanations, my story came out. Falteringly, feeling more vulnerable than I ever had before, I began to share, barely aware of her coming over to me. Placing her warm arm over my shoulder, she whispered to me. "Look, start at the very beginning, not here, but way back when you were little. I want you to tell me everything…I don't care if we sit here all night."

I retold my life, year by painstaking year. The physical abuse distressed her, but it was the mental torture …seen through her eyes I wondered how I had withstood it. By the time I had finished the dawn filled the empty streets.

I skimmed over the details of Sarah's death, still unable to share them fully.

"And you've not been home since?" Dismay was written all over her face. I didn't protest when she pulled me closer, stroking my hair and making soothing noises as though I were still the neglected bairn I had described to her.

It was as if, just like the Tower on the card, *all* my barriers had come down. And we had shared almost three bottles of wine. "I've not really been alone, Lorna, no…" She was looking at me steadily. *Did I dare…?*

It came out in a rush, the secret I had kept so long. "Have you ever heard of the *Darna Sealladh*, the second sight?

"You mean like those old Highland seers who are supposed to be able to predict the future? You're not telling me you…?" Incredulity made her almost move back from me. Or was it fear? Whichever, it was soon replaced by utter glee as she wrapped me in a smothering embrace. "I always knew you were different, Ally McPhail, but I never thought for a moment you were as strange as all that. Tell me all about it. What do you see? Is it visions? Spirits? Tell me everything!" I was angry at myself now. I had betrayed the Gift. How could Lorna be expected to understand this blessing I had been cursed with?

She sensed my hesitation immediately "Don't welch on me now, Ally– help me understand it." I knew she wouldn't be happy until her curiosity was satisfied. Lorna had a positive hatred for anything unexplained or unfathomable. No withdrawal would be possible once the interrogation had begun. Shifting to a more comfortable position, I was still determined to play it down.

"It's no big deal, Lorna, really. It's much the same for me as switching on a TV is for you. They are there for me to watch should I wish to. But if I choose *not* to see them I can pull the plug almost, knowing they're waiting for me. They can't escape, you see, any more than I could or would wish to go join them, or be fully in their existence."

As I thought, Lorna wasn't satisfied with such a superficial reply. "But it's not TV, Ally, it's so much bigger than that." Taking a hearty sip of her wine she savoured the taste, before adding keenly, "It's like ET and Peter Pan or Alice in Wonderland all mixed up together. It's everything I'd like to experience and more. Can you teach me Ally?"

She had no clue what she was asking.

"Sorry, Lorna. It's not something you're taught."

"What do they look like, Ally? Do they all look the same?"

Did Lorna want total honesty? Or was this just more curiosity?

"Not how you'd imagine, Lorna. It's not all tinker bells and funny little men with exaggerated hats and pointed shoes."

Her enthusiasm refused to die. "So what *are* they like? You have to give me that at least. It's bad enough that they're there and I can't see them, when I'd love to!"

That glorified image she had couldn't have been further from the truth. "You say you wish for the gift, but you should be thankful it's not yours. For once you are in their grasp, you see them for what they really are. Image shifters, changing shape to suit their moods. They display their good humour in sheaths of finest threads. But just as quickly they can turn grotesque, tattered and ragged, or deformed and skeletal. Worse, if they become angry." I shivered mentally.

"Sometimes, Lorna, they can frighten you. They're trapped, confused by time. They know neither happiness nor sorrow, nor fear nor elation. They're simply there, eternally, wondering at us, often laughing cynically at what we're striving to do. They've seen it all, you see, watched it all down the centuries, since time began and they'll continue to watch longer after we're gone. There is no time as we know it there. They exist on a different plane. The way I see it, it's as if they've been swallowed whole, sucked through the looking glass. Joining them in their own realm and being accepted there was just a …rite of passage. I couldn't not do it, though I often didn't – don't – want to. "

I was angry then, hating the fact that I joined them there alone.

Lorna was looking at me, bewildered. For the first time I was seeing her upset. I softened my tone, realising she was sad for me, because *I saw* what she did not. "The ones I'm talking about, the ones who really frighten me are few and far between, though at times I'm forced to meet without warning." I didn't dare tell her about the others, those terrifying ones that tried so often to seek me out. I guarded myself against them, refusing for the most part to acknowledge their displays of strength. Draining my glass, I picked up the bottle and poured myself another, just to buy myself a moment. In my mind's eye, I revisited them, unable to prevent my mind from conjuring up images of things I could not afford to dwell on. The image changers harboured thoughts. Thoughts that transferred to me and weighed heavily - lustful thoughts, or thoughts of death, desire for the suffering of others. Just a glimpse of them could cause Lorna to lose her mind. Sometimes I was aware that they were fracturing my own thinking.

Sometimes, when the weight of them grew very heavy, it was as if splinters of my soul were sharding their way into my mind.

Lorna refused to let it go, despite my discomfort. Surely, she sensed my pain? It was not simply a tale. It was my life being ripped apart.

"What purpose do they serve Ally? There has to a rational explanation?"

"There is no rational to that which existed long before man. How can you conceive the two are somehow connected? There is no line to cross, no barrier to see, but it exists none the less. No time, no matter – the laws we live by don't apply. Unless you think I'm imagining it all?"

The kohl around her eyes was streaked, her eyes a little bloodshot. "You must admit it's a bit out there, Ally. I mean, if we told the others at work they'd think you were mad."

That cut close to the bone. Terrified of her response, I asked the question I had long feared. "Do *you* think I'm mad Lorna?" *Was* there something wrong with me, something *visible* that people could sense?

For a breathless moment, she looked at me. "No Ally, I don't. I believe you. I believe because I want to. I look at you and I see somebody very different to anyone I've ever known. You have this *look* about you…" She reached over to hug me tightly, trying to comfort me in my strangeness. "You've always been honest with me, spoken the truth, so how can I not believe you?"

Part of me wished I could take back my truth, say, "I was just having you on." But to deny it would bring ill. "You won't tell the others will you? It's hard enough trying to fit in here. That would be cruel, Lorna." And I knew there was a streak of cruelty in her. The unspoken accusation hung in the air.

"Don't worry, Ally, I've no wish to hurt you. I'm your friend – always. Never forget that."

That last drink, and my gratitude, had me throwing my arms around her. "I'm so grateful to you Lorna, not just for this. I've never told you this, but when Sarah died I thought I'd never trust another living soul. I thought I would spend the rest of my life lonely. And you changed that."

Leaning my head drunkenly against hers, I was whispering now."I prayed the *bean-nighe* would take me. *I swear, I taunted her night after night by the Seat but she* never sought me out. My despair turned to frustration, then to anger and bitterness. I don't know where my life would have headed, what path I would have followed if you hadn't rescued me."

Lorna laughed, more to soften the hurt I had felt then than to hurt me now. "Dear Lord Ally, how you go on, all I did was show you around a bit."

"That's all it was to you, but to me it was a lifeline. Stopped me drowning in my own misery. You saved my life." I was slurring now. "Maybe someday I'll do likewise."

It was good to hear her laughter, despite all the feelings within. "Not anytime soon I hope. This conversation has turned rather morbid, Ally. No more wine for you. "

The bottles were empty anyway. We fell exhausted into Lorna's unmade bed, Lorna captivated by all she'd learned and I …oddly relieved to have shared my truth.

We failed to see it yet, but those hours had bonded us together more strongly than ever before. Confiding in Lorna grounded me. The pain of loneliness, the fear of having only myself to rely on in this world, disappeared for a time.

That night I slept peacefully.

Chapter Five

It hadn't been wrong to tell her. Even with a hangover, I felt *liberated* inside, as if old fears had been wiped away. As I stepped off at the bus stop closest to the office, I felt mellow, unhurried. People bustled about their very ordinary business. I wondered at the new sense of calm I felt.

That was my mood – that *tranquillity*, that sense of peace, when I saw his face for the first time.

He appeared out of nowhere. Our paths literally crossed.

I actually stopped, just to look at him, feeling the pull - almost physical – the sense of being drawn by him. The sensation threw me. It had never happened before. It was as if I was *compelled* to follow him, pride overpowered by a fear of losing him in the surge of commuters. I *had* to find out where he was going. The suddenness and severity of the urge both amazed and terrified me. Following him into the morning sunlight he seemed almost vision like. It was the strangest feeling until, straining my eyes to find him, I knew exactly *why* I was feeling such a connection. He reminded me of the *Connall*.

All those years on the Island, my guardian spirit had been kinder to me than any mortal ever had been. Little wonder I had grown to love him. Despite his prediction, I had not forgotten him, just grown to accept that we couldn't be together as we had been. And now this man, who resembled him so physically, had besotted me instantly and completely.

Part of me was afraid to follow him, to speak to him, in case the resemblance ended in the physical, in case he wasn't worthy of standing in the Connall's shadow. And part of me knew I didn't care.

As we turned into the complex where I worked he disappeared. My wonder turned to panic. How could I have lost him? How would I ever find him again? And yet he had turned in here. Was it too ridiculous, too sublime to think he worked in the same building as me? There he was, climbing the steps ahead of me. I followed, shaking, trying hard not to make it look like I was stalking him.

Up close, the resemblance to my childhood saviour was less striking.

He had the same confident air as he strode ahead of me, the same sense of ease with himself. His body was lean and fit. Everything about him was neat, particular almost, his suit well cut, his shoes polished. I wasn't the only girl who noticed him. As we walked through the foyer, other women turned to admire him. He seemed oblivious.

Terrified to lose him again, I hurried past several women I worked with. Distractedly, I noted their confusion at my hurried, 'Hello', but I had no time to explain. I didn't even know why I was pursuing this man, almost despite myself. All I wanted was to be close to him.

He walked straight to the lift, and then stood, waiting for it to open. I stood alongside him, hoping he couldn't hear my shallow breathing, staring at his reflection in the shiny metal which protected the lift shaft. In it, his hair was raven black and shiny, his eyes the deepest brown. His mouth was perfect, his face clean-shaven. I could smell his scent as I stood there next to him and it was as though I had been roused from a deep sleep. With it had come an awakening of all my senses, heightening them to a new level. Until then men had held no real interest for me. Now I was mesmerised. I took in the shape of his hands, the strength of his jaw line, the sheer magnetism of his body. I thralled at the new emotion he stirred in me, even as I named it. Desire. That was it; I wanted to be his.

The lift doors opened, we stepped inside and took up our positions, side-by-side, but slightly apart. I stood silently, desperately hoping he would say something, anything. He smiled at me, once, as he left the confines of the small compartment, a glorious smile, a smile so vibrant, so beautiful I fell in love with a man whose name I didn't know.

I was at my desk, feeling bewildered and excited, when the others arrived, ready to start another day. Office life was so dreary, any hint of gossip was seized upon. They were circling, ready to pounce with a hundred questions. My emotions already out of kilter, I decided to head off any questions before they even began.

"Morning, Molly. How are you today?" I asked, in a voice far cheerier than even I expected. Dear Molly our supervisor was the Miss Prim of the establishment. Everything done by the book, always on time, policies had to be adhered to…Yet she had a sweetness of nature I had come to appreciate.

"Very well, Ally, since you ask," said Molly, unravelling the scarf she was never seen without. "And you? You looked a bit *strange* earlier as you passed us."

If only Molly wasn't so damned easy to talk too. "Actually, Molly, I'm feeling a bit befuddled."

Molly frowned, pausing with her fingers on the buttons of her jacket. "Befuddled?"

"Earlier, when I passed you all, it was because I was desperate to find out who he was."

"Who *who* was?" asked Molly, puzzled.

How could she not have noticed him? "Don't joke, Molly, the guy who passed you just before I did."

Molly's sweet but she's not the sharpest tack in the box. She sat down heavily, replaying the earlier episode in her head. "I swear Ally, I didn't see anyone else. I thought you were on your own."

"Oh Molly, it was only seconds ago. I was right behind him…"

"Sorry Ally, I wish I could say I saw him, but I can't. Perhaps Sue or Vanessa noticed."

Hearing their names mentioned the two women looked our way. "Morning Ally, you looked in a hurry to get to that desk of yours." No one liked Vanessa, not really. She was a bitch both in character and in work related matters. She thought nothing of treading on toes if it served her own purpose. She reminded me of a bloodhound. A bloodhound dressed in a too-short skirt. It was as though she could smell a good piece of gossip…

Much as I hated divulging my crush, I needed *someone* to verify how amazing he was. I tried to play it down. "Actually," I said, fussing with my hair, a ploy I often used to cover up my confusion, "I'm trying to find out the name of the guy I walked in behind this morning."

They both looked at each other in confusion.

"You must have seen him? Tall, dark, off the graph handsome… how could you not? Are you just trying to wind me up?"

Molly smiled. "Ally, how could you think such a thing? If we'd seen him we'd say so. Surely you saw how surprised we were when you rushed by. We thought we'd offended you in some way."

What was this, some April's Fool joke? But her confused expression told me she was telling me the truth. Vanessa was already shrugging the incident off as further proof of me being even more 'strange' than usual.

Reapplying her already too bright lipstick, she grimaced at her compact mirror. "What's the story with this guy anyway? Why were you in such a rush to follow him?"

I wished then I had kept my mouth shut. If she got even an inkling of how I was feeling she would no doubt find him and set him straight on my 'weirdness'. He would never take me seriously then.

I lied. "I'm not looking for me. Lorna wanted to find out more about him, you know what she's like."

My explanation satisfied her. She started droning on about last night's telly. Half-listening, my mind returned to the image of his face. I had to find him. He had gotten off two floors down. I needed an excuse to go there. The offices throughout the building were open plan. If I could come up with a reason for visiting his floor, I might be able to spot him from a safe distance. With any luck, I'd know some of his colleagues and could spear them for information. I was already walking towards the lift when I thought to swipe some paper from the photocopier, so that I wasn't roaming around the building like a complete stalker.

The activity level on his floor took some getting used to, the endless clicking of fingers on keyboards, the continuous flicker of the monitor screens. It was good to know some people actually worked in the building: I recognised a few faces, high profile managers with egos to match their status, but he was nowhere to be seen. Phones rang, people bustled about from one section to another. Everyone appeared focused. And the one face I wished for remained hidden.

I did a complete circuit, taking in several departments. Heads turned as I passed. I smiled sweetly, praying no one would ask what I was doing there. Having gone full circle, I admitted defeat.

He must work in the Executive, otherwise I would have seen him. I left, feeling cheated. I sat staring at my in-tray, knowing there were things I should be doing. But I couldn't put the thought of him out of my head. What if I *did* find him? What then? I had never made any attempts to attract a man before. The taunts of my childhood weighed so heavy, I had forgotten I was a creature whose hormones now dictated procedure.

Lorna had arrived late as usual. She was used to me being quiet, but even she picked up on my mood when I had hardly spoken for much of the day. For some reason, although I shared so much with her, I was unwilling to tell her about my mystery man.

I counted down the minutes till five o'clock. Lorna tried to jolly me out of it in her usual bubbly way. "What d'you want to do after work? Pub?" She jumped up onto my desk, unconcerned by Molly's prudish tut-tutting as her skirt rose up to reveal even more leg. She messed with her hair, fixing loose strands, knowing full well, no one around had the nerve to chide her. They'd get a tongue-lashing if they dared. Lorna was used to getting away with murder. No one wanted to be on the receiving end of her sharp tongue. Her conduct had earned her verbal warnings thanks to a teller of tales both faceless and nameless we were both sure was Vanessa. If Lorna ever found out for sure, the repercussions would be endless. Once she held a grudge, it never diminished. Time held no meaning for her.

It didn't seem to be holding her back at work any. Lorna had far greater ambition than me. If the opportunity arose, Lorna took it. And that, ironically, was her undoing. She had been passed over time and time again for being too pushy. Every time it happened, she said she wished she were more like me, saying I had 'what it took'. Could she not see how terrified I was at the prospect, how I feared the spotlight? I'd even been asked to take part in a publicity campaign for the company. The thought of having my image splattered across buses and on the side of buildings – I dreaded what it would bring about. The *taibhsean* would be drawn by my discomfort, *taibhsean* I had no wish to provoke or disturb. I knew nothing must draw attention to me, otherwise the precious freedom I had would be shattered. I had no wish to be known by the masses, as Lorna did. My life was complicated enough.

Lorna broke my reverie. "I've had a nightmare day, Ally. I really *need* to go for a drink. What do you say?"

I was still so focused on *him*, on feeling physically deprived by his absence, that I had to force myself to speak. "Sounds great, I have everything I need with me. We can head straight from here if you like?"

She jumped off the desk, giving a flash of her candy pink knickers. Then she was off.

We met up after clocking out and headed straight to the toilets, glad to find them empty. We fooled around as we always did, our laughter loud, as Lorna liberally practiced her impersonation of Vanessa as she applied several coats of make up, firstly on her own face, then on mine. Try as I would, I still hadn't mastered the art. I liked it all the same. It gave me a mask to hide behind.

We quickly dressed in our minimal outfits, polluting the room with clouds of CFC gases from our hairspray. When we were done, I stared in the mirror.

There were moments like this when I hardly recognised myself. Apart from my hair, which I had learned to tame into glossy ringlets, there was very little of the 'Island Aluinn' in my reflection. I looked no different to countless other young girls in the city, but I couldn't help thinking how the Islanders would disapprove of me, of the way I was living my life. I looked like Lorna, almost her clone, but for me it was an outward disguise. She was still everything I wished to be; confident, beautiful, daring, sexy.

Deep inside, I was the same; nothing had changed.

When Lorna had pronounced herself satisfied with our transformation, we made our way towards Princes Street, through Leith, then along Lothian Road towards the Grass Market. Our usual pub-crawl.

How many times had we taken the same route on a night out? Yet as I saw myself reflected in a store window, for a split second, I saw myself through my mother's eyes – cheap, tawdry, whore like. I felt embarrassed, almost as if her eyes were upon me. Illogical as the thought was, it accompanied me often. Why should I fear her reactions any more? But no matter how long I had been living my new life, I still believed someday she might arrive to march me straight back home.

Thoughts of my mother disappeared amongst wolf whistles from every hot bloodied male we passed. With heightened confidence, we entered the first pub on our route, *The Auld Hundred* in Rose Street. Despite my bravado, Dutch courage was still the order of the day. When I had the first drink in my system I always relaxed, ready for anything.

The bar's décor was far from tasteful, but it didn't matter. We would have stayed supposing it was drab and empty. There was no one there, except a couple of older men in workmen's clothes, hands etched with plaster and grime, engrossed in a game of space invaders. The drink was all we were after.

The lounge had one of those new-fangled large-screen TVs playing all the latest up to the minute videos. We enjoyed our drink, excitement building in us. The barman eyed us up, a pet hate of mine. His eyes were like slits in his lecherous face. He even wet his lips with his tongue when we came in. Repulsed, I moved my seat, giving him a fine view of the back of my head. Lorna laughed, understanding my action, but not fully understanding my annoyance. She smiled at him, always hopeful there would be a free drink headed her way.

She leaned towards me, teasingly. "You're in a strange mood today. Lighten up, Ally, we're out to enjoy ourselves, remember? Good time girls, that's us!"

I moved closer, so that only she heard, my voice no more than a whisper. "Lecherous old goat. I don't know how you can bear to give him the come on." Everyone sets their own standards, and Lorna knew mine were higher than most.

She pulled a face, making me smile. It instantly defused the awkwardness. "Look, you're not stuck on your little Island now! This is Edinburgh. People don't mind how you behave here. Do you honestly think they'll care?" Lorna ducked down low under the table and gazed back up at me, whispering in a mock-frightened voice, "Or is there some mysterious force, watching you out and about enjoying yourself?"

I stiffened, full of regret for having told her, though I knew she meant nothing by the remark. I shrugged. "I can't help how I am. Things happen here that would never be allowed where I come from."

"Well then," she smiled, placing her hand reassuringly on my shoulder, "I think you should think yourself very lucky that you're here and not there."

If only she knew how right she was. I loved her spirit, her joy in life. She was in so many ways the opposite of what I had grown up with. Why take that away from her with tales of things that had to be experienced to be understood?

I took a slow sip from my glass and smiled at her. "I count my blessings every day I'm here." Even voicing the thought was difficult, as though I was broaching some unwritten taboo by criticising the Island. "But you heard me last night, Lorna. It's *hard* to shake off the old ways. I lived under rules and restrictions all through my life. It's hard to let go."

She had seen me like this several times in the past, mostly alcohol induced. After last night, she knew better than to goad me. She pulled another face, her way of making light of my reply. Without malice, just to lift my sombre mood. "Poor Ally," she teased. "Tell you what; let me buy you another drink to make you feel better."

Watching her undulate her way sensually towards the bar, I took it for granted she wouldn't be asked to pay for her drink, even if she was made to pay for her arrogant friend's. As usual, she took her time, flirting with the barman. Her laughter was infectious, but not as pleasing to him as the ample cleavage he was ogling. I sat lost in my thoughts, barely conscious of the solid oak door opening, the movement of air touching my cheek.

Lorna rejoined me, inhaling deeply on a cigarette. "What a sleazebag, but at least I got my drink," she smiled, tapping its glowing tip into the ashtray. Turning around, she waved her glass in the air by way of a 'thank you'. "There, he's happy now. As if I'd look at him, baldy auld pervert."

We laughed at his vanity, and toasted Lorna's skill in using his gullibility to her advantage. She was amazing. "I wish I had more of your confidence," I groaned.

"I've worked hard to perfect this role, Ally. You have to fake it to make it. You're gorgeous; you should work it more." She seemed satisfied with her nugget of wisdom, inhaling again and blowing smoke circles in the air, satisfied she'd had the last word.

"Excuse me?"

We both turned towards the voice.

It was him.

Here, as if by magic. Asking if we could help him.

I gazed at him, dumbstruck. Lorna had no such inhibitions. "Hello there. What is it you want to know?" she said, in her sexiest voice. I sat there like a sack of grain as she chatted animatedly to him, her body language making her attraction clear.

She *liked* him. Lorna liked him too. My whole body was crying an alarm as I watched the two of them together. If she wanted him I stood no chance. But I would fight for him, even against Lorna, I knew that. Watching his dark head lower to hers to catch what she was saying, I knew I would risk our friendship without a second thought.

If he didn't notice me soon I'd erupt. Why couldn't I say something? If I didn't speak soon, join in, my behaviour would seem not just sullen but irrational. But my head was competing with my body, which was screaming for me to just throw myself at him. I wanted him so badly, I was convinced he could sense it.

Another thought sideswiped me. What if he didn't like either of us?

Lorna leant forward, the better to display her 'prize assets' as she called them. I was jealous, angry, and terrified, all at once. "You can join us if you like." At her invitation, he took a seat between us, easy confidence spilling from him, but with such a lack of arrogance, no one could have been offended. I stared at him, transfixed, but Lorna had all his attention.

"My name's Cormac. I haven't been in town very long." Watching him run strong, slim fingers through his hair I was mesmerised how it automatically fell back into perfect shape. "I don't know my way around, so I'm hoping you two girls could give me a few pointers, where to go and what to avoid. You could save me a lot of wasted time and energy."

Lorna answered for us, twirling a lock of her hair round her finger as she mapped out all the cool places to go. I was glad, sure I would have made a complete fool of myself if I had tried to speak. He was so handsome, so secure in himself. I wanted him to look at me, but at the same time, I was terrified. Insatiable, I watched all his mannerisms, the tiny dimple in his cheek when he smiled, the way his thick dark hair was moved... I wanted to reach over and run my fingers through it, feeling the richness of it. His beautiful brown eyes stayed on Lorna's pretty face. I hated her then.

Up till now he had avoided looking at me completely. Was I overreacting, or was he refusing to make eye contact with me?

I was bewildered for another reason. When I met new people I usually had an innate sense of them, their history, their nature, what lay ahead for them. I didn't seek the information, it simply came to me. Its absence was glaring now. For some reason I could neither see ahead of nor behind this man.

It didn't feel wrong, just mystifying. Perhaps the strength of my feelings was clouding my *sight*. Whatever the reason, it made him more intriguing to me. I waited impatiently for him to acknowledge me, but he was utterly engrossed in Lorna. If he didn't turn and talk to me soon, his own behaviour would be bordering on rude.

Nothing.

Livid, I stood up and headed towards the *Ladies*. Angry thoughts circled my mind.I was annoyed with Lorna, but mostly with myself. *Why couldn't I just open my mouth? Why wouldn't he talk to me?*

The pain of his rejection was like a physical thing. I lashed out at the solid wall with my shoe, instantly regretting it as the pain connected with my head. Yet in a strange way, that pain was more acceptable than the emotional turmoil I was in. I paced backwards and forwards across the tiled floor, cursing myself for behaving like an imbecile.

I caught sight of myself in the mirror. All I saw was stupidity. "You're a fool, Aluinn McPhail!" I scolded my reflection. "He must think you witless."

Just that morning I had marched round his offices for a tiny glimpse of him. Yet there he was, not two feet away from me and I had sat there like a wet weekend.

Several deep breaths later, feeling a little calmer, I retouched my makeup. By the time I had finished I mustered up enough courage to go back and join them. I was determined to speak to him.

But he was gone. The only sign he had ever been there was an unfinished pint glass, ironically left next to my own drink. Totally deflated, convinced I had missed my one chance, I sat down heavily. Lorna seemed cheery enough.

"He was nice, dead chatty. He asked your name by the way."

Angry at her simple assessment of him, I could barely force the words over my lips. "He did?"

"He works beside us, can you believe it? Said he'd seen you there. Imagine, a gorgeous guy in the building, instead of all those po-faced, middle-aged, fat-bellied, leering halfwits we normally have to contend with."

Lorna calmly lit another cigarette. "Here's a laugh. He said you must like your job because you were always too busy to notice him! Can you imagine – you loving your job. That's a first!" She laughed as she finished her drink. I found myself laughing too, my mood instantly lifted. I moved forward on my seat, unable to hide my excitement.

"When did he see me?" Even as I spoke, I knew I sounded too enthusiastic. Lorna sensed my eagerness, and eyed me suspiciously.

"He works in Auditing, next door to old Saunders. He saw you when you went in to take those memos up. He works as a something or other, I can't remember. He said it so quickly, I didn't quite catch it," Lorna said satisfied.

"No wonder I never noticed him! That old goat always gives me such a hard time, I'm scared to look anywhere but at my feet." I could feel myself blushing. Lorna stared at me closely, as though she had tried to answer the question before she asked it. "Why did you go diving away like that? Cormac told me to apologise to you. He thought he'd intruded. "

She spaced her words evenly, as though she sensed I was hiding something. "You feeling okay?"

I shrugged, thoughts tumbling through my head. If he had asked about me, surely that meant there was hope? Had he been too shy to talk to me, and taken my silence as lack of interest? It must have taken courage for him to approach us in the first place. And I had sent out all the wrong signals. But at least I knew now knew where to find him. I'd find him, try and clear up any misunderstandings.

Lorna, bored now, wanted to move on.

We hit the town. Most places we went, people recognised us, and moved up to let us sit with them. I had no conversation, thought only of him. As soon as was decent, I made my excuses and left.

Chapter Six

The following morning I had somehow managed to procure the agony of a hangover. I forced my unwilling body up off the bed, steadying myself on the edge, working up the courage to take those first, unsteady steps towards the toilet. The sheer effort for the simplest of tasks was excruciating. Movements out of synch, dressing became a feat of co-ordination. The beating inside my head was excruciating, made worse by the knowledge it would be hours before it felt tolerable. The thought of applying makeup was just too much to contemplate. I grabbed my sunglasses, checking Lorna was awake before I closed the door of the flat.

On the bus to work everything around me was loud and intrusive, the constant drone of the engine, the kids chattering, the radio playing thumping music I had enjoyed the previous evening. On top of that, there was an obnoxious, pimply youth bragging about his exploits the night before. I wanted to scream at everyone to shut up, but that would have required too much effort on my part. Even the thought of it caused tiny stabs of pain inside my head.

I got off the bus early, desperate to be free of the confines of the bus and glad of the fresh air. I needed a chance to distance myself, to think for a few minutes before work. There was no great rush. I had arrived early. If I hadn't made that effort of will when I first woke, seized that one surge of energy, I would most likely have been laid in bed all day, coiled tightly into a ball, promising myself I would never, ever, do that to myself again.

My pay packet wouldn't have been able to stand the loss of a day's wages when I first joined the company, so I had made myself an unwritten rule then that being hospitalised was the only reason for missing work. You could just as easily let the hangover wear off there, where you were being paid to be. Still, I was thankful no one was about as I made my way to my desk. I set it out in such a way that I would look busy, even if I had to head for the loo, to rid myself of the evidence of my 'enjoyable evening'.

The office began filling around me. The painkiller I had taken appeared to have smoothed away the mere edges of the discomfort to a more humane level. By first break I felt half human glad to have made the effort, rather than staying in bed, all guilt ridden and sorrowful. Lorna met up with me in the canteen for coffee, looking even worse than me. Her face was devoid of makeup, her hair tightly scraped back into a ponytail, instead of the usual, immaculate bob she favoured. She was wearing dark glasses like mine. Who did we think we were fooling?

"I see you made it in then."

She lowered her glasses, revealing her tired eyes, and then quickly pushed them back again. "Only just. Why on earth didn't you stop me taking that complete idiot home last night, Ally?"

I had forgotten about the guy. Poor Lorna! As far as my memory served, and it wasn't exactly crystal clear, I had tried to do just that. "I warned you at the time, but last night you thought he was gorgeous."

We squeezed into an empty table, far enough away from the usual crowd.

"I must've been really bad." She sunk her head onto the table and soothed away the pain with a gentle massage.

Gingerly I removed my glasses. Squinting at the sunlight, I was pleasantly surprised to find I could bear it. "Don't be too hard on yourself, Lorna. I'm feeling lousy as well, even if I did manage to go home on my own. How much did we drink?"

Lorna drunk her coffee slowly before she replied, "Quite a bit, and of course Mr Hyde bought us a few."

"Hadn't turned back into Dr Jekyll by morning then?"

Lorna raised her voice slightly. "I wish!" Immediately she put her hand to her head, as though hoping the pain would magically disappear. "No such luck, I'm afraid. Thankfully, he was so out of it he fell asleep before me. I kept my pride intact. If I'd slept with him I'd really be feeling bad! Saying that, he did have the cheek to try his luck this morning, then cursed me for putting him out of the door before I got ready for work!"

Her laughter was infectious. I laughed with her, rejoicing in her honesty. She was so straightforward, never took any nonsense from anyone.

My stomach still out of sorts. I only managed a small amount of the black coffee, pocketing a plain biscuit for later, once my spirits had lifted.

"Good morning, ladies. Do you mind if I join you?"

I recognised the voice immediately, turning towards it instantly. There he stood, smiling that beautiful smile.

I sank down in my seat, aware I looked seriously worse for wear. Lorna answered for us both. This time I was glad; there was nothing working its way from my brain to my lips. I did manage to keep looking at him though, and caught his eye for the very first time. I even managed a smile, suddenly forgetting I was still under par. He smiled back, seeming pleased.

The longer I looked at him, the more I became aware that I couldn't break the hold of his stare. I was transfixed, spellbound. I held his eyes. I wanted to be the only one he looked at. The only one he wanted to be with. I needed to know everything about him. I vowed under my breath that if he was ever mine he would never leave me.

He seemed reluctant to break our eye contact too. And before he did there was something in his eyes that told me I had the power within me to captivate him. But when would I have the chance to try?

He put out his hand. I took it. He held mine slightly longer than necessary, and my cheeks reddened because I knew then he knew how I felt. To hide my embarrassment I spoke quickly. "Good to see you again."

I pulled my hand out of his grasp, turning my eyes downwards. Picking up my cup, I turned away slightly, looking out of the window, as if something of interest had caught my eye. He and Lorna had a short conversation. I did my damndest to pretend I wasn't listening. Finally he turned back to me. "I don't suppose there's any chance you two will be repeating last night's indulgence again soon?"

I was so glad Lorna was there. If there was one thing she couldn't resist it was an offer of a good night out. She had sensed it coming, but played for time. "Oh I don't know, that depends what offers we get, doesn't it Ally?"

I turned to face them, trying hard to appear disinterested. I could virtually hear my heart thumping. I would have sold my soul to know where he would be, without asking outright. I wanted to encourage his interest, but there was a big part of me afraid of …what? Rejection?

It would be more than that if this man, this living reminder of the only happy part of my childhood didn't want me as I wanted him. I swallowed hard. My cheery reply surprised even myself. "Friday's usually the best night to go out. I'm not sure what we're up to. It all depends on whether Lorna's feeling better or not."

Cormac took her improved health for granted.

"Good, that's settled then, you can be my tour guides for the evening, drinks on me. I really don't want a repeat performance of last night, though. All I want is some good company, people who aren't afraid to let their hair down," he said, looking so goddamn sexy, it took my breath away.

Unfortunately, he seemed to be having the exact same effect on my friend. It was as though I was fighting a secret battle, one my enemy didn't even know had begun. When Lorna smiled, her entire face glowed, showing her perfect teeth. I watched her as her tongue protruded, just a tad, just enough to hint what she'd like to do with it. How I hated her then, gripped by a jealousy I had never experienced before.

"Then all I can say is, you've come to the right place; I'm sure we can muster up enough energy between us, can't we Ally?" Lorna looked directly at me.

"Why not, and since it isn't pay week, what else have we got to do that is more exciting?"

"Great, then we'll meet at eight in *The Auld Hundred* again. How's that?" Lorna asked.

Cormac smiled directly at me. It hit me right in the solar plexus. I smiled back, knowing I could no longer be afraid to be myself. I knew his parting words were aimed more at me than at Lorna. "Excellent. I can't wait to see you later."

Once he had gone, I sat wondering, how on earth I would ever get through an evening in his company without making a show of myself. A bottle of wine between us before leaving Lorna's flat would help. I'd even decided which of her outfits I would borrow.

Getting ready was still an ordeal. It was the thought of his eyes on me. I wanted to look extra special for him.For some reason I wasn't able to tell Lorna. Normally, I confided every waking thought to her. But this was too private, too new. She might embarrass me. Nothing would spoil this night.

By the time we walked into the city centre Lorna was getting a bit sick of my need for reassurance. "For the hundredth time, Ally, your outfit is hot. You're mega-gorgeous. What's with you tonight?" In my head and in my heart I knew with utter certainty that this night had the power to break me. The more I thought about him, the more nervous I became. I had always been terrified of things I had no control over. And I had never felt so powerless.

Lorna had had enough. "Lighten up Ally. What's the matter with you? If I ignore the head nods, you haven't answered me once since leaving the flat. What has you so distracted? It doesn't have anything to do with *him*, I suppose?"

"Who?" I tried to sound casual but it was clear she hadn't fallen for it.

"Alright, Ally, you play it your way, but you don't fool me. I know you too well, remember." She stopped to touch up her lipstick under a streetlight before looking me straight in the eye. "I've known you a wee while now, and I've never seen you like this. You haven't fallen for him, have you?"

I turned on her, surprised at how indignant I sounded. "Don't be daft, Lorna. I hardly spoke to him. He's probably already got some one else. "

She laughed loudly. More than a few people glanced our way.

"Since when did that matter?"

Instinctively I went on the defensive. "This time it would."

We walked a short distance, neither of us talking, until Lorna broke the heavy silence.

"Look, Ally, it's ok. I didn't mean to upset you. At least I've got you half talking again."

I stopped and turned to face her. We were being honest now. This was my chance to lay down a few ground rules.

"Lorna, please don't embarrass me in front of him. I want to at least *try* to seem normal, or at least not a complete idiot!"

"Reading you loud and clear," she said, executing a mock salute. "I promise I won't do anything to wind you up. Now can you please turn back into the real Ally who likes a fun time?"

I grimaced, sorry I had made the start of the evening so difficult. Taking her arm, I marched off down the narrow cobbled road. "Sorry for being such a prat. First drink's on me."

The place had started to fill with strangers, all anticipating a good night on the town, dressed to kill and dying to pull. Cormac hadn't arrived yet. There was still time to compose myself. I couldn't believe how eager I was to see him again.

Time passed. Every time the door opened, I felt my heart leap into my mouth. The anticipation of his eyes on me kept me riveted to my seat. Sitting with our friends I was quiet, waiting. Lorna had given up on me and was looking elsewhere for some *craic.* Suddenly my eyes were drawn towards the oak door, and sure enough, in he walked.

He met my gaze at once and smiled at me, just with his eyes. The rest of his beautiful face didn't move, and yet his eyes told me all I needed to know. He felt the same. Until that moment, he had been as nervous as me. He was there at last, and everything was as it should be.

"Hi, sorry I'm late. I got held up at work." As he made his excuses, he casually threw his overcoat onto the back of a seat.

Lorna let him off easy. "We've only just arrived ourselves, haven't we Ally?" She was more aware than I had realised. There was a change in her. She had backed off, as though she knew how much I liked him. My spirits lifted.

Determined not to be the quivering wreck he had seen so far, I spoke first. "What do you want to drink? It's my round. " He ran his fingers through his hair, a habit I'd come to look for, as he considered his options. "I'll have a..." He paused before smiling. "I'll let you guess what I like," he said.

"Only if you promise to drink it if I get it wrong."

"Promise."There was a flash of something in his eyes that made me glad to escape to the bar. A few minutes later, I returned to find himself and Lorna deep in conversation. They both looked at the glass I was holding out to him. He seemed surprised. "Well done,

Ally. How did you know?"

The barman had remembered him from the previous evening. I half lied. "I'm psychic." As he reached to take the glass from me, our hands met. All the clichés about bodies tingling at someone's touch – they were true. For a second I wondered how good it would feel to lie in his arms and I couldn't make eye contact with him. It was almost as if I was afraid he could read my mind.

I distracted myself, putting my purse inside my bag, taking time to fasten it. By the time, I had placed it under the table; I had some semblance of control again.

I had no desire to spoil the chase for him.

The atmosphere was lively, the pub full of beautiful people determined to make the most of the evening and their youth. Young girls dressed provocatively, guys strutting like virile bulls, every man in the room ready to score. Once the alcohol fuelled their systems, they would become reckless in their search for a mate. Determined always to love a man's soul before I loved his body, tonight the air felt charged. I felt charged.

Gradually the tables around us filled until we were forced to shout over the din. The alcohol had loosened my own body. I became braver, looking directly at him and for longer. Cormac was feeling it too – I found his eyes on me often.

Lorna was mingling freely. Left on our own, Cormac and I spoke little, happy just to be with each other. I wasn't surprised when Lorna came back to say she was going on with friends. I made a mental note to thank her later for making it so easy.

As soon as she left, it seemed everything around us disappeared. No people, no noises, no distractions…Without saying anything Cormac took my hand. It felt good, it felt right. He looked into my eyes, like the answer mattered. "Do you want to go on somewhere too, Ally?"

I stared back wide-eyed, totally besotted by him and not caring now that he knew it. "Anywhere," I replied.

We walked along Princes Street. The night air cooled my hot face. It felt good not to be crowded by heaving bodies. It felt even better when he put his arm round me. We walked slowly past the bright shop fronts. Such a simple thing, but the moment was perfect. My body didn't want to leave his, not for a second. To part from him would have caused me physical pain. We were lost in each other, in the synchronised movement of our bodies, in the warmth the other generated. I knew almost nothing about him, yet I knew all I needed to know. There was no confusion, no embarrassment, and no game playing.

"I've really enjoyed being with you this evening, Ally." It was as if he had read my thoughts, and had no fear of sharing his own. But his next words surprised me entirely. In halting syllables, in my native Gallic, he said, *"Tha mo bheatha air a dhol bun os cionn bhon chiad latha a chunnaig mi thu."* Hearing the words, him telling me that his life had turned upside down ever since he met me, felt…miraculous. And in my own tongue – instantly I was transported back to the Island. Back to the *Connall* again.

Unable to conceal my delight I whispered, *"Ciamar a tha thu comasach air a bhi cho filenta nar canan?"*

Cormac looked slightly embarrassed as he reverted back to English. "I don't speak Gaelic at all, I just shared a room at Uni' with a student who taught me a little. I thought you'd be impressed if I made the effort…"

"It has been a long time since I've spoken my mother tongue, Cormac." The thought suddenly saddened me greatly.

"Ciamar, a Aluinn? Innis dhomh."

I kissed his cheek, but it was too early to explain why thoughts of home made me sad. I snuggled into him and responded in English. "Let's just walk, Cormac, and enjoy being together."

We walked on, past the Head of Leith, along the straight road where the elegant Victorian houses framed the otherwise modern intrusions of roads, and streetlights. When he stopped in front of a very smart looking building, I thought he wanted to kiss me, but instead he pointed up towards the second floor windows.

"This is where I live. I promise I'll behave myself if you come up. I'll be so good you can even stay the night. I have a small spare room but it's comfortable."

I was totally thrown off balance. Here I was, ready to give myself to him, for the first time ever. "I see. It's nice to know you find me so attractive."

My assumption clearly amused him. It took him a minute or two to regain control, he was laughing so hard. "I want you to know I have respect for you, that's all." Looking into my eyes he whispered, "I can wait for as long as it takes to win your heart."

I melted, wanting the words to be true, not just some smarmy chat up line. I wanted to tell him he already possessed it, that I had no longer had control over my emotions. But some instinct prevented my mouth from forming the words that swam around my head. I was suddenly embarrassed. "For all I know you're a total womaniser and this is a sophisticated ploy for getting girls into bed." I looked at him, praying it wasn't true. He already had the power to break me.

His arms around me tightened. It was as if he sensed the real reason for my nervousness. "We've got all the time in the world, Ally. I'm not going anywhere. Come on up." He grabbed my hand and pulled me through the gate.

"This is your parents' place, right?"

He laughed again, and shook his head.

"So how come some one as young as you can afford a place like this?" I looked up again, taking in the sheer size of the apartment. "The rent must be colossal."

His reply was without arrogance. "I don't rent it Ally, I own it." He laughed. "Let's just call it a family heirloom. Are you always so direct?" The look he gave me said it didn't matter, didn't mean anything. We were all that mattered. Now. This moment.

I pushed all doubts aside. Nothing would stop me from being with this man who had drawn me so completely from the beginning. I followed him inside and up the intricate spiral staircase, which would not have looked out of place on any lavish film production set. Opening the door, he led me into his apartment. He walked slightly ahead and now it was my turn to laugh. He reminded me of a proud peacock, ready to display its finest feathers.

The sheer elegance overwhelmed me. I had never seen anything like it. I wandered around, letting my fingers linger over the furniture. "Is this all yours too? It looks like an antiques showroom. But everything looks new."

He was pleased, I could tell. "All genuine, I can assure you. My family have always taken great care of the possessions. I get angry when people have no respect for their heritage."

"You sound so serious when you say that. I almost had a flashback of living with my mother," I said.

"So, your parents were careful people too?"

"I never knew my father, but my mother was enough of a disciplinarian to keep me in check, believe me."

"That's the second time you've hinted there was something painful in your past, Ally. Won't you tell me about it?" In two easy strides he was beside me, cupping my face in his hands. Still looking into my eyes, he pressed a soft kiss on my lips.

"I will, Cormac, but not tonight. Let's leave the past in the past for now."

He laughed, "So, what? Did you murder someone?"

I purposely turned away, so he couldn't see my face. Sarah filled my mind, and the stab in my heart was unbearable.

"You're a funny wee thing. I've never met anyone quite like you." The way he said it made me raise my head. I knew I was giving my feelings away but I couldn't help it.

He reached out and took my hand. "You and I are so alike, Ally. You just don't see it yet."

His voice was serious. "What do you mean?" I remembered then that what I didn't know about him was endless.

Sensing me pulling back, he pulled me to him, soothing me. His voice was so calm, whispering to me so sweetly, all I wanted then was to be near him. I wondered for a second whether the alcohol hadn't affected my senses. I had never felt so drawn physically to a man, felt so wanted. I needed him, and sensed he needed me too.

"Patience, Ally, we've all the time in the world. And we're in no hurry this time…"

This time? What did he mean?

"You really don't trust me, do you?" he laughed, relinquishing his hold on me, but I had unsettled him, I could tell. Instantly there were messages coming from somewhere, telling me to be careful, reminding me I was in a situation I had no power over. Taking a step back, I shook my head, but in the same instant, he pulled me to him, lowering his head to take my mouth. As he kissed me, touched his beautiful mouth to mine, all the uneasiness passed. When he pulled me closer into his arms, I surrendered.

How could something so effortless make me want to cry tears of joy? Bliss. No conscious thought but of him and this moment. Was he feeling the same as me? This *elation*?

When he finally pulled away from me, I had already accepted I was lost. Any reservations had left me. Whatever he wanted was okay by me, now and always. When his head arched down to meet my lips again, there was no resistance. I kissed him passionately, my body alive in a way I had never known or felt before. When he deepened the kiss, a desperate urge rose in me to quell the passion he had wakened. Shocking myself, I pressed my body against him, urgently, timeless instincts controlling my movements. He led, I followed, with no sense of time or space until we clumsily collided with the sofa. Still we rolled together, my body under his as he angled his mouth over mine to possess it more fully.

His hands rose to my breasts, caressing them almost reverently. His thighs pressed against mine, pushing upwards against me, responding with another thrust as I pushed back on him. Suddenly he withdrew. I looked at him in confusion. For a moment, he was unable to meet my eyes. Why was he refusing what I was so clearly offering?

Mortified, I followed him reluctantly as he rose and pulled me to the room he had described to me earlier, with its comfortable single bed. Opening the door, he stayed in the hallway, looking down at me, his eyes on my lips.

"Goodnight, Ally. I'll wake you in the morning and take you home."

I was too taken aback to even speak. Normally evenings ended with me fighting off unwanted advances. This was so strange, so formal, so …frustrating. I didn't *want* his respect, the veneration he promised. I wanted him to take me to his room and make love to me, all night long and all tomorrow if the notion took him.

Till then I had always been a little afraid of lovemaking. I had never been able to imagine any joy in two people becoming one. But that night, I longed for his touch, wanted him to conquer my body. It screamed with disappointment at the pleasure it was being denied. Surely we could…? I moved towards him and caressed his face in the darkness. He stood there, looking down at me, showing no emotion at all.

When he kissed my forehead and left me, I felt more alone than I had ever felt. I wanted to follow him, would have, if the thought hadn't come to me that perhaps he wouldn't want a girl who would be so easy. Unsure, I wasn't prepared to risk it.

Why not wait? Wasn't it wonderful I had found a man who respected women so much? I found that I couldn't convince myself of my good fortune.

Would he have been shocked at the thoughts circulating my mind for the rest of the night? I left the curtains open and lay awake, imagining him in the next room. Was he asleep, or lying awake wishing, like me? I must have fallen asleep at some point. By the time morning arrived Cormac had to knock on the door quite forcefully to rouse me. For a split second, I couldn't think where I was.

But I knew I was deeply relieved. It almost felt as if I had passed a test, as if he would like me even more now. I jumped out of bed, eager to begin the day in his company. Halting a moment at the window, I peered out at the traffic that had already built up below. No noise penetrated the thick glass. From my vantage point, the city looked like a silent movie.

I made my way out onto the plush passageway, looking for a bathroom. I stopped at Cormac's room, and took a sneaky look. His bed was a dishevelled mess. Perhaps he had spent a sleepless night too.

I showered quickly and emerged a short time later, feeling refreshed. I had no choice but to wear yesterday's clothes, which looked less than appropriate in the cold light of day. Following the sounds of clinking cutlery, I found Cormac preparing breakfast in the oval kitchen. He half turned towards me. "Good morning. I hope you slept well?"

"Yes, fine thanks, although I look a bit of a state."

He turned around fully, and studied my crumpled appearance. He, I noted, was his usual beautifully turned out self, every inch the gentleman. "I've seen you look better, but then I've also seen you look much worse."

I had been trying to make some semblance of order out of my unruly mane, trying to trap the locks escaping in thick spirals from brushing against my face. Instantly my brain was in turmoil. When had he seen me look worse than I did now? It dawned on me.

"Yesterday, you mean?"

"The morning after Camilla's bash. You looked so rough I actually thought about leaving you alone."

He laughed so hard I knew he was teasing me. I couldn't help but retaliate.

"What made you so sure I'd be interested in you anyway?"

Catching my wrist, he pulled me to him and kissed me deeply. "Be serious. How could you resist me?"

I laughed too, but inside I was thinking *how right you are*.

It had never felt this way before. I had never felt grateful just to spend time with a man, to stare at his face, to soak up every detail about him. I wanted to remember everything about Cormac, felt a need to be with him with such urgency it was as though my very life depended on it. Taking my place at the table, I watched him ravenously as he finished making breakfast, trying to make it less obvious but knowing I looked like some lovesick puppy. When he eventually sat down, he took my hand.

"Will you go out with me tonight? I want to take you out somewhere special. Don't worry, I'm not going to get you drunk and drag you back here. I want to do this right, give us some memories. Will you let me?"

I wanted to scream at him, "I don't need romance. I need you to love me." All I managed was, "Great."

He seemed satisfied. "That's settled then, I'll take you home and I'll pick you up at eight again tonight…Wear something sexy, so I can really show you off."

"I'm glad you didn't say demure or I'd have had to let you down gently."

He reached over, took hold of my other hand and pulled me towards him until our faces almost touched. Softly he said, "Don't even joke about it. This is too serious for that. Promise me, Ally."

"I won't Cormac, I promise."

He smiled then, as his lips brushed mine gently. I was on fire immediately, but he pulled back, quickly changing the subject. "I think we'd better eat this before it gets cold."

*

The gloom hit me as soon as I opened the door of our flat. As usual, it was deserted on a Saturday afternoon. Abandoned clothes lay in the hallway. The living room was strewn with uneaten meals left to congeal. Newspapers and odd shoes lay haphazardly around the worn chairs. They all knew the mess irritated me. It irritated me even more when I went around tidying up after them.

I crossed to the kitchen, to be met by a sink of dirty dishes and hardened grease. For once, I paid them no heed. They could all damn well clear up behind themselves, when they got back. I headed straight for my room, and raided my wardrobe. I wanted to look extra special.

Minutes later I found myself studying my reflection, wondering if what I was feeling had made me look any different. After my shower that morning, my hair looked beautiful, unruly and bountiful. I gathered it high, and then I let it fall. Whichever way I wore it, it looked good. My crowning glory. Even in Edinburgh, it still drew stares, which strangely increased my insecurity.

Cormac, I decided, would never again see me looking anything less than my best. I floated around the flat for the remainder of that day, playing corny love songs which suddenly held new meaning for me. Even more than the physical feelings, he excited me in other ways, his friendship, all that he was. I had found someone I could share everything with. I was no longer so alone, locked inside my own imaginings.

My *sight* was still absent around him. Normally I knew who would harm me or cause me discomfort. My basic instinct for self-protection had been heightened ever since the *Connall* had left me. It had been bothering me, that my gift seemed to leave me when I was around Cormac. But another part of me reasoned it was only right – why would I *need* a sense of self-preservation, if he would protect me from now on? Perhaps these overwhelming emotions I was experiencing had simply obliterated it.

Back in the flat I tried to review last night's events. Blurred images appeared from time to time, ideas which I struggled to formulate, but they remained strangely out with my grasp. When I tried to make sense of my unease, my head swam with images. I tried to untangle my emotions. The harder I tried, the more aware I became that there was something formidable happening here. My thinking was distorted by my emotions.

For the first time in life, I had a chance to be happy, really happy. I wanted him so badly.I knew he wanted me. It all felt so fresh and wonderful, yet I ached with an exquisite pain I couldn't articulate. All I knew was that I wanted the feeling to last. I never wanted to lose the newness of it all.

I had given no thought to Lorna, or what had happened to her after she left. Suddenly, she was there, in the forefront of my mind. What had happened to her last night after she left me?

I hated and loved my gift in equal measure. All those things I saw without wanting to, but when I *needed* it to show me where Lorna was, to see if she needed me, it deserted me. Since Sarah's death, I sometimes feared my gift too.

I hoped Lorna hadn't regretted leaving me with Cormac. Part of me still felt guilty. I had a feeling that things would change now. There would be restrictions on our friendship because of what I felt for him. My heart suddenly weighed heavy, afraid of the changes that would occur, recognising how my dependence on her had shifted. But I was powerless to prevent it; I wanted him. Lorna could never make me happy the way he did.

I decided not to phone her. If she were angry with me for not getting in touch, she would let me know.

Chapter Seven

I grew impatient for him. I knew I would have to remind myself to breathe when I saw him, become dizzy with the sheer effort of steadying my heartbeat. It would always be that way. Though I was frightened, it didn't diminish the joy. I spent hours trying on outfits. Despite Lorna's assurances that women all felt the same insecurities, I knew growing up on the Island had deprived me of confidence in the way I looked. I would never be adequate in my own estimation.

Hearing a car draw up outside, I pulled the thick curtain back slightly. It was a taxi dropping somebody off, looking very much the worse for wear as he staggered across the street. I grew impatient. *Did the whole world live by a different clock?* I paced the floor, then went back to the mirror, checking my reflection for the hundredth time. I looked hard at my face reflected in the glass, trying to see what others saw. Despite the compliments Cormac had given me I felt the way I always did - nondescript.

A few seconds later, a loud knock sounded on the door. My heart leapt to my mouth as I rushed to open it. He looked more handsome than ever.

He took his time, looking me over from head to toe. Strangely, I was more than happy to endure his appraisal. He savoured the moment before he spoke. "You look beautiful, Ally." Then he put his arm protectively around my shoulders and led me out to his car.

We ate in a French restaurant I would never have dared to go in without him. I was relieved the portions were miniscule, too nervous to eat. He had been quiet the previous night. Tonight he had stories to tell. Stories about parts of the world I had only read about, river rafting in New Zealand, trekking in Australia, mountaineering in Norway…Not boasting, sharing the experience with me. It made my narrow world seem very small.

I watched him place his glass of chardonnay to his lips, his tongue touch the rim of the glass. The sight was so erotic I burned with longing. When he moved closer, I could smell the sweetness of his breath, feel its warmth hot on my neck, then just as quickly he withdrew.

"So what about you?" he said, readjusting his napkin over his lap.

What could I say that would interest this man? Tell him about my lonely childhood, or my dull office job? "There's really not much to say, I'm pretty ordinary." He was watching me keenly, but I was well versed in distraction techniques when it came to discussing my unorthodox childhood. "Let me fill you in on the seedy goings-on at work."

An anecdote about members of staff being caught enjoying each other on CCTV amused him. I was surprised he hadn't known about it. The footage had been enjoyed by half the workers in the building before they found out.

"So that would explain why they hardly give each other the time of day now. Is it true about the Area Manager, being given cocaine by the office junior?"

"He almost went to an executive meeting high as a kite, but they just caught him in time."

He smiled. "So what other gossip do you have, Ally, since you clearly have no wish to tell me anything about yourself?"

The heat rose to my face, and my eyes flew to his. There was no anger there, just compassion. It was as though he sensed some of what I had endured. Still I balked at wasting the evening by giving the memories in my head room. "Honestly, there's nothing much to say. I came to Edinburgh several years ago. I've worked in the same office ever since. I like my life now, Cormac. Especially now our paths have crossed. "

He seemed satisfied. "Keep your secrets for now, Ally. I can tell there are things you want to forget. I want to help if I can. I've not felt this way about someone before – protective. I like the feeling. Very much."

As we looked at each other I wondered if tonight would be different, if we would be committed to each other in a deeper way.

Despite his reassurances that he would respect my privacy, my mood for the rest of the evening was sombre. In my mind, I kept going back to the Island. Somehow there was a sense that my refusal to share it with him had drawn an invisible barrier between us. I longed for the waiter to bring the bill, so we could leave.

We went back to his apartment. The moon shone through the huge bay windows, bathing the room in its silver light. I stayed Cormac's hand as he moved to turn on the light, pulling his head towards me in a slow arc, kissing him with all the passion I had repressed all evening. I could feel my emotions overflow. He pulled me close, caressing my body in a way he had controlled till then. He traced a path with his tongue along my neck and down towards my breasts, lighting the passion in me. I tilted my body towards him, unbuttoning his shirt with trembling fingers to reveal his chest, running my hands along the manly contours of his body, fascinated by the feel of him under my hands. Our passion grew more urgent. I could feel his maleness hard against my belly. Shameless, I pushed my torso into him. He pulled me further into the room, and down onto the rug in front of the fire. Moments later, his hand slipped under the fabric of my skirt, to the heated skin between my legs. They parted willingly to welcome him. I could feel his rising frustration as he fumbled with our clothing. For the next few seconds my nerves were screaming, "Now! Yes! Now!" Just when it seemed inevitable that our bodies would take over, begin the rhythm too powerful to prevent, Cormac pulled away.

My body was still pulsing from his touch. How could he be so... cruel? I couldn't understand. Cormac said nothing, not even 'sorry'. I lay there in the dark, utterly dejected.

It was *normal*, surely, for two people who lusted after each other to follow their desires? I had been prepared to see it through; I could not, would not walk away when my heart was his.

It was too much, this second rejection. Had I done something wrong? Suddenly his hand dipped to the softness of my belly, and I felt his mouth on my neck. "I'm so sorry.If I hadn't stopped there I would never have been able to forgive myself."

So it wasn't just me feeling this mindless compulsion? A tear rolled down my cheek. He kissed it away. Turning back to him, I skimmed a row of kisses along his chest. He caught my chin in his hand and brought my mouth down to his mouth, fiercely. "We had better just lie still for a while, or I'll not be responsible for my actions. I can want to wait, Ally, till it's right. I want to prove to you that this relationship is not just about sex."

As we lay there in the darkness, I listened to the beat of his heart under my ear, felt the warmth of him, smelt the smell of him. I thought of all those other women I saw every weekend. The ones who threw it away left, right and centre to anyone who was willing. If Cormac was the one for me, and I believed he was, then I was prepared to wait, to prove my virtue to him, if that was what he wanted.

It was not easy. In the next few weeks I was often carried away past a certain point, but always Cormac would pull us back. As time passed, I was grateful to him for it. The mere touch from his hand, a single kiss, became more meaningful than any moment of passion I had known till then. At other times I went to bed angry and more frustrated than ever. In my blackest moods, when everything seemed to shatter my inner peace I wondered why I had to endure this torture when Ally had numerous partners more than willing to satisfy her needs.

We settled into a pattern, meeting frequently. There was a rightness in Cormac's company I had never experienced such before. At moments, it was as though he looked into my soul. Often we said or did the same things at the exactly the same moment, and laughed to see the other's delight. So why was there something holding me back from telling Lorna about us? Part of me wanted to share this precious thing I had found, but I was afraid she would laugh at me. I told myself I didn't want anything to jeopardise us. I was almost convinced she had found out anyway; she acted oddly around us when we were together, even in a group.

The weeks passed. Still I hadn't found the right moment to tell her. It grew awkward. Just seeing us together seemed to irritate her. Cormac and I even avoided sitting next to each other in her company. Instinct still told me to keep them as far apart as I could. There was a tension there still, probably based on her initial attraction to him. And I feared that. How could they fail to be attracted to each other? I thought them both perfect in their own way. Together they would be amazing. No wonder I saw her as a threat. I only prayed that she would never act on it, out of loyalty to me.

He was so good about it, understanding that Lorna just needed time to adjust to our friendship being something more than that. Cormac even suggested we keep things cool in her company until I had found the right time to tell. Somehow, it felt like a dirty secret till then, something to be hidden away. Time passed and things stayed as they were - for fear of confrontation, I suppose. She seemed to be drinking even more than usual, which helped our subterfuge. When she was tanked up, it was easy to slip away. But it bothered me, this barrier. Just not enough to do anything about it.

I was so happy with Cormac, it made me reassess my friendship with Lorna, truth be told. I began to wonder if I hadn't been living in her shadow. I felt myself growing away from her.

This wasn't the only confusion in my life - there were days over the next few weeks when my view of the world seemed blinkered in other ways. Normally so clear-sighted, I felt my perception of people and events muddied. It confused me, this lack of insight. Without it, I realised just how dependent I had been on this natural awareness. I found it strangely terrifying. With this growing sense of confusion came a growing sense of my dependence on Cormac. There were days when I felt my feelings for him almost eating me alive, feeding off my insecurities.

When Lorna and I were alone together things were alright. Saturdays we still got ready together at her flat. I liked that time alone, just us. Everything seemed different; normal, for it was easy being happy with her. I liked that time alone, just us. Everything seemed normal. Lorna had turned the small bedroom into a smoke haze, as usual. Opening the window, I turned to smile at her, waving the clouds of smoke away. I found her looking at me sullenly. "That's right; take away the only enjoyment I have left. I'm hardly getting any sex, food's shit, but hey, take my fags, see if I care!"

"You're way too honest, do you know that?"

Lorna moved closer. I knew she had drunk more than I had. It appeared to have loosened her tongue. She put her mouth to my ear and whispered, "Actually, I had great sex last night, the best ever, I swear, but I'm not giving details."

"Who with?" I asked, intrigued.

"Ah," Lorna pouted, tapping the side of her nose, "that would be telling, plus it's a secret."

"You can tell me, Lorna. You know I won't say a word if you say not to."

Lorna looked uneasy. "Ah promised I wouldn't say," she said seriously.

She didn't look in any mood to take advice. "Fine, if that's the way you want to play it, when you're ready I'll be waiting." I hoped she wasn't getting into deep waters, but why upset her on a night out? This was our time and I wanted to make the most of it.

Her strange mood had lifted – she was up for a good night. There was no one I would rather party with than Lorna. She gave me the confidence I needed to go out there and have fun. I never worried about how I looked or what I wore with her. We were above the rest, somehow, in a world of our own. No one reached us, unless we allowed them into our tight circle.

Much later, having toured the usual haunts around Rose Street, we took a taxi to the Grass Market. The nightlife there was always loud, rough and ready. By that time, we had lost our inhibitions enough to walk irregularly all the way up the hill onto the High Street, till we reached The World's End pub on the corner.

Lorna had really hit the drink by this time. Her temper was the worse for it and she wasn't happy with my choice of venue. I had arranged to meet Cormac there.

"Why have we come here, rather than going on to a club? I want to disco until my legs ache. Come on Ally, it'll be fun. Much better than this! Look, we only need our entrance money. It's not as if we need anymore drink, plus the dancing is the only exercise I get, apart from 'sex'ercise, get it?" She motioned with her body the difference between the two.

I laughed, wishing I'd had the chance to discover the difference for myself. But Cormac's stance hadn't changed. I noticed several lads eyeing up Lorna's finely toned body salaciously, and I felt sick for her. It was hard staying quiet as they edged closer to her. One even came right over and simulated sex with her. She thought it was hysterical as I grew steadily angrier. It had never bothered me before how little respect was paid the act itself. I was turning into a prude. How ironic, considering the frustration building up inside of me.

I dragged her off to diffuse the situation. How often had I gotten myself into a position like that, but never seen the danger, engrossed in having a good time? It was a miracle we hadn't been attacked by some loser. Thinking I had spoiled her fun, Lorna was louder than ever. She wanted her own way and didn't care who knew it. "Please Ally, this place is boring; I want to dance. Look, the crowd's about to leave, are you coming or not?" she said.

"I don't fancy it tonight..." I got no further.

All hell broke loose. She gripped my shoulders with more strength than she realised and bawled in my face. "Oh, come on Ally, you can't let me down. Not tonight!"

I pulled away, wary of her now. "Please Lorna, don't make a scene. I just don't fancy a club tonight. There are more than enough of our mates here. Surely I don't have to go if I don't want to?"

She erupted. It wasn't just about tonight anymore – it was about all the other times as well. That was it, a big fight in public. I was angry.

Lorna let her glass fly, not entirely in my direction but close enough to make me take notice. Several others at a table close by tried to restrain her, but she lunged at me. It was a side of Lorna I had never seen. The alcohol had taken away all her inhibitions.

"You're never there for me anymore! Where do you sneak off to every weekend, Ally? Who is it you're spending time with, 'cause it sure ain't me!" Her voice slurred. She lost her balance, knocking a chair into the table behind and covering people in drink. Far from being angry, they were plainly enjoying a good slanging match.

Not entirely sober but far from drunk, I was mortified at having my dirty linen aired in public. She regained her balance, by which time a crowd had gathered. I seriously wished I could disappear, but I had to wait for Cormac.

"Come on, tell me." Lorna spun around, extending her arms to the crowd. She swayed as she turned full circle, almost toppling over, then steadying herself. "Tell us all, 'cause I'm not the only one who's noticed the change in you, eh girls?"

She turned to include the tight group behind her. Most of them I recognised, but some of them were strangers to me, Lorna's 'new' friends. I tried to calm her, but she was so drunk I had already lost the battle. "Look Lorna, we can discuss this tomorrow, when you're sober. It's really no big deal..."

My words trailed away. I stood and waited for another onslaught, but instead I heard Cormac's voice. At first, I thought I dreamt it inside my head until Lorna looked behind me. Her face literally fell.

"What's no big deal, Ally?" he said.

I turned too. Maybe my smile was a bit too welcoming. Lorna went off on one. "Now you're here, maybe you'll talk some sense into her. I want to go clubbing but she's not up for it, yet again!" Lorna roared.

He shot her down in flames. "I don't see it's any of my business. It's entirely Ally's decision."

You could see a switch trip in her head. "But *is* it her decision, Cormac? How come *you* always turn up at the end of the night? How come you always know where we'll be? How is it I never notice you leave…either of you?" Lorna threw her arms in the air before as she bellowed, "Would somebody like to tell me what's going on? Is there something happening here I should know about?"

I tried to pacify her. "Look Lorna, we don't have to row about it. I don't want to go that's all."

Lorna looked genuinely upset. She stared at me, as though she no longer knew me at all, "But you love to dance, or at least you did before he showed up!" I could see the last penny drop. "I've been so stupid, how come I never saw it?"

Lorna slumped into a vacant seat at a table close by. The colour drained from her face. I wanted to make everything all right between us. We had been best friends for so long. Now this secret had placed a divide between us. Why hadn't I been honest from the start?

I had wanted to keep Cormac all to myself. Deep down I had been afraid Lorna's beauty would take him from me. I wished with all my heart I could have turned back the clock. She would have understood; she would have been pleased for me. Why had I not included her in my happiness?

I had disrespected our friendship; Lorna knew it, drunk as she was.

She reached for my hand and pulled me down near her. Her eyes misted over and she looked genuinely upset. She spoke so very quietly, I strained to hear her. "Listen, there's something I really need to tell you…."

"Ally, get your coat we're leaving!" Cormac said behind me.

I turned and faced him, confused. Lorna was obviously distressed.

"I can't leave Lorna like this," I pleaded.

"She's not alone. She's with that crowd she always ends up in. What's the point of trying to sort things out with her when she's so drunk? It'll only escalate again." He grabbed my arm and literally pulled me, none too gently, through the throng. "She'll be fine, let's get out of here." People complained loudly at our passage. It was only outside I could make myself heard.

"What the hell did you do that for?" I screamed. "Lorna is totally off her face!"

"She was just going to turn cruel and vindictive – that girl tries to control you, can't you see that?" He put his hands on my waist, pulled me closer, his voice gentling. "Trust me, Ally; you don't need to hear whatever she feels she has to say. I promise you, by morning, if she remembers this at all, she'll thank me for it."

All I wanted to do was go back inside and console her. Something had upset her. I knew her too well not to recognise the signs. Besides, what she had said was true. I had neglected her lately. She had every right to be angry. I vented my frustration on Cormac.

"People have been controlling me all my life and now you're doing it too! She's my friend. Friends have arguments. Do you have a magic wand to remove every single bad thing from my life, Cormac? I need to experience life for myself, not live it second hand, like some bairn in need of protection!"

He put his hands on my shoulders, looking deep into my eyes. "But I do want to protect you Ally. I love you." Then he walked away. Just a few paces, then he looked back. "If you insist on going back in, I'll leave without you."

I was dumbfounded. He was *blackmailing* me.

A terrible silence fell between us. It lingered for the longest time.

I could feel the anger that had built up inside me, but I was so staggered by what he had said, I couldn't speak. *He loved me.* Inside my head thoughts spun wildly.

He held out his hand, tilting his head and looking at me with such *need.*

He was right. There was no point. Lorna was drunk.

No matter what the outcome, it was out in the open. There would be no more lying now...

Chapter Eight

"Why don't we take a break, go away for a few days? It would do you good to get some perspective. Put some distance between you and Lorna, see her when you get back?"

"How do you think she would feel if I ran away, afraid to face her?."

"You could say it had all been fixed beforehand? How about it, a trip abroad? Give us space to be ourselves." His kiss was electrifying. "If we're going to cement our relationship, move it to the next level," he whispered, tracing the curve of my breast with his fingers till I could hardly breathe, "I don't want it to be a fumble your average Joe Bloggs would be happy with. I want it to be special, so you understand the seriousness of our union."

"You're a bit too deep today, Cormac. I have enough to think about already."

"I'm only saying what I should have done a long time ago. You're special to me Ally; I don't want to mess it up." Then he kissed me and all thoughts of Lorna disappeared.

The rest of the weekend passed. As time drew closer to seeing her on Monday morning, I felt ashamed, almost dreading finding out if I still had her friendship or not. Cormac couldn't seem to understand my dilemma, why I was so teary and out of sorts. I had half hoped he would take me to his bed to comfort me, but his resolve was firm – we were going to wait, make it special. But it was getting harder and harder. To make absolutely sure, he dropped me back at the flat.

Once alone, I could finally admit to myself that I had done the wrong thing. I should have sorted things out with Lorna there and then, apologised. What was wrong with me these days? I had become so selfish. I locked myself away in my room and cried until exhaustion overpowered me. I dreamt of another time, long since past. When I awoke images lingered I could neither comprehend nor shake off. In my dream I had seen three hundred of the blackest *fithich,* guarding the Island's shores. Huge ravens, bloodstained and weary. Somehow I understood they were fighting against those who had come to claim the Island for themselves. I watched their battles, watched the slashing and maiming as the great bird creatures slaughtered huge armies of *Na Gadheil o shean,* highlanders of old. The great bird creatures showed no mercy, forcing their routed foe to flee before disappearing far below the earth again, drawn down by a power far greater than their own.

I awoke bathed in sweat, my heart pounding. In my dream, I had been somehow amongst them. In their victory, they had welcomed me, their cumbersome frames strangely agile. Moving closer, they had swept me up into their dance, round and round captive to their throng. But when I was in their midst they had seized me, held me fast in their claws, their talons sharp with spikes exposed now below the coarseness of their feathers.

Somehow, in my dream, the ravens became mixed up with Lorna's defiance, her embarrassing me, the crowds of people around us, jeering. I woke with a feeling of terrible sadness. The vision of those beings, the awareness of their existence wove on through my mind, tormenting me. The old gifts that had deserted me for several weeks often came to me in my sleep. My new weakness strengthened them somehow. I was unable to keep them at bay in my dreams. They could not be held back. I woke often fearing they had broken free from the confines I kept them in, threatening the layers of sanity I had so carefully constructed. At moments like that I knew that my feyness, so carefully controlled, would set me apart forever.

When I awoke the second time, I felt calmed. The night terrors had not destroyed me. I felt somehow reassured that events would work themselves out. There was no movement yet from Lorna's room. I assumed she hadn't yet risen. Vexed not to be able to explain or apologise before work, I left earlier than usual. Walking to clear my mind, I chose the pathway around Arthur's Seat. I often felt drawn to the place when I was sad, wanting its connection with home. Its ruggedness never failed to solace me. It was as close to the Island as I could find, reminding me of the northern part of my homeland, where the sheerest cliff faces were too steep to be mastered. How I longed for my Island still, its forest moors and soft creeping grasses, its rocky glens and talus slopes. My soul had been at peace there, in a way it would never be at peace anywhere else. Despite what lay in its depths.

Legend had it that the Island could disappear at will into the mists, lying unnoticed by seafarers. Here in the city the Seat seemed invisible too – how many in the capital were really aware of the glorious mountain in their midst. Like my Island, once known as *Beinn Theine*, the fire mountain, the Arthur's Seat was volcanic. It seemed to have erupted out of the earth below the city. The buildings strewn at its feet looked like lego bricks in comparison to its strength. Its majestic beauty was home to many *taibhsean* who had chosen to take up residence in its splendour.

My lonely childhood had deepened my awareness of the natural world and of those who lived within it. As a bairn on the Island the spirits had been real to me, so much that at times I had doubted my own sanity. Today I no longer cared whether they existed out with my mind, or solely within it. I saw them for what they were, and was no longer afraid of what they might teach me. Truth be known, I was happier in their company than of my friends who took life so much for granted. It was easy enough to stay clear of the menacing ones. More difficult were the bewildered *taibhsean* who had been misplaced, forgotten in place and time. I felt compassion for them. They understood little of what they witnessed around them. Part of me wished I could take them back with me to the Island, to enjoy its tranquillity.

Sometimes I used the *taibhsean* powers to lift my mood, but not too often. Playing with them was dangerous. They held no grudge against me, but their timelessness vexed them. Contained in this world, unable to move on, they took their sport in watching man try to prove he was master of himself. Our antics seemed so feeble to them, cloaked as they were within their otherworldliness. I knew their strengths and gave them due respect. Who was I, after all, but a *Fiosaiche Gun chli,* a lowly seer, who hated her gift?

Mischievous weather spirits followed me that morning as I walked slowly up round the Seat. When I sat for a moment at the small lake they unsettled the ducks and swans there. I could see them grow restless at having to share their domain. One by one the birds left the water to them, gradually moving to the other side until the mischievous entities had the entire run of the pond. I watched them, knowing that onlookers were surprised by the choppiness of water on a calm day.

Needing its strength, I lifted my eyes upwards towards the peak of the jutting rock face again. Its massive strength never failed to move me, so out of place within city limits, surreal amongst so much concrete. Nature's strength revealed. Yet this rock lacked the thunderous noise and pungent smell of the sea. There were no tumultuous waves peaking at its base, no swell, nor waters ebbing away slowly from its grandeur. Would it never leave me, this longing for home?

Others were drawn to the ancient site that morning too, unaware of the spirit creatures that walked its paths. How could one explain that such phenomenon were an every day occurrence for me? That they followed me wherever I went? That at times I used them to my advantage, if another had treated me unkindly? For all my life we had simply co-existed. It was only when I had begun to want to be with Cormac that I had begun to set up boundaries. I could see that now. They had seemed to accept the change. But in the last few weeks, especially at work, they had been trying to get my attention. It seems something had irritated them.

Some *taibhsean* had congregated on the grassy banks at the feet of the monument. It suited them, of course, being part of such a noble place, with little intrusion from mortals. When I approached they sensed me immediately, waving to me, beckoning. But things had changed. I was no longer a child - I had responsibilities now. They looked sad when I waved my regret. But I was not sorry. Part of me felt vulnerable around them these days.

My path was suddenly slowed by a congress of ravens, their presence like a dark shadow on the otherwise clear morning. Something about them sent fragments of fear shivering through me. I turned instinctively towards Colton Hill, glad of the wind singers congregating there. They had hidden themselves from me all these weeks. But that morning they were there in abundance, floating on the air currents, adapting lightly to the ever-changing conditions. How I envied them that ability. They must have sensed my distress at the ravens, for they moved closer on the wind, using it to speed their arrival. Within seconds they had circled my body, until I stood shrouded in their energy. I felt my feet lifted slightly from the ground. For a second I thought they might topple me, but they were merely greeting me. They were so childlike, with no cruelty in their hearts, or vengeful thoughts. But anyone who awoke their anger received different treatment. Then they became hideous, took on deformed shapes, tormenting and punishing the offender. I humoured their antics, knowing they had the power to set other *taibhsean* upon me.

Without a word from me the wind singers moved towards the ravens, gathering speed. The birds cawed angrily, before flying off in dark formation.

*

At work my day stretched out in front of me. I sat at my desk, dreading Lorna's arrival. Knowing her as I did, there were two ways she could play this. Either makes a beeline for me, chatty as ever; ignoring our disagreement the other evening…or else she would be like a she-devil, ready to rip my throat out. I had no idea which way it would go. I tried to compose myself by preparing for the worst.

Bang on time, she stood in front of my desk. Waves of shame washed over me. I couldn't bring to myself to lift up my head and meet her eyes. I instantly blurted out an apology. "Look, Lorna, about the other night…I'm so sorry."

Her voice was confused. "What have you got to be sorry for? You didn't do this."

I looked up and she slid off her dark glasses. Both eyes, severely blackened, the purple swelling around them threatening to take over her cheekbones. In a few days, no doubt it would succeed. All my petty concerns disappeared. "What happened to you? Lorna, I feel terrible. I never thought you were in any danger when I left!"

She slipped her glasses carefully back over the bridge of her nose, so as not to cause any more discomfort and leant over the desk, so only I could hear her words. "Don't go all guilt laden on me. It's not your fault - it didn't even happen on Saturday. It was last night. When I hadn't heard from you I was angry. I decided to go out on my own. I started drinking. By the end of the night, I was paralytic, Ally, really guttered. Some slime ball decided to follow me. If a couple of men hadn't been passing, I mightn't be here at all today, talking to you. They scared him away, whoever it was, and took me to the police station. Truth is, being so drunk, my body was relaxed when I fell. Otherwise I might not have fared quite so well." She was trying to sound brave for my sake. "Told you one day it would pay to be plastered, didn't I? There's not a lot the police can do, except give out all the usual warnings. Big deal, eh?"

Vanessa passed by my desk, then scurried back to get a better look. "What's happened to you then?" Vanessa stood waiting for an answer, hands on her rather wide hips and her bosom overflowing from a crudely designed floral number. I knew she was about to be severely disappointed.

"Nothing for you to worry about, you old bag!" Lorna hissed. Vanessa stood staring for several seconds, just in case Lorna relented. When she realised no more information was forthcoming, she shrugged her shoulders and stalked off.

"As if I'd tell her anything! No doubt there'll be a few choice comments but I'll just have to rise above them. Nine day wonder – I'm not scared of that gossipy old bitch. I'm not scared of anything. "

Lorna's words hung in the air. I was still reeling from the shock of her injuries, so they took a minute to register. What a strange thing to say. "What's going on, Lorna? You must have been scared – when it happened? Look at the state of you."

She drew so close I could smell her breath, not too pleasant even now. "I need to talk to you. Thing is Ally, I didn't tell the police everything. No one would believe me, or else they'd think I'd really lost it."

I could see she would explode if she was couldn't tell me soon. I dragged her off to the toilets, locking us into a cubicle. I was amazed when she started crying, great racking sobs I could barely believe were coming from my beautiful, strong Lorna. She cried for long moments, trying to talk, but the tears and her fear stopped her. Slowly, the tears subsided and her story came out. "I can tell you, Ally. *You'll* understand." Sobs racked her, lifting her shoulders as I pulled her to me, comforting her. "I didn't see anyone – I don't *know* who did this to me. Just... just before it happened I felt a great rush of air, like a huge flapping, powerful surge and then something hit me, smashing down into my face..."

As she said the words, I recalled my dream. Those bird images had been interwoven with images of Lorna. My weakened instinct had been trying to warn me, but my bond to Lorna was too strong. I could have screamed with frustration. What *were* those things I had sensed? Why had those strange beasts hurt her? "What are you saying? That whoever struck you wasn't on the ground? They hit you from a height, from above you?"

"Kind of..." Lorna reddened, clearly embarrassed, "I know it sounds impossible...I was drunk, but not drunk enough not to remember. I didn't *see* anyone near me. Nothing.. Even those men who found me didn't see anyone running away." Lorna paused. I felt her tremble before she began again. "They didn't lie," she said leaning closer to me. "They didn't see anyone running away because *it* lifted itself up and disappeared before they got there." She was sobbing again now. "Even though I know, in my head, it's ridiculous, whatever it was that hit came from nowhere, from thin air."

She looked at me with such a pleading in her eyes, I felt sorrier for her than ever. I said the words she needed to hear. "I believe you, Lorna."

She tried to smile. I realised then the pain she had in her facial muscles. "I needed to hear that. I'm sure there's some rational explanation – but until they catch whoever did it, I think I'll just stay home for a while – or at least till this dies down." Lorna touched her cheekbone gently but winced in pain. "And even then I'll not be walking going out alone. You'd better be careful too, Ally."

She was genuinely concerned for my safety. It seemed only right to come completely clean, so she wouldn't worry about me. It was long overdue.

"Lorna, I need to get something off my chest too. I *have* been seeing Cormac." The words hung in the air between us. "I like him...a lot."

She took a step back, cutting me off. "I get it. You two are an item and I'm out of the picture, right Ally?"

I could understand her reaction. She looked genuinely hurt. I wished I hadn't waited so long to tell her, but there would never have been a right time. "You're my best friend, Lorna, but we always knew we would meet someone. It doesn't have to mean the rest of our life stops, does it?"

Even after her weeping, I might have known she wouldn't show her true emotions now. Her sarcastic tone wounded me deeply. "You tell me, Ally… you're the one in the relationship, not me!"

I was not about to have another catfight. "This is bad timing. I'm so sorry, Lorna, for what you've been through. If I'd been with you it would never have happened. Look, I'll see you in the canteen at lunch. Please don't let this come between us Lorna."

There was both hurt and resentment in her voice. "I think I should be the one saying that to you, don't you think?"

I watched her leave, torn up inside. Why had I not read more carefully into that strange dream? She was my best friend. She could have been raped, murdered or both. I had a sense of having been let down by the instincts I had relied on since childhood. Would they soon leave completely? Would I have to rely utterly on my own resources? How else could I explain the way my *sight* had abandoned me in the last few weeks? The gift I had hated for so long suddenly seemed very precious.

I shook myself mentally. I had long ago accepted that I had no control over the past. I was determined to keep her friendship, especially now. For the first time I realised that I needed space away from Cormac, regardless of what my heart told me. As I watched Lorna walk away, I felt my outlook change. It was as though I had found a reason to stand my ground against Cormac to protect our friendship. I had to be strong, prove to him I was no walkover. It was as if my head was back in control, my autopilot deactivated. I spent the morning guilt-ridden, the feeling worsening as the morning progressed. I watched the hands of the clock crawl towards twelve thirty, anxious to see Lorna, show her I meant what I said.

I took the stairs to the canteen, thinking I'd be quicker. Starting my descent, I heard the door below bang shut. In that second fear rocketed through my body. Instinctively I held my breath, holding tightly onto the banister, peering over the landing to see who was there. The stairwell was empty. No footsteps. Cursing myself for being spooked by Lorna's story, I sped down the flight of stairs to the canteen, sighing in relief as I reached the door to the next floor.

My fingers never touched the handle. I was grabbed from behind, and spun around so quickly my head swam. All thoughts of screaming were lost. By the time I had instructed my body to panic, a hand was held firmly over my mouth, and I had been pushed back onto the wall. I looked straight into the eyes of my attacker, feeling terror. But there was no brutality there, just a pleading expression that emphasised his fear. He placed his finger over his own lips, urging me not to call out.

I closed my mouth. He removed his hand.

Fear had blinded me. I recognised him. He was not a stranger, though it had been more than five years since I had seen him. I would have known him anywhere, by the scar he had carried since childhood. It still ran the length of his cheek but didn't detract from his handsome face. He had always had the bluest eyes on the Island. Almost uniquely amongst the people I had grown up with, he had never been part of the unkindness of my childhood. The last I had heard, he was working the trawler with his uncle Cavendish.

"Calum, you scared me half to death."

He spoke rapidly in Gaelic. I struggled for long seconds to decipher his meaning, but his words were so confused, I had to stop him. Surely he couldn't be saying what I thought he was?

I had to take control, for if we were to reach any kind of understanding somebody had to. In the tongue of my childhood, I stopped him. "Calm down, Calum, I can't make head or tail of what you're saying. Start again, nice and slow. Maybe I'll fathom why you're here."

He stared at me, and then wiped a hand across his forehead, removing a fine trace of sweat. "I was on my way up to your floor to see you. I gave the front desk some spiel about us being family. I needed to talk to you."

Knowing he would never hurt me, I relaxed. "You're lucky you caught me. I was on my way to…"

Immediately he silenced me. "What I have to say is important, Aluinn, so don't waste time. That man downstairs told me I only have ten minutes. He only let me in to give you news of your mother."

His words put the fear of God in me, but I was not about to show it.

"You've to come back, Aluinn, back to the Island with me. There's not much time…your mother's dying."

Dying?

But to go back? The very thought filled me with panic. The words were out before I could stop them."I won't go, Calum, you can't make me."

His words rushed out. "Stop shouting! Every sound echoes in this stairwell. At least come somewhere and talk to me, so I can explain. Don't tell anyone else I'm here. I mean it, Aluinn, not a soul."

I tried hard to grasp his words. Part of me still couldn't believe he was there at all. Why had he travelled all the way down to Edinburgh, to find me? I pacified him. "I can't think straight. I'll meet you after work. Be outside the building at five o'clock. Follow me when I leave. I'll go into some quiet café, and we can talk then. Is that agreed?" I wanted him gone.

He relented."I've little choice, have I?" A nerve flickered in his cheek and his eyes held mine, searching me.

I needed to get away. His news of my mother – the thought of her dying had staggered me - more than I wanted to show. Panic started to rise in me. "I've got to go, my friend will be wondering where I am. She might come looking for me,"

"RememberAluinn, not a word to a soul!"

I would have willingly sold my soul to the devil to see him leave. "I promise."

With that, Calum disappeared downstairs, only too willing to be gone, now he had passed on his message.

A man I trusted had told me that my mother was dying. Yet somehow I couldn't believe him. I wasn't a heartless person. Despite her treatment of me, despite the beatings and the neglect, she was still my mother. Not to return, to ignore Calum's message, would make her lose face before the entire community. But that wasn't the real reason I was so shocked. Once it reached the ears of those back home that I turned my back on my own I would be shunned. I could never again return. Their rejection of me would last forever. There would be no forgiveness nor absolution, only shame.

I gathered my wits about me, straightening my clothes and pushing the pins back into my hair. I took a deep breath; I couldn't talk about my encounter with Calum, and that meant I would have to lie to Lorna.

She almost pounced on me as I walked through the door.

"Where've you been? Look, Ally, I know I gave you a hard time this morning. I'm sorry, honest. I was feeling bad and I took it out on you. We're okay right?"

My tension disappeared. "We're fine", I smiled. And then I lied. "I got caught up in work, that's all."

Lorna returned to her table. I was almost sure I wouldn't be able to eat anything. "I've been thinking, I could put my injuries to good use, Ally," she said, hungrily biting into her sandwich and speaking at the same time, "I'm going round to mum's tonight; might get a sympathy vote. It could take the heat off after the last time I went home." I doubted it. Lorna's family put the 'd' in dysfunctional. They all drank too much, rowed too much and did little to mend the damage. She didn't talk about them much, just often enough for me to know her family had the power to hurt her where others couldn't. I never intruded or tried to give her advice – What would I know after all about a happy home life? And why give her more grief. We'd been through enough already.

Ignoring my silence, Lorna stirred her half-finished coffee. Her manner changed a little, seemed more formal. "Cormac came in, only for a minute. He asked for you, but said he couldn't wait." From the stubborn look on her face, I thought she had probably given him a hard time. I said nothing. The last thing I wanted was another argument.

Lorna seemed put out by my silence. "He was in a hurry. Something important had come up, but he would see you later."

If I was annoyed then it was nothing compared to my next reaction.

"So, Ally, tell me all about it. Every little sordid detail - your nights of wanton abandon with the man of your dreams. Start anywhere you like. I'm all ears."

Chapter Nine

True to his word, Cormac caught up with me as I left the building that evening. I had thought of little else but him. I leant forward and kissed him warmly. "Hi, I missed you at lunch, where did you disappear to?"

"Am I to be at your beck and call all day, woman?"

"If that's your way of excusing yourself…"

He laughed as he put his arms around me, pulling me close and whispering in my ear. "Don't worry, I'll make it up to you. We've lots of time, a whole lifetime." He lifted my chin, so that our eyes met. "If you want, that is?"

When he kissed me everything else went out my head. When he offered me a lift home, I automatically accepted. There was a nagging feeling, as though I had forgotten something important. But it refused to come to mind. Whatever it was it could wait. He pulled up in front of the flat.

"I've people I need to catch up with but I'll see you tonight," he said, flashing his perfect white teeth. He leant out through the open window, pulling me inside. His kiss was passionate, rough even, before he gently kissed me goodbye.

I watched as he drove away, feeling strangely low. It was only when I was inside the flat that realisation dawned. In my excitement at seeing Cormac, I had forgotten all about meeting Calum. Why had he not called after me, if he saw me leaving? He should have tried to get my attention.

A little voice in my head said maybe it was better this way. Maybe he would just take it that I had just decided not to go home with him. Maybe he would just leave me in peace. What did I care for that tiny place so far away? How could I even consider going back to it, when I had had to fight so hard to leave it? And at what cost?

It was lonely without Lorna for company. I hoped her parents would be easy on her. Feeling disturbed by my meeting with Calum, I was angry at myself for having gone back on our agreement. I had always had a lot of time for him, and it would have been fantastic - the chance to talk to someone from home. Hear the news, how everyone was doing. For all their unkindness, at some level I still wanted things to go well for them all.

When the phone rang, I was pleased it was Cormac. He had returned to work; the noise of a copier hummed faintly in the background.

"Sorry it's taken me so long to call. It's not easy working up here in the Gods, you know."

"No, but the pay's a lot better," I laughed.

"It has its perks I suppose. Get your party gear on. We're going out to a rather suave do. It doesn't start until 9pm, so you have enough time, right?"

I glanced at my wristwatch.6.45. I supposed I might just be ready in time. "Fine, sounds great. What time will you be here?"

I could imagine him laughing at the panic his next words created. "Give me an hour."

The connection died.

An hour? That wasn't long enough to do all I needed too. Grabbing some wipes, I smeared at my face. There was no way I could wash my hair. Instead, I piled it up, wild and high. Cormac liked it like that, said it emphasised the creaminess of my face and shoulders. All I knew was that it made me look immediately younger. I stared at myself in the mirror. Without my make up it was easier to see the old Aluinn looking back out at me. I had striven hard to bury her, but she was part of me still. Almost in defiance, I pinned my hair up, jabbing the long locks tight to my head with a multitude of pins, enough to withstand a hurricane.

Desperate times called for desperate measures. I went into Lorna's room, something given normal circumstances I never did without permission, but I was frantic for something to wear. Ripping open her wardrobe doors, I gazed at her finely tailored clothes. Though only on slightly higher pay, Lorna cared much more about her appearance than I did. The investment she'd made in it certainly made a substantial difference to her wardrobe. Thankfully, her new little black dress was hanging just where it should be, elegant enough to be smart, yet funky enough to be wearable.

Ready with time to spare I was slightly nervous. If Lorna arrived back early and found me in her new dress, having had a row with her family, who knew how she would react. And I dreaded to think what would happen if she and Cormac arrived together.

A car horn sounded outside. I almost flew out the front door, only just remembering to lock it. As I made my way over to his shiny new car, Cormac opened the window and whistled. "You look sensational!"

I walked towards him, confident for once in my own allure. "Perhaps we should just go straight to your place?" I joked. "Or hadn't you noticed my overnight bag?"

He raised an expressive eyebrow before turning the key in the ignition. It suddenly occurred to me I had no idea where we headed, but it didn't matter. I was with him again.

As we drove out of the city, I closed my eyes. An image formed in my mind of Calum's pleading face. It was so real to me that I almost told Cormac about our strange meeting. But I had made a promise, a promise to one of my own. Inwardly I cursed Calum for becoming the cause of dishonesty between Cormac and I. Because of it I was quiet for the rest of the journey. As Cormac drove, I listened to the music, taking in the views as we passed the city limits. Once we were out in the countryside, I was enchanted to see the sea again. Far off to begin with, gradually the coastline grew, until the road ran along grassy slopes, which swept downwards to sandy beaches and the gently lapping waves.

It was like home. Such a strange feeling, being linked to a place by the illusion of another. Overcome with homesickness a longing stirred in me so strong I had to close my eyes against it. It was only then I realised that I was depriving myself of the joy of looking at the sea again. The coast road was breathtaking. I saw another, parallel coastline far off on the other side. We were heading through luscious greenery and heavy croplands. The rock formation that sat out in the Forth raised my spirits to another level. It was like seeing a familiar face from the past and the thought came to me, *Would it really be so bad to let Calum take me home?*

If I went I would miss all I had come to love, especially the man who sat by my side. But what if I were to share it with him?

Once again Calum's face sprung into my mind's eye. I had promised him I'd tell no one of our encounter. The words I had wanted to speak died on my lips.

"How much longer, Cormac? What's the name of the place we're going to?"

"It's a big old house in North Berwick. I'm positive I mentioned it." His eyes never left the road, which twisted and weaved constantly.

If there was one sense that never failed me, it was my memory. "If you had spoken of it I would know, and wouldn't need to ask again."

"We'll be there shortly. Should be a nice evening – quite elaborate affair. Lots of stuffed shirts, I'm afraid. I don't mind if you bat your eyes at some of the men, as long as I know you're going home with me."

"Cocky, aren't you? And what if I meet someone there who takes my breath away?"

The car swerved slightly. He was angry. I realised now that he was often angered when I showed my stronger side. His reaction was usually to play me at my own game. He slowed the car slightly, watching my eyes. "In that case, do I have a free rein to flirt with all the beautiful women who'll be there?"

"Please yourself." He had called my bluff. I was livid. The very thought of him with someone else sent me spiralling off into a tailspin of jealousy. Seeing he had hit his mark, he was gracious enough to speak first. He couldn't stand the silence between us any more than I could. The thought gave me a small satisfaction. In a way, I had won.

"Let's just try and enjoy the evening. It's a stupid thing to row about – how about we forget this conversation ever happened?"

"What conversation?"

He laughed. "Good timing, if I do say so – we're here." And he manoeuvred the final bend in the road. We passed through large wrought iron gates and pulled into a driveway. Hundreds of miniature roses from darkest pink to near white lined the road to the house on either side.

The car stopped. "Big house" had been something of an understatement. It could have been a grand hotel. People were walking up to the steps, greeting each other formally. I was suddenly nervous. Cormac must have sensed it; as he handed his keys to the valet, he put his arm around me.

We approached the middle-aged couple who stood at the door, welcoming their guests to their home, dressed in finely tailored evening clothes. The woman looked almost regal, adorned in the most dazzling jewels I had ever seen outside of a shop window. Diamonds encircled her slender neck. She had a proud look, not quite haughty, but there was no softness to her features. The man too lacked warmth. He stood erect in the doorway, his whole demeanour signalling authority and ownership.

This was obviously a business function. I had to make an effort for Cormac's sake, if not my own. At least I had observed their dress code. Whether I passed their other criteria was a different story. When they turned to me, their smiles seemed forced. As the woman looked me up and down my face flushed with indignation. That feeling of being judged which I had left behind a long time ago was there again. I realised this couple had the same power over me, the same ability to make me feel vulnerable.

"Take Ally inside, darling. We'll catch up with you later." The woman's hand on Cormac's arm, as much as her easy endearment, took me up short. How well did he know these people? Was this a family party rather than the business function I had expected? I looked at him, confused, but he was already greeting people.

The men and women in the room he led me into clearly didn't suffer from my lack of self-assurance. They exuded wealth, that easy sense of entitlement. All my old insecurities came flying to the surface – along with my prejudices. These people were the epitome of everything I hated. Instantly I sensed their judgment of me. With their breeding had come snobbery, distaste for those below them. Somehow – was it my own fear that told them? -they had already sensed I wasn't 'one of them'. I fought hard to control the resentment building in me.

A tiny voice began in my head, telling me to get out of there. How could Cormac bring me here amongst his kind with no warning? How could he be so inconsiderate of my feelings? In my eagerness to please him I would have come that night. With forewarning I might have coped better with this quiet hostility. Their eyes betrayed it, even as they reached out their hands to shake mine. Cormac moved easily from person to person, greeting them warmly. I felt panic rising within me.

To these people, *his* people, I was as nothing. They belonged together, held secrets to which I wasn't privy and never would be. Their poise, their casual acceptance of the grandeur around them – I'd never develop that in a thousand lifetimes.

I loved this man with such ferocity it terrified me. Would he see me now through their eyes? I told myself I was being paranoid, but the feelings refused to subside. Instead they grew, and with them came a new realisation. I rejected these people just as fiercely as they rejected me. Long minutes passed. I strove hard to control the revulsion that swept through me as I was passed from hand after hand, being subjected to further scrutiny. Not one kind word or welcoming face.

I had become the outsider again.

Their rejection of me brought back untold unhappy memories. My own people had not wanted me. What hope had I of being accepted here? My higher self was on full alert, warning me to get away.

Cormac was moving amongst them easily, oblivious to my discomfort. "I'll just go and get us both a drink." Ignoring my mute plea, he left me alone, vulnerable. The bar was only a few metres away, but it could have been miles as I stood alone, watching these people watching me.

I sensed a darker side to them, an undercurrent. My weakened senses couldn't unravel all that was hidden, but I knew enough to question Cormac's decision to spend time with them. Were my flagging instincts weakened, misguiding me? Yet the sensation of evil was growing stronger.

It *wasn't* just my perception of them that was at fault. I found no worth in these people. It wasn't just my fear that was separating us. They *were* vain, *were* hostile. As I stood there, waiting for Cormac to return, I had an overwhelming sense of the ugliness of their souls – real loathing for anyone not of their ilk. The force with which my mind and body were jolted, the energy surge, felt as though a thousand volts had electrified every single part of my anatomy. I lifted my head and squared my shoulders. My instincts were right - why expose myself to their arrogance and hostility? I had worried that Cormac was too good for me. Standing there, I began to see what he appreciated in me. I had no need to hide behind any man. I had character, qualities these could never hope to attain, despite their wealth and breeding. I had no need to prove myself to anyone.

The truth, of course, was that I was afraid.

I had to leave. My gift which had deserted me all these weeks was protecting me now. It willed me to head for the door. Cormac was still some distance away. He seemed mislaid to me. A group of earnest looking people had encircled him, hanging onto his every word. He turned to me, a plea for understanding in his eyes. My heart surged with love for him.

I watched him make his way towards me. Dozens of eyes followed him over to me and were focused on us. They seemed to be looking at me in just the way the Islanders had, as though I had no right to be there.

"Cormac, I'm sorry. I need to get out of here. Can we go?"

"Go? Ally, we only just got here!" He raised his eyebrow in disbelief.

"I don't feel comfortable, Cormac. Everyone's staring at me. "

He looked angry now. "You're being paranoid, Ally. These parties always take a while to warm up. As soon as my parents have finished greeting everyone, things will become less formal."

Those people at the door were his *parents*? "Why on earth didn't you tell me before now?"

He laughed shortly. "Your overreaction, Ally, is *exactly* the reason I didn't tell you before." Putting his arm around me, he turned away from the other guests. "My parents are very private; they wouldn't want anyone gossiping. When we have a quiet time with them later, you'll be properly introduced."

Something stirred in my heart, an overwhelming feeling that things were not as they should be. Why couldn't he understand how hurt and angry I was at being deceived? It gave me the final courage I needed to leave, no matter what anyone thought. "I want to leave. Now!"

I hadn't meant to speak so loudly. Other guests were looking our way. Cormac stared at me, not understanding, furious at me for making a scene. Since my earliest years I'd had the ability to cloud my innermost thoughts. I used it now – instinct, self-protection.

"Don't be ridiculous. My parents would be insulted."

His arrogance angered me more than anything he had done or

not done till then. "I have no intention of staying a minute longer, Cormac. I don't like being looked over like some prize cow, assessed to see if I have the proper credentials for the job."

He grabbed my arm, steering me further away from crowd. I shook him off, determined to stand my ground. It seemed every eye in the room was on us.

He regripped my arm, it was agonizing. "Ally, you're behaving like a fool. Come and have a drink. It'll help you relax."

"I shouldn't be here." The fear was growing stronger, controlling me. I could *feel* their disapproval. It almost overpowered me. "I need to go!" I shouted.

He looked away from me, embarrassed. I turned to go, my movements suddenly heavy, painful. Time seemed to slow down, weighting me with its bleakness. He wasn't coming with me.

Would he ever forgive me? He had the right to be angry. But I had no choice - in that moment, Cormac had been somewhere far off, separate and lost from me. He had been different with them, less caring, caught up in being a part of them.

On the road outside the house, despite my anger, I knew I had made the right decision. My instinct hadn't failed me - there had been something deeply disturbing about those people. Behind all the grandeur and affluence I had sensed danger, as clearly as I had on the Island. Even outside the boundary gates, the thought of those people caused my body to tremble. Everything I had sensed was real, but how could I explain that to Cormac? I had known my own security to be under threat. How could I ignore the signals? It was as though my sight had been re-energised by the episode, reawakened.

I had no money and no transport. Out on the deserted road, I realised I had lost all sense of direction too - it was the curse of the seer to be confused by time and place. Fear flickered in my belly.

I urged myself to be patient. Turning left, I started to run along the width of the road. The night was dark. There were a few houses set together, none quite as grand as the one I had left. The narrow road wound away from me. Though I was putting distance between myself and it, my sense of danger wasn't lessening. I ran until cramp reached up and seized my inner thigh, the pain so searing I cried out. I had reached the near deserted streets of a town.

Up ahead were streetlights. I sensed there was safety here for others, but not for me; my gift told me I was more vulnerable than ever. I had *made* myself vulnerable. Hearing steps behind me, I looked back. A large group of youths, dressed in identical tracksuits and caps, was following me. I sensed their threat, their instincts. I felt the fear grow in me. I was half naked, in heels too high to run in. Their hunger surrounded me.

I ran through the darkness, blindly. And then it rose out of the darkness beyond me. It was as though my mind had conjured up my Island and brought it there to me, captured it so vividly that it merged perfectly with the night sky. I held my breath, afraid it would fade like the other sights the *Darna Sealladh* gave me. But it stayed there, strong. I stared at it, exhilarated by its force. But somehow frightened too.

Now instead of running from the men, I called to them. "What's that land mass up ahead?" I needed to know that it was there, that I hadn't imagined it. I sensed its connection to the Island. It reminded me of all I had left so far behind.

They jeered, thinking I was drunk. "Have you never seen the Law before? North Berwick Law."

It *was* real, my sight hadn't misled me.

The men were getting closer, calling to me to wait for them, to come talk to them. My heart was hammering – where was Cormac? I had been so sure he would come after me. For him to find me, I had to stay on the road. It turned and broadened into a street with shop fronts, closed save for a pub. Seeing me quicken my movements the men shouted insults, their jeering laughter loud on the night air. Taking off my shoes, I started to run again, as fast and as hard as I could, running as I had not ran since childhood.

I stopped at a sign post, almost crying with relief when it read Edinburgh. Sticking out my hand, I walked slowly backwards along the kerb, hailing whenever a car passed, but no one slowed. The men were still following me – giving me a little distance, calling out to me, enjoying my fear. In the night tiny beads of light grew larger. Another car. Headlights swathed an arc through the darkness. Determined to have the driver stop, desperation made me step out into the road.

As the car halted, I was suddenly afraid.

The fear disappeared when I saw Cormac's face in the semi-darkness. "Get in, Ally, please," he said with a calmness I had not expected, "I told my parents you were feeling unwell and made your apologies." I couldn't look at him. "Where do you think you were going, just for curiosity's sake?"

I would not grovel, regardless of my feelings for him. "I was going home."

He shook his head, "Hitch hiking's not a wise thing to do, not around here anyhow. It's only been a few years since two girls from Edinburgh were left murdered in this area; the killers were never caught. Their bodies were badly mutilated."

He was trying to frighten me into getting into the car. I hadn't asked him to follow me. My pride balked, yet how was I to get home without him? The warm interior beckoned me, the soft brown leather waiting to welcome me. Still I hesitated.

He spoke again, breaking the silence, "Get in, Ally, please."

The crowd of young men roared their anger as I opened the car door. Cormac moved off. For long moments we spoke not a word. My hair had almost come undone. I removed the few remaining pins and let it fall wild over my shoulders. It gave me back some of the strength I lacked. How could he not sense the evil in that house? I had clearly sensed that his parents were part of it, been aware of the malevolence within their make up, just as surely as I sensed his love for me. Cormac turned and smiled at me. I regarded him gravely.

His people might not accept me, but Cormac would never wish me harm. Throughout the journey I remained silent, glad Cormac did likewise. Better things be left unsaid for now. I feigned sleep, relieved and thankful he had come for me. We arrived at his flat. He showed me to my room again. I felt like a small child, being punished. But I made no resistance, going straight to bed. Drained, I slept soundly.

No more dreams, no more apparitions.

Chapter Ten

By morning yesterday's fear and anger were just hazy shadows.

Pain drummed behind my eyes, robbing my spirit of calm. I listened. There was no movement in the flat. Passing Cormac's room on my way to the bathroom, his door stood slightly ajar. His bed had not been slept in.

Had he gone back to his parents' place as I slept?

I should have insisted he drop me at my flat. All those times I let him make decisions for me, allowing him more and more control. Little by little I had given over the power I had sought so hard to win. I refused to be manipulated. I had had enough of that to last several lifetimes.

And yet I knew myself – without him I was able to be alone and content. His absence this morning had me distraught.

I felt weakened in energy, empty. My stomach cramped with hunger. I hadn't experienced hunger pains since I had left the Island. Growing up my need to be free had meant many missed mealtimes for my growing frame. Although never underfed, I had always felt hungry.

The food was like sawdust in my mouth. Where was he? There had been dozens of attractive women at the party. What if he had left because he could no longer bear to be with me? Even the thought of it had me pushed far beyond the realm of pain. My reason told me he could no more bear parting from me than I could bear being away from him. Yet if that were true, why had he left me alone?

There was something wrong with me, I realised. My thinking, the thoughts I had always relied on to comfort me, were causing me pain. My panic turned to anger as the front door opened. Still dressed in clothes from the night before he looked strangely untidy. I had never seen him dishevelled before.

I had a sudden sense of myself for a moment, as he had seen me last night – a young woman, ranting and afraid, leaving his family gathering with no way to get home. No wonder he hadn't believed me capable of disappearing into the night.

"You're awake. I hope I didn't disturb you earlier?"

I tried to sound calm. "Morning. Where have you been?"

He looked at me in the oddest way, seeming to hesitate, as though trying to discern my true feelings. I kept him at bay, refusing to let him inside my mind. When he spoke, he stumbled over his words. "I fell asleep on the couch last night. When I woke I had such a crick in my neck I had to get up and walk about. Decided to go down for a paper before getting breakfast," he said, waving the broadsheet I'd failed to notice. He smiled that smile.

For first time it displeased me. It seemed to come too easily. It was too perfect, too practised. How many others had fallen for that same vanity of his? Perhaps he had used that same smile elsewhere? An overwhelming fear washed over me, fear that he would betray me, would give to another the love he had withheld from me. Jealousy…I had always considered it a ridiculous obsession. Now I knew it would destroy my mind, if I allowed it room to grow. I had long felt threatened by another emotion, the fear of being not good enough for him. Now the fear was of being replaced by someone else. I knew then the real reason I had kept our connection hidden from Lorna. I had seen her as a threat.

I couldn't hold back the words, "So you haven't been anywhere else then?"

Sitting down at the kitchen table, he opened the paper forcefully. "Where else would I have been?"

I forced myself to remain calm. "I thought perhaps your parents' house?"

He folded the paper. I watched as it was doubled, then narrowed again. He beat his palm with it, his sarcastic tone barely disguised. "And let them know I had lied to them about you being ill?"

So my behaviour was neither forgiven nor forgotten. He slammed the paper onto the small table and stood up fiercely, his face menacing. "Your behaviour appalled me yesterday. I wondered at one stage if you hadn't lost your wits."

My greatest fear, that I was or presently could be insane had finally been spoken by another. "If you felt that way, you should have just taken me home to my own place." The words were a mere whisper.

He deliberately misunderstood "You don't like staying with me? Is that it?" He was cheapening and twisting everything, diminishing the hurt I was feeling. He rose, glaring at me, towering above me. For the first time I felt threatened by him. Suddenly his expression changed. "Whatever you're thinking, just say it, Ally. I don't want you keeping anything inside your head. It's hard enough for me to understand you without you complicating things."

I lost it. All those suppressed thoughts came roaring out in a rush, tumbling out in one tumultuous torrent of pent up frustrations. "You embarrassed me in front of your parents, you insensitive bastard! You didn't even introduce me properly. What kind of a message did that send out to your folks? What happened to *us*, Cormac, the couple? I thought you said you loved me? If you did, you'd realise how I felt last night." I didn't want to play his game any longer. "What kind of a relationship is this, Cormac? What are you getting out of it exactly? Clearly I'm not good enough to be introduced to your family. And it's not sex you're after – we're still in separate rooms." I was almost weeping now.

He looked sad, almost defeated. "I see. I thought I was treating you the way you deserved. But if it's a quick romp between the sheets you're after, let's go, I'm all for it."

With one stride, he had lifted me into his arms and was carrying me into his room. Kicking the door open, he threw me on top of the bed. My heart was racing. In spite of our anger, I wanted this.

He looked down at me for a long moment, then walked away. I heard the front door close behind him.

I lay there for the longest time. The rejection was more than I could bear. Finally, I cried. Gathering my belongings I left.

I knew he wouldn't come after me this time. I had overstepped the mark, spoilt everything. Despite everything he had said, I had cared too much, far more than he had. Lorna had been right after all. I had been eaten up by him. No wonder she had felt abandoned. Suddenly I was desperate to see her, to confide in her.

Outside the sky had darkened as I stood waiting for the bus back into the city. Defenceless against my own dark thoughts I allowed myself to fill up tender melancholy. I was lost in my pain, unaware of the dark blur beside me until I felt the first sharp claw connect with my face. Still lost in the mist of my unhappiness I reeled under its impact, struggling to recover as the bird's talons tore at my scalp. Its sharp beak broke the tender skin of my hands which I had raised to protect my face. The attack seemed to go on forever; it was as though the moment were frozen in time. Hot shards of pain tore and ripped at me. It was trying to get at my eyes! I screamed as the black form tried to engulf me, fighting desperately to find strength within myself, to regain control. Then, just as suddenly as it had arrived, the raven flew apart from me, and went off, cawing madly. I stood alone, terrified it might return.

There had been no one to witness the bird's savage attack. As a bus drew alongside me I climbed shakily inside. It was headed in the wrong direction, but all I cared about was getting inside, being safe. All I could think of was getting to Lorna. Had the attack she had suffered been like mine? That had been no ordinary bird – it had had the strength of a man.

Unsteadily I took my seat, and sat peering out of the window, trying to make out its dark shape in the morning murkiness. When I had finally convinced myself it wasn't following me I sat checking my hands and face. My jacket had protected me from the worst of it, but the slight scratches on the back of my hands and my cheeks bore no witness to the pain of the attack. I could see the other travellers staring at me, my shakes, my quiet desperation. Judging me, oblivious to the turbulence in my heart. We stopped at traffic lights and a sudden thump on the glass doors of the bus had us all jump in our seats. They hissed open to reveal a young man, his face half concealed within his jacket. He thanked the driver for stopping, almost colliding with a small child standing in the aisle in his anxiety to get on board. The child howled, distracting me. The bus moved off in shuddering starts, rejoining the slow-moving traffic. As I looked up at the large windows of the houses we passed, a hand touched my shoulder. I turned, praying it would be Cormac. Instead, there stood Calum.

"What are you doing here?"

In all that had happened, I had forgotten about him. He sat down next to me nervously eying the other occupants of the bus. Apart from a couple of young children, they paid him no heed. When he talked, it was a mere whisper. I strained to pick up his words, humouring his paranoia.

"You forgot about our meeting? I followed you. I've been watching you; where you go, what you do. I had a hunch you'd be coming back to his place last night." *How long had he been spying on me?* There was an unspoken accusation in his words. It made me uneasy – how could he understand? Everyone's eyes were on us as, speaking the Gaelic on an Edinburgh corporation bus. Now they knew me to be the same as him. Knew that I had been acting only, playing at being one of them. It was true, I knew it now. All I had wanted was an ordinary life, not fantastic or magical. And I had wanted to be inconspicuous. Now I was different again.

In my soul, I resented the man next to me. Calum hadn't just seen me, the way I carried myself, my liberty. He had seen my dependence on Cormac. The way I had behaved around him. I felt somehow ashamed. Yet as he sat beside me, I could see no judgement in his blue eyes.

"I'm sorry," I said, angry with him, although I knew I was at fault. "I really didn't mean to let you down; it was a genuine mistake. Let me make it up to you, I'm in no hurry now. Why don't we go for that coffee? Look, there's a café over there."

As soon as I had made the suggestion, I was livid with myself. What had gotten into me? Once off the bus, Calum hurried slightly ahead. So much had happened in the last hours – my emotions were still on a rollercoaster. Whatever the true reason for Calum being here, I had to go along with things for now. If a red warning light started in my mind, I would find the strength to make my excuses and leave.

We reached the small café. I settled at a corner table, hidden away from the window. Calum was talking with the young girl behind the counter. It was obvious the girl found him handsome. She flirted openly, obviously hoping I was a sister rather than a girlfriend. She threw me a smile, then laughed again at the joke they were sharing.

When he joined me, my coffee had already cooled. He smiled at me. I had given little thought to Callum over the years, separated as we were by time and place. Yet as he sat in front of me, it seemed as if no time had passed at all. I had always been fond of him, but that fondness didn't make me any happier to see him now. He was *their* messenger. I would hear him out and wish him a safe journey home.

It would be enough.

"Guess I got sidetracked," he said, winking back towards the girl who gave him a wave. He reverted again to our native tongue. "Pretty girl though." I found myself relaxing a little as the sounds washed over me. Immediately it was as though speaking English had been false all these years. Somehow less than it should have been. I studied him from under my eyelashes. The girl had been right to flirt with him. I had had a soft spot for Calum myself. Had he known back then how I had felt about him? How I had lain sometimes in the whin bushes, watching him work with his uncle? The thought brought a flush to my cheeks. He seemed not to notice. Instead he asked a question with a directness I would never have suspected him of, "Why leave like that, Aluinn? Surely there was no need to run away?"

"I didn't run away, Calum. I just left. I needed to find out what was out here, to see if I could be a part of it, be accepted." Suddenly I was angry, then angry at myself then for showing my irritation. "I thought you said what we have to discuss is urgent?"

"I *told* you why I'm here. I'm to take you back with me."

It had been a bad morning. "I don't need your or anybody else's interference in my life, thank you, Calum."

His tone changed. "Your mother's really very ill, Aluinn. There's no more time to delay. Unless you don't want to see her again."

I was shocked by how little I felt at the prospect.

Reaching over, he placed his hand on top of my own. "I'm sorry." He paused, for he had seen first hand the abyss between my mother and myself. "I know it wasn't easy for you, but how will you live with yourself if you don't go see her now?"

The strangeness of the previous night dulled into nothingness. "Are you sure she's dying?" The word stuck in my throat like a thorn. "Is there nothing they can do?" Hearing the pleading in my own voice, I almost burst into tears. *If I went back, what guarantee would I have that they would let me go again? And the pull of the Island itself was so strong. What if I couldn't find the strength to leave?*

I stirred my coffee. The thick froth split then slowly disappeared into the dark liquid below. As I stirred, I visualised my mother's emotionless features. And then a new thought came to me. *Would she stoop so low as to trick me into coming back?*

Calum was a decent man. Surely he would tell the truth? *If he gave his word to me that she was really ill...*

"Is it no more than a sick excuse to get me home again?"

He shook his head. Before he had a chance to speak, I vented my anger, suddenly unable to limit it. "I won't go back, Calum. I'm happy here, for the first time in my life. I have friends, a good job, a life of my own. I could never be happy there again."

I had raised my voice, but didn't know until I saw the two middle-aged women looking at me from the table across the way in alarm. I tried to smile to put them at ease, but they both appeared startled. And then I understood why. I was Island Aluinn once more, my fiery hair flowing wildly. Looking threatening.

I stared into Calum's face, full of remorse for my outburst. He was not the cause of my upset. He didn't lift his head, just sat stirring his coffee, unaffected by the attention I had drawn on myself. When he had collected the froth on the spoon, his lifted his chin and looked straight at me. "You're right, I can't make you. But your mother's going to die, whatever you decide."

He looked for all the world, as if he had just delivered a report of the weather. Instead of this great, cruel, fact.

Old childhood fears resurrected themselves, rearranging themselves in my subconscious, re-evaluating all I had left behind. I arranged those memories alongside newer ones of my life in Edinburgh, and felt very afraid. How could those two separate parts of my life ever coexist? I feared they never would. At home, I was controlled still by tradition and pride. But the thought of being shunned, of never again being allowed to return to the place of my birth...that thought filled me with dread.

One day, when my life was content, when my search for my own identity was over, I had meant to return. A voice in my head started screaming a warning, saying I wasn't ready. Yet in spite of everything I knew and feared, I understood that I was going home.

There was no way to avoid that pain in the future otherwise.

Suddenly I was filled with utter conviction that this was the right thing to do. I would return to my Island, say goodbye to the ghosts of my past. What would happen on my return I didn't know. I understood only that I couldn't disgrace my mother or myself.

"How soon do we have to leave?" I already dreaded the answer, whatever it would be.

He smiled at me, to show he understood. I was glad it was Calum, who had come for me. He was not a bad memory. Many a time he had broken up tussles between Morag and me, protecting me. He was a good man. I wished he had noticed me back then. Perhaps he might have changed things, saved me the pain I had known since?

When he had said he understood, it was not an empty statement. In his eyes I could see that he well remembered those days. There, in his eyes, was the reason I was yearning to go home.

Making plans for the trip back was a welcome relief. I had been forced to banish thoughts of Cormac. In time, perhaps that pain would ease too.

*

I left having said goodbye to everyone who mattered, purposefully avoiding Cormac. The thought of a meeting face to face was unthinkable. Back at the flat, I wrote him a letter, saying I couldn't see him again. I lied willingly, letting him think me callous and cruel. Let him believe I was as disinterested as I pretended to be. As I formed the words, I pictured his face as he read them. Let him put me out of his mind. Let him wish never to see me again.

Cormac had been in the dark all this time about my life. Why muddy the waters now? It was a tortuous kindness. If I abandoned my principles, despite those long lonely years on that Island, I didn't deserve ever to have set foot on the place again. As I packed my few things, I tucked away my true emotions, hiding from myself the plain truth that I loved him.

I told Lorna of my plans. Her towering dislike of Cormac made me sure she would keep my secret. Something made me hold back from confiding more – how the raven had attacked me, how afraid I had been. The moment had been so terrifying, I couldn't bring myself to remind her of her own ordeal. Besides, our truce was so fragile. I couldn't tell her how much I missed him, that there was no joy in my freedom. I was in limbo. By tomorrow, I would be far away from the city. Feeling restless and discontent, I decided to go into town, to gather up a few last memories. I walked the length of Princes' Street, happy to be hemmed in by the masses of tourists creating their own memories of the city. Behind me streamed a long procession of wind singers, wailing furiously. I sensed their unhappiness at leaving them. The edgy rawness I felt was reflected in their antics. I chided them for interfering, as busy traffic slowed to a halt, delayed by their meddling. Tomorrow I would leave and the bustle of the city would continue. How small my birthplace would seem. But as I walked its streets, I knew Edinburgh had never given me the same joy in my soul.

To escape the whispering *taibhsean* I jumped on a bus. It seemed they understood my need for peace, for they did not follow. They had already made their disapproval of my decision felt. I followed the walkway around the gates of Holyrood Palace, the streets there full of tourists enjoying the beautiful spring day. Pictures were taken, happy memories caught forever. How I envied them.

New life was everywhere. Mothers pushed newborn infants in expensive buggies, or carried them under their hearts. Toddlers ran around on the grass, laughing and screaming their joy at being alive. I had wanted so much to be a part of what these women had.

Once more I stood at the foot of the Seat. The weather spirits were there in force, more than I had ever seen before. They had come out in great numbers, alerted by others, afraid to draw near for my mood had blackened. I was angry at them. Did they not know that this was my last visit? I had thought they had had grown to love me, feyness and all, wanting to experience my pain as I sensed theirs. As they gathered round me I went to them in spirit, apologising for my ill humour. I gathered succour from them, focussing inwards, shutting out any distractions. I saw once again my Island, the lush spates of pines and conifers, protected by the North hills. The beauty of the peaks belied their treachery. In my mind, I flew over them, to the blue-green water that lay within the South Bay. How I longed to see it all again. If only I could find a way to live in harmony with the others who had made their home there, I would be content there always.

I prayed the *sight* would give me the courage I so badly needed.

Chapter Eleven

Rain threatened as I journeyed home, but I could see it clearly in my mind's eye, the coastline, the jutting landmass that would appear out of the mist, terrifying and magnetic. Despite my fear of the Islanders, I knew I had a greater fear – that I would never be able to leave.

My mother was like the Island itself, solid rock, hard and cold. She demanded the respect of others, seemed not to need their love. She neither gave, nor received any. Her forbidding appearance helped her, made it easier to keep the many secrets I knew she carried in her heart.

This was the real reason I was returning. If she was dying, part of me felt the need to witness that she had truly gone, that she could harm me no more. If I balked, she might haunt me always. This way, finally, I might be set free. She should have nurtured me all those long, hard years. The traditions of the Island were far stronger than any law on the mainland. As I had grown to womanhood, I had realised that only their control of her kept her from treating me more cruelly than she did.

Needing comfort I pictured Cormac then. My mind revisited every encounter we had shared. I saw his face so clearly, every detail recorded in my memory. How he had mesmerised me. Every minute since my departure from his side had been pain. Had he thought of me at all? Or was my own agony wasted?

He had made no effort to contact me, and why would he? I had made my intentions clear.

Lorna had done little to comfort me. I refused to dwell on it. Perhaps she was glad it was over between us.

Calum and I spoke little on the journey up towards Oban. There was nothing to discuss; I was going home and Calum was taking me, as he had promised. I had accepted my fate for now. Leaving the last major town behind, I lost my sense of anonymity.

The long, winding roads which led through the very heart of the Highlands, were so beautiful. Then came sheer drops hidden by greenery that fell down to the blue waters. The glens looked uninhabited but I could make out small cottages hand sewn into the patchwork of colour. In the highest reaches the grassland died out, turning golden yellow, reminding me of beaches devoid of sea or shoreline. This was cruel terrain, fit only for sheep to graze. My *sight* travelled to times of old, with no roads or lighted paths, nothing but mile upon mile of barren ground and rough terrain.

Then the vision was lost to me.

Finally, we arrived in Oban. Calum parked in the car park behind the harbour, talking readily now, as though we were on an outing. Perhaps it was a distraction technique, I thought suddenly. Our legends were full of tales of young women abducted under false pretences. Was that my fate? Was I to be duped because a childhood friend understood the pull of the Island and all that was waiting there for me?

Cursing myself for my own paranoia, I lugged my belongings towards the harbour wall and was instantly uplifted by the sight of the sea. There were dozens of people walking about, and others waiting to catch their ferry to their next destination. I watched life as it should be lived, people free to do exactly as they chose within the boundaries of the law. My gaze was drawn upwards far above the harbour to the magnificent circle of stone columns, built on solid rock. Drawn to its symbolism I used my seer's gift. Sure enough, there among the stones were the *taibhsean* who claimed the structure, dwelling there as unchanging as the stones they protected. I turned away, apologising for having disturbed their serenity.

Calum joined me with some fresh scallops from a small hut within walking distance of the ferry. I had not had such fresh seafood for so long. It seemed strange to my pallet, yet I relished the taste. The sun shimmered on the gently lapping water. I had never felt so downhearted.

I watched the ferry approach, a tiny shape in the distance. I watched the sea below it, stuck by its awesome blackness. How deep was it, the water? For a split second, I wondered if it would be so bad, simply falling into the dark depths. It might be a kinder evil than what I had yet to face.

The ferry was taking shape, cutting effortlessly through the water. Within minutes the true size of the huge hull was apparent, the name

'Clansman' lettered on its portside. Time stood still as all the cars were driven off. But then one by one other cars were driven on, led by travellers heading towards the various Islands. The ferry operators knew better than to offer daytrips to my home. It was not often they were required to reroute.

The journey was calm. With every sea mile that passed, I moved further away from all I had left behind. My heart was both weary and sad, my grief at losing Cormac weighing me down like the anchor that issued from the ferry's depths. I felt my heart swelling as land was sighted an hour later. Land. My land.My emotions were in chaos as we steadily approached the familiar harbour.

As the engines stopped, I had a moment of clarity. Perhaps, if we had spoken once more, Cormac would have made me stay. We had been separated by nothing more than my foolish pride.

I said a silent prayer, for the strength. Only Calum and I descended. I made my way down the wooden gangway to the waterfront mooring. As I stepped off and away from the ferry, I was seized with such dread, I swayed, grabbing onto Calum's arm. I turned, intending to run back up the gangway. Calum seemed to sense it, for he took my arm and literally dragged me off.

Once again, I had lost control of my life. I had lost my identity; I was Aluinn of the Island once more. We walked along the jetty and onto the harbour's cobbled street. In my ears the voices of my childhood echoed, the taunts, the scoldings. I broke loose from Calum's hold, turning to retrace my steps. But the ferry was already churning through the waters, anxious to be on its way.

It was then I saw her, walking towards me. As she came nearer, I felt sick with apprehension. As her cool grey gaze came to rest on me, I knew my mother was no more ill than I was. From a nearby building McGregor appeared, moving to stand uncompromisingly beside my mother, his hard features set in a stony expression. I recognised the look, had seen it often enough before, when he was determined to beat me. What surprised me was how he had aged – his skin looked sickly, sallow.

I was jolted by the realisation that I was unafraid of him. For I had 'seen' his end. Nothing he inflicted on me could be worse than what lay ahead for him. The image of it was incomplete and had no timescale. There was no real setting either, merely broken segments of utter certainty. Was my sense blocking the truth to protect me? I cared little, he was a vile woman-hater.

"Good to have you back amongst us again, Aluinn." His sarcastic tone caused ripples of approval in the people who had gathered around us. He played well to his audience, who lapped up his theatrics. "Tell me, what have you learnt since we last saw you that merits such betrayal?"

I stood tall, determined to be unafraid of their small mindedness.

"I discovered, Pastor McGregor, that away from this place, people think for themselves and that life is sacred."

McGregor laughed, surveying the crowd who tutted, mirroring his incredulity. He draped his arm around me in a display of showmanship.

"I see you use their English better than your own tongue now. Why don't you tell us about the lost souls you met out there, floundering without values and traditions?"

He was trying to humiliate me.

"Your view of them, Pastor, is coloured by your intolerance." He had been educated on the mainland, had experienced freedom. "The vast majority of mainlanders just want to get along the best they can. To live their lives freely, whichever way they choose. It's called a democratic society."

I could hear the whispers of anger around me. "You've obviously become more assertive, Aluinn. I like that." His breath was hot and damp on my neck. I almost retched. I dreaded his hands on my body. Instinctively I pulled back. Aware of my discomfort he stopped his course and lowered his voice slightly, perverse pleasure evident in his voice. "I can wait, Aluinn. You'll change your mind, in time."

"I'll not be kept here against my will."

"That's what I've missed Aluinn, your fighting spirit." He laughed. "There's more than one way to change someone's mind. It doesn't necessarily involve striking a blow."

As he looked at me, his vile tongue running along his bottom lip, I knew exactly why he had wanted me back on the Island. He meant to lie with me.

"I'd die first," I spat. McGregor roared with laughter.

"You'll change your mind, *chi thusa*, you'll see."Once again his laughter roared loudly. The real promise came as a whisper that only I heard. I watched as he turned and left, patting his henchman on the back as they shared a moment I had no desire to understand.

He had always been a threat to me, even as a child. That day at the quarry he had been held back only by my mother. It was the only time she had ever protected me. I could see her face yet, mottled in fury, hissing at him to leave me be. "She's not yet age." Her words had hung heavy in the air. McGregor wasn't used to the Islanders standing up to him.

Perhaps she couldn't face using her abortionist tools on her own daughter…

It seemed now he was intent on claiming his due. Watching him walk away my mind was screaming 'NEVER'.

Cormac's face appeared in my mind's eye. Strange, in all the madness which surrounded me. I drew comfort from him. I smiled then, knowing that although we were apart, Cormac was still my salvation. He had shown me what love was. Had I never laid eyes upon him I might never have experienced it.

I had been so terrified of McGregor I had forgotten my mother. She stood before me now, angered by the fleeting smile on my face. Did she think I was mocking her? She studied every detail of my hair, clothing, my make-up. The hot sting on my left cheek caught me completely off guard. It took several seconds before I connected the loud cracking noise with the searing pain. I had forgotten the rules. Her thick Gaelic spat into my flushed face, determined to humiliate any atom of me the blow had left untouched.

"Glan d'aodann, a nighean, mus tig thu a-steach do mo dhachaigh-sa!"

Using my sleeve to wipe the 'muck' from my cheeks and lips as she had ordered, my eyes filled with hot tears. The last remnants of doubt disappeared entirely. It was as if the blow to my head had jolted something into place. Back here, I had become her chattel once more, fit only to be ordered and bullied about, given less respect than a favoured dog. Instinctively I walked behind her as she made her way homewards with Calum, the two deep in conversation.

All at once, my senses returned, keener than ever. Regardless of how they treated me I had no other option but to see this through, for my own sake. I had to find a way to stand up to them. If I were ever to make a life for myself, ever to be free of these people, I had to show them that I was strong enough to take whatever they dished out to me.

The Island had remained just as I remembered it, the scenery postcard perfect. Minutes later I entered the only home I had ever known. There was no comfort, no warmth. I shivered. Turning to her resignedly, I formed the question, half-knowing the answer.

"Why have you brought me back, mother?" I pointed Calum's way. "He told me you were dying. That's why I came back. Why can't you just be honest with me? Why bring me back when you hate me so much?"

"Quiet girl! Thur's nah point in wonderin'. I*h*t's done that's auh! Yuh need tae stay here till it's o'er. "

I had some strength left, enough to stand up to her. "Until what's over mother?" The words were out before I could stop them. "I tried, so hard all those years to make you love me."

No reaction. I paused for a second, to find the strength. "How can you treat your own child like this?"

Silence.

Not daring to look up and see her wrath I went on. "All those years, I thought it was normal, that it was my fault. But I've seen enough now to know it's not. Mothers should protect their daughters from harm, not inflict it on them."

She silenced me with another sharp slap across my cheekbone. The shock of it jolted me into silence.

"Calm down, yur hysterical. Aw yur talk is nonsense. Ah cannae chainge the way things a*h*r."

Tears filled my eyes once more, watching in silence as they dropped, silent, onto the material of my jacket, leaving tiny stains. "Just tell me why, anything, just something that will make it bearable." She offered no answer, just started picking up items that lay around. I waited patiently for her anger to subside, remembering the ritual. She would speak only when she was ready, not a minute before. "Ye had a man friend on the Island I hear – walked in the path of temptation. Yur tae stay in yer room for a while. Folks are awreadi askin' questions. I want ye to stay awae fae them. It's fur yer own good. Not another word, deh ye hear mih?"

A cold shiver ran through my body. Had they found out somehow about Cormac? Calum might well have told them I stayed at his flat. Had they assumed our relationship was intimate? Was she afraid I was pregnant and wanted to keep me hidden till she could be sure? I almost told her she need not have worried, that I had already broken with him over my stupid pride. But if there was one quality my mother and I shared, it was stubbornness.

Perhaps they were surprised that I allowed myself to be led to my old room. I was disheartened and weary. The room was a tiny box with a skylight, no view. All my childhood, I had hated only being able to see a small square of stars at night. I lay down. Now I was confined to that small space once more, with no idea how many days I would be forced to endure it. My only hope lay in finding the strength to survive their tortuous games. Sadder than I could ever recall having been, I sought solace in my memory. I had spent my childhood in the hills, away from her, away from all of them. Wakening every morning, I had rushed through my chores, anxious to be away. In my head I returned to the joy I found there, to the solitude and beauty that sustained me.

My thoughts were disturbed by muffled noises below, filling me with frustration. I had no idea who was down there, or what was being discussed. No doubt I was the main topic of conversation. They had gone to considerable effort to bring me back. A new thought sprung to mind, one so terrifyingly shocking, I refused to give it room. Yet it refused to give me peace, reoccurring constantly, although I pushed it aside.

Lying there on the bed I allowed myself to face the truth. What if I had been brought back for McGregor ...like a lamb to slaughter? When I was a bairn, I had been no match against his strength. Even now as an adult, I had but one weapon against him – shunning. My body remained weaker than his. He was the monster that dwelt within every dark place, feeding off my innermost fears and weaknesses. As much as I hated being shut away, if it kept me from his clutches it wasn't too high a price to pay. I would rest for now. See what they had in store for me. Then I would flee.

Footsteps approached, dull thuds on the old wooden strapping. My mother. Her deceit had killed any last trace of feeling I had for her. The only thing she had ever done in my favour was let me live. My seers' gift could not make her out. The bond was too strong.

The door opened on the turn of her key. She entered her, height overwhelming in the enclosed space. "Ah've brought ye food tae eat. Eke it oot, mind, ah've tae go awa'. Thurs nae point makin' ah racket." I watched, as she placed the tray on the bed. The contents looked unappetising but I knew I would eat it rather than face her wrath when she returned.

I refused to look her way, not wanting her to see the hurt in my eyes. The bravery I had brought back with me had almost disappeared. Motionless, I watched as she placed a rusty bucket in the corner. It was for my use, I realised, a crude toilet. I had no illusions now. She meant to keep me trapped there.

I hated her then, more than ever. I was powerless, with no way to escape except into my head. My fear was that if I went there to often I would stay there. I had no option but to sleep often and pray that my isolation would end before the fear turned my wits. The key turned once more. It had been purgatory as a child. It was worse now, knowing that life existed beyond this place.

When I was sure she was gone I fell to weeping. I must have slept then, for I awoke feeling strengthened, physically and mentally. The sleep had strengthened me. I would rely on my inner resources, think only of pleasant things, my friendship with Lorna, and the feelings of worth I had found at my workplace. I would remember all the good times, all the new things I had learned, going over them in my head. Anything but think that of how I was being deprived of my freedom. Or wish that I had never returned. Or replay that last morning with Cormac, seeing the anger on his face.

As the days passed, my fury at my mother grew. She must be keeping me away like some unclean thing, till she had proof I wasn't with child.

I could not find the grace within me to forgive her. Another day. My mind drifted.The child in me returned to soothe my soul. Once again I relived all the joys of imagining. I was a free spirit. I saw the child I had been, running wildly through the rugged countryside, splashing in burns, watching seedlings raise their heads in the morning sunlight. That magical world had awoken my spirit then. It gave me the feeling now that I would survive, regardless of what they forced on me. I returned to that world now, still confined in that small space. Every time I returned to reality, the room seemed smaller.

Fear was growing – fear that the turmoil within me would win out over my reason, that my fragile sense of self would not survive this isolation. The watch batteries I had meant to replace ceased to function. Time had no meaning. Days sped forward or reeled backwards. I judged the hour roughly by the shadows on the walls or the patch of stars at night, through the sparse window. Small distraction from the fear building in me. How much longer till she returned?

Everything was so mixed up, my internal body clock confused and disorientated. I almost began to look forward to seeing her. Had I lost my mind? Had she broken me? Was she downstairs, only feet away, enjoying my suffering?

I had eaten sparingly, and only when I could no longer bear not to, but my food supply had dwindled. All that remained was stale bread, scraped to remove the mould.The bucket was overflowing. I had grown accustomed to the stench and the silence. My senses were greatly heightened by my solitude and paranoia. When I heard in the distance the faint but unmistakeable sounds of footsteps, heading directly towards the croft, I listened intently. Fearing to breathe almost as the steps increased in volume. Whoever it was must be outside the walls of the croft.

My heartbeat quickened. Instinctively I held my breath, my sudden fear contradicting my earlier loneliness. Now I felt stark terror. I pictured the Pastor's face, praying it wasn't him, praying that I wasn't about to be made endure something far, far worse than anything I had endured so far. Lorna's assault came to me, her battered face. I knew now that she had been lucky. The thought of being forced against my will…

I heard the faint click of the cottage door. It opened and closed again.

Some one was inside her home. No one dared enter my mother's home without permission. Was it a stranger? Terrible scenarios rushed through my mind. It was not my mother. Her heavy step was unmistakeable. I never thought to cry for help. It was as though I was paralyzed by fear.

They were directly outside the door. I watched horrified, as the handle slowly turned. Creeping backwards towards the bed I shrank against the wall. I waited for the door to be forced. Instead from the other side came a voice I recognised.

"Aluinn? Are you in there?" Calum whispered. "There's a threat against you Aluinn, some one far more powerful than your mother. I need to take you away. You have to trust me. But I need your answer before I unlock this door. If I can't trust you to do as I say then I'll be forced to leave without you."

I had no reservations. I needed to get out of that room. No matter where I found myself, it surely couldn't be worse than that. To breathe fresh air would be enough for me. I had to trust him. He had brought me back here, but only at her bidding. It seemed he regretted it now.

I had little choice. If this was his olive branch, I would accept it without qualm.

I called out, "I trust you, Calum. Open up. "

How could the sound of a key turning cause such joy? But the door stayed locked. It was the wrong key.

My heart was racing again as he fumbled with another key. "I think this is it..." The door clicked open. I grinned. He stood alone. Not some twisted trick then, but a man offering me his hand. All I had to do was accept it, to be released from that space. He was wincing at the stench from the bucket. There was no time to be embarrassed. I urged him forward and followed him down the low staircase. We ran through the back door and headed out over the open fields.

I stopped, winded, taking a second to bask in the pleasure of breathing fresh air, letting the wind fan my face. I raised my head upwards, squinting against the sun. It was too strong for my sensitised eyes but I revelled in its warmth.

Calum was beside me. It had been too long since I last washed. I drew back, embarrassed. Calum seemed to sense my discomfort. Instead of saying anything, he took my hand and held it tightly, pulling me after him. I didn't need much urging. I wanted to be long gone.

I kept pace alongside him, until I realised the direction we headed.

"Where are you taking me, Calum?"

He laughed, unable to hide his satisfaction. "Somewhere she will never think to look."

The fear was back again. "Please don't tell me you're taking me up there.... to the Manse?"

He looked puzzled, as though I should be as pleased as he with the idea.

"Where else? It's perfect; she'd never believe anyone would be crazy enough to take you up there, to the most sacred place on the Island."

He stopped in his tracks. For the first time he looked me in the eye, genuinely concerned for me. "Look, it won't be for long, I'll hide you well. In a few days I'll get you back to Edinburgh, I promise."

He made it sound so simple, but I still couldn't go along with it.

"No, Calum, I'm sorry, I can't do it. My mother is daunting enough to me, but *that place* is... another matter entirely. The truth is, I would rather you leave me where I was than take me there." Calum threw back his head and laughed loudly.

*

My mind clouded over, heart pounding, hands sweating, panic rising. It was as real to me still as the day it had happened. Pastor McGregor blocked my path. His aura was crimson, almost ablaze as the decadent *taibhse* within him tried to escape. But there was no release. Every movement shook it, so it shimmered and moved, alive with the force of its own corruption. I pictured myself as the child I had been then, saw the brilliant light around me. As soon as I noted his nearness, fear changed it, spoiling and tingeing the pale hues with darkest red. There was no way to avoid him this time.

"Where have you been child, out so late?"

"Nowhere pastor. A*h*m goin home."

"Let me take you then, it's not safe for you to be wandering about on your own."

"*Yhe* don't need...."

I never finished for his hand brushed my shoulder through the thin material of my dress. I recoiled in horror but he only moved closer and held fast. He gripped my arm as we approached the hidden walkway which led homewards. My body cried out in terror, but I couldn't force a sound over my lips. Why should he enjoy my fear any more than he was doing already?

I calmed then, refusing to show my distress. To give him that would be unthinkable. His grip was like a vice; he was determined not to lose me this time. How often had he tried to be alone with me? Yet I had always outwitted him. This time I had forgotten to stay safe.

We were a few hundred yards from our croft. My mother always tended her garden late in the evening till I came home. I had often pretended she was secretly watching there, worrying for my safe return. As he forced me on, I prayed she would be there that night too. I screamed out to her, "Mother, help me!"

Afterwards I couldn't tell if the scream had only been heard in my own mind. He seemed not to react at all.

Suddenly my mother's voice could clearly be heard, calling back. "Aluinn, where are you girl? It's late, y*he* shood b*he* hame!"

Her tone was displeased. Instantly the Pastor let me go. I threw myself headlong towards the direction of her voice. I looked back at him. He remained standing there, like a predatory animal. As I ran past my mother, I saw a satisfied smile on her face, a rare sight. But what confused me was that it was not aimed at me, but rather at the McGregor.

*

Calum looked at me oddly, as though he had caught me in a trance. "I'm serious, Calum, take me anywhere but there!"

He could tell by my face I meant it. He stood a moment, carefully considering the options open to him. "I could hide you down at the harbour amongst our nets, but that's most likely the first place they'd search." He paced this way and that, kicking the rough ground in anger and frustration. "Don't you see, Aluinn, I only let you out because I thought I had a way of keeping you safe? It never occurred to me that you might not want to hide there. Have you any bright ideas of your own?"

Even if I had composed a master plan, it would have made little difference. There was no time to reply. Around the concealed bend of the hill, a large crowd appeared. At the very head of the party was my mother.

Seeing her, I was suddenly angrier than I had ever been.

She was headed home, where she believed me 'safe'. Her face changed when she saw me, out in the open, free. The lack of comprehension on her face was almost funny.

Poor Calum was ashen faced. He drew me a look of desperation. If only I had agreed to go with him, his eyes told me, we would have missed them.

I had always thought her coldness aimed only at myself. Now I realised her presence intimidated everyone. They all stood willing to do her bidding.

Because of this last betrayal something in me had broken. I was no longer afraid of her. "You and the McGregor are in this together!" I screamed at her. "You're controlling them, keeping them down as you did me as a child. Why couldn't I see it before?"

One of her sidekicks reached for my arm, but I moved out of reach. I screamed to the crowd that had gathered round me. "If only you could stand outside and see your lives as they really are. This joylessness and fear, they're all her doing…" And there was more than that. Far more. "All those poor women foolish enough to listen to her. Where have all those babies gone, mother?"

The others were silent, looking to her expectantly. It was as though I had physically struck her. She stood perfectly still.

"Where did you put them? Are they buried under the floorboards? Or out in the garden?"

I kept going before she had the chance to silence me, undaunted, ignoring the loathing in her eyes. I would not be made back down. "You've had free rein here all these years. It's time someone stood up to you."

One of those men addressed my mother, trying to rouse her to action. "We telt yhe she'd be our dounfall one day."

"Silence!"

She glared at him with such force he shied away into the crowd. Which left her to focus her attention on me.

I stepped back as she moved her large frame towards me. "From the day ye were born ye were trouble..."

I felt myself start to cower away from her large hands, which could strike out without warning. But she stopped herself, the effort to control her temper visible. "As fur goin' anywhere, ye can get that outta yur head! Yuh think yur saeh clever, dont yeh? I hate taeh be the one taeh spoil it, bit yeh've trusted the wrong one."

How was it possible? Calum had gone against them.

"No, you're lying... she's lying, Calum, isn't she?"

I looked pleadingly at him. He hung his head, unable to look at me. He offered no explanation.

I almost felt sorry for him.

When finally he spoke, his words offered little comfort.

"I'm sorry Aluinn, I've no choice. They *know* things...about me." He moved closer, whispered quickly, "I'm sorry." Then they dragged him away.

I sank to my knees on the cold earth. I was lost.

Her words carried to me on the breeze. I picked out little that made sense. "Y*he* cannae ....that's the way it hustae be ...... Y*he* risked too much, y*he* fool."

Calum's pleading tone, almost disbelief in his voice. "I never knew. How could I have known?" He paused, looking to her for assurance that never came. She stared straight ahead, unyielding.

"No one could have foreseen it!" he shouted.

Confused by their argument, I was convinced Calum had acted out of remorse. Strangely, my mother held out her hand and he took it. I was once again thrown into confusion. It seemed they had made their peace. What did it mean?

The sight of her smile angered me yet again. I hardly recognised the sounds that came from my own mouth. Yet I felt more in control than at any time."You were never a mother to me." I almost spat into her face. I had gone close to her, just to make sure she understood. "I hope when the time comes you rot in hell. You're evil, a murderess. You've killed countless innocents. Why, mother? Is no one on this Island to be happy?" I stopped to catch my breath. I stared into her eyes I thought I saw the truth behind all those tragic deaths. "Did you bury the shame along with their little bodies? Is that what it was all about? Are you protecting their abusers?"

Two of her henchmen reached forward and grabbed me. I was screaming now. "What about the shame you've brought on our family? Think on that for a while. Always right, nobody will ever tell you different. I feel sorry for you, so set in your ways you can't see past your own misery. I only pray, hope, some one stronger comes along to end this nightmare!"

I thought I saw tears in her eyes. But how could that be? She had no feelings; she was a machine. "Yeh're wrong, daughter!"

"I'm no daughter of yours!" I screamed, struggling to free myself from their grip.

She carried on regardless, knowing I was forced to listen. "We who nevur leave, we who are loyal, huv kept our laws. They might no be written down, we might hae no records, but they are more powerful than anything the mainland possesses. Thae outsiders, wi auh their confusion…"

Her face was set hard . She clearly believed herself the saviour of those women she had misguided and deluded over the years. And with no one there to tell them otherwise, she was above their traditions, a law unto herself. And clearly mad.

"Yuh think me evil? Well, lit me tell yuh, au they women came beggin' me taeh help them. If that makes me evil, thin so are auh thae hospitals on the mainland, daein the same, only yeh cauh it abortion an' that makes it legal. Ah've carried oot ah service auh mah days, an' there were few who had taeh be forced taeh make thur decision. Ah'm noh as hertless as yeh think me!"

Did she seriously think I had forgotten life as a girl living under her roof? All those nights I had kept to myself, all those young women who made their way to her door, all those screams … and yet it had been she who had haunted my sleeping mind.

"You can try and justify your actions, but it's still wrong! I saw those young girls, crying, pleading. You never offered a word of comfort. Just as you never comforted me, your own child. Can you stand there and deny you never cared for me?

"Eenufh oh yur foolishness. I dinna need tae explain tae yuh! Tis eenufh ah allowed yeh tae live!"

She had finally said it, admitted it to myself, and everyone around us. I was saddened to my very core. "Why *did* you let me live?" I asked solemnly. "And what of my missing father? Or didn't he want to know you either?"

I attempted to move towards her, but they held me back. All I had were words to aim at her. "For years, I've tortured myself...wondering why you didn't love me. But you're not capable of emotion, are you? It would have been kinder to kill me too. And now the ending's the same anyway, isn't it? There's no way you're going to let me walk free. My fate will be the same as Sarah's. Am I to drown like her?"

Her own words escalated, till they were a wall of sound surrounding us both."Stop yer rantin'! Yhe'll live here amongst us fur the rest of yur life. Now yeh understand, yeh kin never leave. Weh'll auh make sure thit yeh dinnaeh!"

That was to be my fate.

"And if I refuse?"

She turned her back on me, whispering almost, as if she hoped I wouldn't hear. "Yeh'll take yur ain' life, unless ye stay safe."

I felt numbed inside; my courage left me as I struggled to absorb her words. Once again, I was led back to the croft and thrown inside my room. All hope had gone. I lay on the bed, weeping tears of frustration till I was so exhausted I drifted into the darkness.

When I awoke, I looked up gazing at the night sky, thinking about Cormac and Lorna. What would they think when I failed to return? How long before they forgot me? A strange girl who disappeared off the face of the earth. No one would even care.

Chapter Twelve

I resigned myself to each tedious new day, trapped in those four walls. They left me fresh food and a clean bucket. I began my monthly cycle, for which I used old cloths, repeatedly rewashed in peat water. So at least a week must have passed. Here was the proof she needed, the proof I wasn't with child. What more was she waiting for?

In my isolation, I finally understood why Cormac had found it wiser not to give in to physical yearning. Away from him my feelings had grown. I loved him more than I had ever done, though there was no physical contact at all. I thought of him constantly, where he was, what he was doing. Had he spared a thought for me since I had disappeared? I prayed I had left enough of myself in his mind that he would never truly forget me.

Wanting something, anything in that room to change, I moved the bed to the window wall, and so came across the loosened floorboard under the bed. Remembering my own accusations to my mother, I had been almost afraid to prise it open. What would I find there?

They couldn't have surprised me more. Papers. My essays from school. All the happy times with Sarah came flooding back and swept over me. I felt the joy I had felt then. Indeed every single piece of schoolwork, all those commendations I had received from Sarah, including my winning poem. I would write another, for Cormac, to show him all I felt for him. I sat, pen poised, longing for words to come that would appease my soul. But no words came. I fell asleep once more, thinking of him.

Why had I chosen to come back to the Island instead of fighting for him? As a child its tranquillity, its sheer vastness had been my only comfort. I could lose myself in it, taking comfort in its greenness, its open fields and sheltering trees. My captors seemed to know my secret and understand. Did the others feel the same way? Did the Islanders sense that this was the only place they could live with their secrets?

In order to survive on that God forsaken Island I had had to forget. Now I wanted to remember.

The Island hid secrets, stored in the vaults of my mind. Here in my prison memories were released now I had lost all sense of loyalty, all sense of hope. They came back with a vengeance to terrify me. As a child, I had not understood all I had seen. I had understood only that what I was watching was terribly wrong somehow. So I had concealed them in dark recesses, in shadowy places, locked them away and discarded the key. To have done otherwise would have condemned whatever childhood I had left.

I was young, very young, no more than eight years old. I had been playing in the old cemetery beside the Great Manse, a place I had been told never to visit. But I had often wandered up there, sneaked in through the high, metal gates. It was one of my favourite places. No one ever thought to look for me.

I heard voices approaching. Afraid it would be my mother, I had hid behind the tallest gravestone. There was only a small gap between it and the solid stone wall. As I waited, pressed against the cold stone, I realised others had arrived. Soon there were over a dozen people forming a circle amidst the ancient stones. I stayed very still, knowing that if they found me I'd know a far greater punishment than anything I had suffered at the hands of my mother so far. So I stood there, without moving, a small child who hardly dared breathe. Petrified of discovery, I knew I should not be watching, but nothing could have forced my eyes away. Within me excitement burned.

But not for long. Even to my young senses, what they did there was far beyond the portals of right and wrong. Though events unfolded with the full consent of all involved, it made the scene no less repulsive. Seen through a child's eyes, I watched it again, with the wisdom of my years. In my mind's eye they began their slow, ritualistic chant, soothing as a lullaby. The chanting, hypnotic, powerful had me rubbing my own eyes, struggling to stay awake. They kept it up, a heady, rhythmic sound, so compelling I was saddened when the pace of it changed. No sooner had my eyes opened again than it grew more frenzied. Faster and faster. They began to sway, backwards and forwards in time with the sounds. I stood, fascinated, watching them, adults and neighbours, aware they were indulging themselves, having fun, something I was deprived of as a rule. Would they be angry with me if I stepped out to join them? I was just about to move out from behind my protective stone, when I knew to stay hidden.

Bodies then, naked bodies. I had never seen nakedness before, but I knew it was wrong for men and women to show themselves that way. They cared nothing for their shame, moving closer together. Closer, closer, till their bodies joined. Then it began, the moving, from one to another, touching and joining together, until each had been with all the others.

Concealed for so many years in the darkest recesses of my psyche, the memories spilled out. I viewed them from my adult perspective, pitying the child who had watched them happen. A girl was brought forward, preceded by two hooded figures carrying heavy, leather bound volumes. She was surrounded by a guard of tall, hooded figures. I pictured her face in intricate detail, young, fresh and beautiful. I knew her of course, had seen her hundreds of times, running errands on the Island, playing with friends. I had envied her long, straight hair down her back so shiny and dark, so unlike my flame red curls.

My senses took over, as I watched the image unfold. Beautiful, but somehow disconcerting. Saved perfectly in time and memory, her smile was serene at first, bodice unchanging, as if painted on a porcelain doll. Her dress was exquisite, white, the intricately detailed above softly flowing layers, which moved gently in the breeze, revealing her slender limbs.

The next part was hazy. Time had caused the less unimportant details to disappear. Then suddenly the confusion cleared. I saw those who stood around her. Her innocent face held me spellbound. A flash of light crossed the image. I understood the movement to be skilfully swift, watched as the first red drop landed on the neck of her white dress.

The childhood me, had been unable to understand. I understood now.

Another slash followed, then another, in quick succession. The drops merged, spreading quickly, the red seeping into the material, until it grew wet and heavy. When I finally looked at her face again, I wanted to cry out, but the sound stuck in my throat. Paralyzed I watched her death mask above the scarlet dress, the colour flowing outwards…

Their celebration was far from over. What happened next was far worse than anything I had seen till then. Although Cormac and I had never consummated our relationship, I knew it should have been sacred, beautiful, the sharing of two willing bodies. Their disrespect for the beauty of the act turned the beautiful into the profane. There was no joining of spirits, just the satisfying of appetites, the mechanics of gratification.

They paid her no thought, as I stood there, weeping silently for the loss of her beauty. The image faded again, as though time had erased another part of the memory, then returned. As I readjusted the view it was not the girl who held my gaze, but an obscure form beside her frame, limp within her bloodied dress. Something lurked there. My memory swam, the image still too painful even for my willing eyes. I struggled against my own mind to expose the truth, knowing instinctively that here lay the reason for my loathing of them.

Slowly it formed, the fog clearing. I saw...not an Islander...but unprecedented evil. Any goodness in me weakened just by looking at it. There was no mind link. It had no thoughts I could recognise, only instincts. It wanted to survive, to stay alive. It was a creature running out of time, venting its anger on its naïve followers who did its bidding without question. And then I fully recognised it. Just as in my dreams, it held its dark frame upright, its claws glistening as sharp as the finest blade. They glistened within the brilliant flash of light.

The evil within it had turned whatever goodness there had been in those people into bestiality. It dipped forward, filling its beak from the girl's cavernous wound. A follower brought a goblet forward. Lifting it up, they drank from it, in a grotesque parody of a religious consecration. As it lifted the chalice from its lips, the creature changed. Its face was that of Pastor McGregor.

He wiped his lips of excess liquid. A faint sheen of blood formed on his limb, which was neither hand nor claw, the distinction distorted. From the realms of memory it seemed he looked straight at me. He smiled, as the image of the beast passed across his face so fast I could not be sure it had been there at all.

He had always repelled me. I understood fully for the first time why. And he had *seen* me all those years before. That was why he was intent on destroying me.

After they had gone, I remained behind the gravestone, staring at the cold, lifeless body of the girl, callously disposed of in a ditch. When his handyman, Stewart McDonald came to collect the corpse, I ran as fast as I could and hid in the barn on the McGregor's farm. I could not sleep, afraid they knew and would come to carry me back there to meet the same fate.

When my mother found me and took me home the following morning, she beat me severely. And I had relished every contact of her belt on my skin. But it hadn't taken away the pain. I had carried the guilt of that young girl's death around with me all those years. Even now, her name escaped me. It had been murder. They would all have provided alibis for each other, I suppose, had her disappearance come to light. But as my mother had said, there was no documentation on the Island. No journals, no written rules and regulations...Strange that their ways had never been written down. Were they like every sect of 'other' thinkers, had they kept a written record, proud of their debauchery? Perhaps they had. All I knew was that for some reason I had never been asked to be a part of it. I had lived and grown on the Island afraid of everyone, never admitted to their closed circle. It had pained me so terribly at the time, this salvation.

Somehow, I had managed to block it all out, retaining only a feeling that I must trust no one. How else would I have survived all the encounters I had endured with the Pastor, knowing what he really was? And now I had to live somehow with the knowledge my mind had returned to me after all those years. Within a locked room, I simply waited, knowing now that my captors had much more to lose than ever I had realised.

When she brought me my food, my mother gazed at me questioningly, as though she was somehow in tune with the changes within me. I offered her nothing, blocking my thoughts. My new understanding had reinforced my hatred for her; if I found a way of leaving the Island, this time it would be forever. No message, no death would bring me home again. Living without the Island would just have to become part of who I was.

Strange. For the first time, I almost understood how she had withheld love from me. What was the point in becoming attached to anyone so disposable? Would I be the next sacrifice? Was that the plan? The thought chilled me. That girl had been much younger than I, yet no one had intervened. That beautiful, innocent child had simply resigned herself to the death. Had she been so brainwashed she saw it as her destiny? Or so worn down by the ugliness of their beliefs that she saw it as a release? A few seconds -then no more pain?

My own fate was sealed. The only question remaining was *when*?

Dear God, was there no one who would help me?

All those years spent in Edinburgh, anonymous, I had felt isolated and insignificant, but safe. How I longed to feel that way again. Closing my eyes, I prayed hard to no one in particular, trying to strengthen myself from within. They would call in on me soon; check on me.

Slowly I was losing my grasp of reality. All I saw, sensed, felt had become muddled, confused – joined in many ways. Enough, at least, for me to have begun to doubt my own sanity. What if all I was were nothing at all? What would there be left of me then?

However long it takes to prove
I will not sorrow show
For I have yet to prove my worth
Which in time they will know

The rhyme ricocheted around my head, comforting me. It seemed almost as if they were waiting too. But what? Were they waiting for me to give up, to become as placid and willing as that child had been before her death? That would never happen. I was far stronger than they realised. I would not be broken.

Thoughts of Cormac filled my mind. Nothing he had ever done compared to the indignities I had suffered here. The prejudice which had made me reject Cormac's people, was the fear and prejudice of the small minds I had grown up with. Fear of the unknown, which had kept me on the Island so long, fear of death, fear of life...Even now a ridiculous emotion burned inside me, the same principle that had been ingrained in me since childhood – loyalty to the island. It had stopped me discovering the truth for myself.

Noises again, low and muffled beneath my room. I lay flat across the wooden floorboards, straining to make out shadows in the room below. Immediately I became anxious, my palms sweating so I had to dry them on my jeans. Footsteps, heavy steps I recognised as hers. But someone else was with her, lighter, yes, but not necessarily small in build. I swallowed hard, as my door lock clicked open. "Get up girl, y*he* have to go somewhere else!" She sounded put out.

"Why, what's happened?"

She silenced me quickly. "Dinnae start asking questions again, just dae as yur telt! Any playing up wull be dealt wih. Yeh dae understand?"

I walked out and down the stairs, sandwiched between them so closely I could smell their stale perspiration. Outside again, sunshine blinded my eyes unprepared for the severity of ordinary daylight. I blocked the pain, gradually adjusting to the brightness as the same dark haired man who had shouted at her earlier led me roughly along a twisting path. After a few minutes, he stopped and wrapped a blindfold over my eyes. Within seconds, I had lost all sense of direction. My fear discovered a new level. It terrified me. If I had no clue to my whereabouts, how would anyone else ever find me?

I thought again of Cormac's face. Something clicked in my head. It didn't matter what they did to me, where they took me, they merely controlled my physical being. Inside my head, I had my own secret place. They were powerless to stop my thoughts. I would think of him constantly from now on, picturing his face, drawing strength from the memory.

Once I had sat within a coffee shop, waiting for him. The street was busy outside, traffic flowing in both directions. I was aware of a car drawing up. Even before I glanced outside, I knew instinctively it was Cormac. But I pretended not to have seen him, still caught up in the game of playing it cool. Finally, I had *had* to look. It was as though he drew me to him, as if he willed me to meet his eyes. In that one glance, we both knew.

I must have slowed down. My gaoler jolted me back, pulling me over on my ankle. A burst of pain stabbed me, making me call out. Still the brute dragged me blindly on. The touch of his calloused hand repulsed me. My mother marched behind, breathing heavily. I winced several times, stumbling on my already swollen ankle. He only pulled harder, as she roughly pushed from behind. My fury kept me upright and moving.

When they removed my blindfold, I almost laughed. They had

wasted their efforts. I knew the place well. The broch lay only a short distance from where we stood. But laughter would have betrayed me - even in the darkness I could escape from here, knew instinctively where I was. As they led me to the slant of the hillside, I saw something I had never seen in all my years of playing in that place. Obviously, they had prepared for my arrival. He pulled back the rough covering of the dug out and pushed me inside. My mother stood close beside. I wanted to scream at her, but her face held me silent. "Ye'll stay here ahn he'll stay wih ye."

What did that mean? Who was he? Was this the start of a ritual? I pleaded with her, in no more than a whisper. "Please don't leave me here. I beg of you, I'll be quiet, only take me back."

But there was to be no reprieve. As she left I trembled. The man she had left me with was a stranger. I resisted eye contact. Even in my present condition, I was wise enough to appreciate I was young and attractive. Within the confines of that cave, I was vulnerable. I looked around for somewhere to withdraw to, found a place just big enough for myself alone, tucked at the back, out of sight. I supposed it was where they had wanted me to sit anyway. In my mind, I managed to convince myself I chose it of my own free will. Sitting very still within that small niche, not wishing to do or say anything to draw his attention to me, my throat tightened. I prayed that the fear would stay at bay long enough for me to calm myself.

He stayed where he was, didn't attempt to communicate by word or action. I was relieved. What was there to say between us? Two strangers thrust together, locked in that ridiculous hideaway cut into the hillside. I retreated to my thought life.

I had no idea when I slept, yet I must have fallen asleep, for I awoke with a start. My entire body ached with the awkwardness of the angle I had been sitting at. Pins and needles ran down both legs, evidently the reason for my waking. Instantly I regained my bearings, reorganising my mind, chiding myself for not staying alert. The tiny cave was far more worse than my attic prison. I looked around for the man. He was nowhere to be seen. Had that been their intention all along, to abandon me? The thought almost turned my bowels to water.

I picked up a noise outside, a faint rustling. I hoped the footsteps belonged to him. An odd sensation, knowing you would prefer to be raped by your captor than by another, a stranger. I placed my hand over my mouth to stop my panic escaping. The curtain moved. He looked directly at me but said nothing. I settled back inside my cramped space, and closed my eyes. It helped me keep control.

My mind drifted back. As a child I had been fascinated by the festivities on the Island every year. After the summer came the festival - thanksgiving for crops safely harvested. Church traditions combined with older ways - the hilltops alight with bonfires. It was as though the dourness of daily life was cast aside as the Islanders celebrated as though there would be no tomorrow. And now I understood – for *any one of them* it could have been the last time. Any one of them could have been chosen.

There was great feasting at those times, in dire contrast to our normal sparse fare. At festival times I ate things for which I had no name, exotic fruits, richly laden dishes, heavily spiced and served on enormous platters. Even to my childish senses, they smacked of excess. Normally the body was held in check, but at these times, no one seemed to object to the greed it encouraged. So I made the most of it, sampling delicacies laid before me. I ate heartily till it struck me that the other children refrained from eating anything at all. Whilst I was allowed, almost compelled, to eat my fill of the richness laid before me.

As I grew older still, I realised no other child *dared* to touch the food, though they must have been as hungry as I was. From the instant I realised that I was the only child offered the delicacies I stopped taking them. I had no wish to set myself further apart. I sensed I had angered them by my withdrawal. McGregor especially seemed to have difficulty grasping my refusal. How does a child explain that hatred has diminished its appetite?

I understood now why the children were sent to bed. Their riotous revelry always ended the same way – with screams floating through the night air.

Threatened by those images once more, I trawled my mind for happy thoughts. There had only been one occasion when the other children had grudgingly accepted me. My thirteenth birthday, not an insignificant number by any means, but made more so by a particular change in me. On Beltane, the fertility celebration that was a high point of Island life, I bled for the first time. My mother had been furious when I told her.

That year it seemed the celebrations reached their zenith. The wine overflowed. It seemed that twice as many boats arrived on the Island. Although I was suffering terrible aching cramps, my mother had insisted I go, even for a short while. In her words, that year was "an extra special celebration of birth and life and hope." It was the most poetic thing I had ever heard her say.

The day was odd from the first. It grew stranger as it wore on towards night. Pastor McGregor seemed to be everywhere I looked. His eyes never left me. Always unwanted, that day his attention was eerie. He bided his time, until he finally found me on my own.

"Enjoying this fine festival, Aluinn?"

I shook my head, moving away from him.

"Oh? And why is that?" he had questioned, laying a hand upon my small frame. He pressed his palm into my shoulder blade, until the pressure became uncomfortable.

"A*h*m just noh feelin' well," I lied.

He lowered his head until our eyes met, refusing to allow me to avert my gaze. With his other hand, he held my chin locked solid.

"Are you not glad you're a woman now Aluinn? You'll be a fine mother one day."

He knew about my change. The words were no coincidence. He had been told. The weight of his words violated all my senses. I ran. When I looked back, he was gone. From then on I hid from him.

I had never quite grasped how at those times the Island filled with strangers. Then after the festival, they departed, just as suddenly as they had arrived. People had come from far afield to join in the celebrations, every year the same families. This Man guarding me must have been one of them, for I knew all the Islanders.

In the darkness of night, the wind howled forcefully, encouraging the banshees from their rest. Outside the curtain they wailed and flailed, enough to waken the Man, who had nodded off to sleep. He lay across the doorway, blocking my escape. Outside the spirits continued their wailing. It was as though the whole Island sensed my captive spirit. It seemed to me that the world that had nurtured me as a child was mourning. Their sorrow urged me to stay strong, but I didn't dare respond. When their calls went unheeded, they departed. The silence that followed was deafening.

Chapter Thirteen

The hovel was small and damp. My body shivered constantly, never having warmed after the long hours of night, when the temperature had grown so low my breath almost froze within me. My skin had dried. My hair hung lank and greasy. I was grateful not to have a mirror, in which to look upon my sorrowful self. I had lost all track of time. There were voices outside again but the Man seemed unperturbed, as though he had expected company. There had been no one else but him for so long I found the thought of another face disconcerting.

Two women entered. They hardly looked my way, just laid down the provisions they had brought. I watched them avidly, looking for any trace of shame or guilt on their faces. Surely they understood it was wrong to hold someone against their will? Or was their own fear keeping their morals in check? Superstition and engrained fear convinced them they had no other choice in life. All that, in exchange for as sense of belonging. I felt strangely moved to compassion for them. At least I had known freedom, even if it had been for a short time. That taste of freedom had given me the strength to hold on. One day I would be free again. If a chance arose, I would seize it. And if I got away I would never again relinquish my grasp on life. I would take my own path. Their shame was not mine. As I gazed at their faces, there was no happiness reflected there. And in that second I knew I had been a fool to turn my back on the only man I had ever loved.

*

The food was surprisingly fresh. I ate heartily, determined to keep up my strength. The Man sat and scrutinised my eagerness. What exactly was going on in his mind? Disgust at my lack of table manners, or fear that I wouldn't leave enough for him? I soon had my answer. He stood up, crossed quickly the small space which separated us and pulled the basket out of my reach.

I said nothing, having already taken more than my fair share. Had I overstepped the mark, jeopardised the fragile truce between us? I had no desire to antagonise him.

The day dragged on.

I was only allowed a minute's privacy every few hours to empty my bladder, grateful he had given in to my request, not to have to release my waste where I sat. At night I was allowed out into the semi darkness, connected to him by a rope around my neck, held so taut that if I dared move it he would know. I bore the indignity, grateful for the chance to breathe fresh air.

My sleep was so disturbed I was unsure of my perceptions. When I fell into a fitful slumber again, there was no comfort. Childlike voices begged me to be aware. *"Duisg, a Aluinn, duisg...tha feum again ort fhathast...thoir an aire..ni e do dhochann."* The words swam around my mind as my eyes opened - *Wake, Aluinn, wake. We need you still. Beware ...he will hurt you.* Their voices still carried on the cold air as I sat bolt upright, startled. The Man slept more soundly than I did. He had not heard the others who lived so close yet worlds apart.

"Who do you speak of? *Who* will hurt me?" I implored. In the darkness, I could not see their shapes, yet I followed their whispering voices, darting around the blackness

"Am fear a thig gad iarraidh...Bu leatsa riamh e....chan iarradhmaid ach thu a bhi air d'fhacill." "The one who comes for you, who has always been yours. We wish only to give warning, *A Aluinn, chan'eil sinn sabhailte en seo...bha thu coibhneil ruin... cha diochuimhnich sinn a-chaoidh.* Aluinn..... we're not safe here......you were kind to us...... we never forget."

They were gone, leaving me more confused and alone than ever, my heart beating erratically. I was sure I had understood their message. They would have witnessed all McGregor's acts, would wish to protect me against such a man. He would not rest until I was his.

I would surrender my very life first.

In the darkness, I cried silently, but inside me a voice urged me on, strengthening my weakening resolve. I was not to give in, but to wait in readiness.

Had I not defeated him once before?

*

How many hours was I held in that dark place?
The waking hours went slowly, the nothingness oppressive. My

thoughts grew more clouded inside my mind. Had I understood the reason for my captivity I might have had some perspective. Without it, I found myself teetering on the brink of insanity.

The never-ending darkness was destroying me. I began to refuse food. My body craved no sustenance. Energy deprived, I could feel my hope of escape deserting me.

My gaoler had been busy, making a makeshift drainage system within the cave. My last tie with the outside world was severed. Ironically, this last indignity deprivation gave me back some of the spirit I had lost. Any chance, I swore to myself, I would flee. I had to regain control of my fate. Out there, alone in the dark, escape would be treacherous if it were past nightfall. But avoiding discovery in the daylight would be nigh on impossible. There could be no welcome for me anywhere on the Island. No one would give me sanctuary.

I sat utterly still, confined within that small space, screaming inwardly. Waiting, waiting for my chance.

When the Man looked my way, I neither acknowledged nor ignored him. We had developed an understanding. No words had passed between us in all that time. My anger was directed his way. He was my warder, the obstruction that kept me separated from the outside world. A creature of habit, yet he never went outside to either take the air or relieve his own body functions whilst I was awake.

The thought was clear, sudden. I knew where I would go. I would feign sleep. When he left, I would seize my chance. I would go that night.

Terrified of betraying myself in my excitement I acted tired, knowing he was safe in his routine. I had been so passive, no one expected me to try and escape.

Strange all those hours remembering my childhood, all those haunts, and now one of them was to be my sanctuary again. As my mind had wandered over the past, I had recalled a breathtaking, magical place, a wonderland, filled by hidden waterfalls within a treasury of green so lush I was staggered by its diversity. When I had last been there, there had been no natural pathway though the age-old slopes had been cut out to allow access in the most difficult spots. If my memory was true, I was not far away from the place where the defile began. I only prayed I had read my bearings rightly. As far as I was aware, no Islander had ever bothered to make the journey up through the gorge. If I managed to stumble upon its narrow entrance, I would at least stand a chance.

It had rained often in the last days. I was often aware of it as it fell. I had no illusions about the conditions I would meet higher up the gorge. The earth would lie waterlogged, especially around the waterfalls.

When I fled I would need some form of concealment, and quickly. There would be only a few minutes before the Man discovered my absence. Then they would be down in droves upon the area to seek me out. I was more than willing to take my chances. Instinctively I forbade my mind to consider how frightened I would be.

I laid down as I did every night and pretended to sleep. My fear now was that my body would betray me, that I would actually drift off. I listened for any movement, the slightest noise coming from his direction. It seemed I was out of luck. He wasn't going anywhere. I had never allowed myself to consider the possibility of it not happening.

My eyes grew heavy. Just when I had all but given up hope I heard a faint rustle as his body rose off the ground. Silently he made his way over to me. He touched my face, his fingers cold, his stale breath warm on my cheek. His touch repulsed me yet I remained silent. It seemed I had convinced him; he left my side.

I waited, frightened but determined.

When I opened my eyes, the rough curtain lay slightly open. I crept forwards. What if he stood directly outside? Pushing myself through the fear, I stuck my head outside the hessian barrier. I could barely make out my own hand in the darkness. My gaoler was nowhere to be seen. I breathed the unobstructed air, feeling the heaviness leave my lungs, gulping in huge breaths of its clammy coldness. The wind roared around my body, unprotected from the elements, the sudden rush welcome. There was no time to think any more.

I took off, running as fast as I could for as long as I could, until my chest tightened with excruciating pain. Cooped up for long days, I had no stamina. On I ran through the night, waiting for his shout, his steps behind me. The pain hit a new level as my lungs struggled for air. I stopped, desperately needing to get my bearings.

Enough distance had been covered. I stood on the ridge of a hill. Far off to the North I made out the lights of the Manse, with the small harbour lights far away in the opposite direction. I said a silent 'thank you' to the powers that be; I had been right. I was near my old haunt. Excitement grew in me. If I reached it, then and only then, would I allow myself some hope. I thought of Lorna and Cormac, silent tears running warm down my cheeks as I ran ahead blindly, trusting my instincts to find the path. But it was luck more than intuition that had me find the old stile marking the opening to the gorge. Another second and I would have passed it. Whilst the rest of the Island showed the influence of man's hand, these summits still stood clear of his influence, untouched, unaltered.

The higher I rose, the warmer the air became, warmer by several degrees than down in the glen. The summits saw more rainfall than the valleys below; the ground was wet underfoot. I was petrified of falling, but I had to press on or wait for my captors to catch up with me. The moon shone brightly, its beams passing through the high trees, guiding my way. An owl rose up in front of me, startling me with its song flight, rising twenty-five feet into the air with a rattling call I was sure could be heard for miles. Fear froze every bone in my body.

As I moved through the woody scrubs and bushes, climbing higher and higher I remembered the long hours I had spent in my magic hiding place. I knew the area like the back of my hand. If I was still free by daybreak I had a chance. Scurrying along like a frightened animal, I refused to remember that I still had no way of getting off the Island. Callum would help me, if I could find him. I would not be beaten.

Loud noises carried in the wind; they were behind me. There was not as much distance between us as I had hoped. On I climbed. Something rustled to my left. Desperate that they had discovered my route so quickly, I shrank against the bushes. The movement of my body disturbed rainwater balanced on its leaves. Icy wetness invaded seeped through my clothes and onto my face. Panic threatened. I tightened my hands around the strong stems that were balancing me. For long moments, I crouched motionless. Suddenly I slipped, unable to hold the awkwardness of my position any longer. I landed squarely on the hard cold stones.

Horrified I waited for dark shapes to form, and drag me back to that prison.

But no one came.

My legs were cut in several places. Angered by the pain my frustration built to a new level. It spurred me on. Raised voices down the valley told me I was not alone in my frustration. Being outsmarted by a mere girl had clearly angered them. Even now my spirit fought to understand, my soul sensed their deep resentment towards me. What was it about me that deserved their hatred? I had done no wrong. Fear quickened my pace but I was tiring quickly. I had had no food for days. My feet ached as I struggled over the difficult terrain.

Noise close by brought me to a halt, crouching low behind foliage, just slightly off the rough path. I steadied my nerves. When I heard someone call my name I thought I was losing my mind. Was this it? Had my sanity finally left me? Cormac was calling me. Those hill spirits were playing a cruel trick against me, but I would not be fooled into believing their cunning. They hoped only to ensnare me for their own sport. Cormac had no reason to search me out, nor did he know where I was.

Still I heard his voice; he called out. His voice seemed to be getting closer. I shook my head to free my senses. Once again, his voice carried on a cold rush of the east wind that battered my fragile refuge. It seemed to draw nearer. I was seized by an image of him, a forceful awareness of his spirit close to mine, so clear it was almost reality. I steeled myself against it, hoping the *taibhsean* would sense my refusal. I would not be taken in, would not be beguiled by them. I would not be tempted into giving away my hiding place.

"Go away, stop taunting me," I whispered into the darkness.

It was strange - they made no appearance. Still I remained silent, too afraid to move ahead for fear of what they had drawn near.

Then I hear his voice again.

"Aluinn, please come out; I know you're here."

Still I hesitated, confused. Those wicked spirits were tormenting me. Why?

"Trust me Aluinn, I mean you no harm."

Had I lost my mind completely? I had not slept soundly for so many nights.

Another rustling, this time even closer. My body tensed. They had come further up, whilst I was distracted by the strange illusions inside my own mind.

A sharp crack near to my left. I held my breath. Out of the shadows, a lone figure appeared, walking through the undergrowth. Slowly I discerned the outline of his physical shape. My spirit rose. Cormac. "Aluinn, please, we don't have time for this. Show yourself." I stood up. I had no sense of whys and wherefores, all I wanted was release from the being without him. He turned abruptly, as though instantly sensing my whereabouts. Quickly he covered the distance between us.

I thought *He'll protect me* as I moved out of the shadows and ran towards him. So many questions needed answering. *What was he doing here – how had he found me? How long had he been on the Island? How was it possible?* But in the second he reached out and pulled me to him, all I thought was that I loved him. Safe in his arms my body took strength from him. He loved me; his coming after me had proven it.

"Thank God you're safe. I've been desperate to find you. Surely you heard I was here?"

Could *he* be the reason for my imprisonment? Was Cormac the reason they had hidden me away?

"How did you even know where to find me?"

"Lorna let something drop after you left. I kept on at her, till finally she told me you had travelled home via Oban. I had to come, Aluinn, had to find out if you were as unhappy without me as I was without you."

All the agony I had suffered left me. "I was a fool to come back."

Cormac held me at arm's length, his handsome features serious in the moonlight. He held my face gently. It comforted. "I'll explain everything, as soon as we're sheltered. I have somewhere safe for us to go."

Without my saying anything, he knew I was on the run. Cautiously, we moved forward again. Through the last of the concealed ground we approached the peak. The north side lay open and exposed, leaving us vulnerable. As we cleared it, we heard angry voices on the night air. We'd been spotted.

There was nowhere to go. Cormac wrenched my arm. He was pulling me towards the voices! I resisted, terrified of being betrayed again. He forced us out into an overgrown field. I was about to run when I found the ground beneath my feet was wet. My shoes sank into it. I recoiled in disgust. Cormac pulled me on a few paces and then gripping my shoulders, he forced me downwards, till we were engulfed by leaves and sharp stalks. Something touched my face. I resisted the urge to cry out. It was soon gone in the darkness.

The voices had grown louder. They were so close now, we might have reached out and touched any one of them. My mother was amongst them. She spoke, her tone flat, uncaring. "We've covered both ends. Either she's tricked u*h*s and d*h*ubled back, else she's stull oot thur, hidin' somewhere i*h*n the dark. It w*h*ull be light soon enough. W*hu*'ll catch her then."

The others muttered agreement. "Find her whe mhust, she could r*h*uin everythin' w*h*ih that m*h*ooth oh hers! Stieh here a*h*t the top. Ah'll set u*h*p at the bottom an' thin y*h*e kin sweep the whole lot. And mind check the falls – she might be floatin' face d*h*oun i*h*n yon w*h*atur!"

I shuddered at her casual cruelty. Cormac held me close, sensing my pain. My own mother wished me dead.

Why was I still so hurt, so betrayed when I knew what she was capable of? I had always been a burden to her. It occurred to me that she sounded every bit as frightened as I was. If she was afraid she could be beaten, then it was possible, somehow, to do just that. All I had to do was survive until then.

A sudden coldness swept over my body. Cormac pulled me tighter for a minute, then took my hand, ready to pull me on when the coast was clear. I felt the burn of his flesh on mine and took comfort from it.

Chapter Fourteen

We stayed hidden amongst the darkness for as long as we dared. Long enough to be sure of our next move. Daylight would soon be upon us. It would be easy enough for them to catch sight of us then.

If it were humanly possible, he would get me off the Island. I trusted him completely. A thousand questions whirred round my head. *Had he already experienced their strangeness? Would he understand? If he had been allowed to stay on the Island, for whatever reason, did that mean he had been accepted by one amongst them?*

Finally we decided to risk it, following a path which wound around and away from the high ground. The terrain became even tougher. Large rocks hindered us. We clambered over them. There was no time to find another route. Besides, 'they' would already have blocked the more predictable paths. I was ready to endure any pain, any difficulty. If this was my road to safety, so be it.

Without warning Cormac sped up. In my surprise I almost called out to him. Dumbfounded by own stupidity, I knew I had almost exposed our whereabouts. The threat still surrounded us, and my slip made me more aware, more cautious. With that sixth sense heightened between us Cormac stopped long enough to beckon me on. We reached the brow of a hill, covered by a spate of trees. He pointed out a small cottage that sat quite alone.

Breathing heavily I took it in. I knew the house was occupied, not just from its peat fire, which sent grey curls of smoke into the dawn sky. Although it had been so long since I had been on the Island, I had never forgotten the *cailleach* who lived there. She was one of the few on the Island who ever had a kind word for me. I had not gone there often, and certainly not by that route, but the old woman had sometimes welcomed me as I passed on my travels. Once, on a day when my mother's sharp tongue had caused me to flee up to the hills, she had taken me in and fed me, bidding me forgive my mother, that she had been angered by some transgression on my part. Though we had only spoken a few times, I hoped it was the same woman. I did not like to think of her passing.

Cormac spoke for the first time. "We have to cover open ground to get to it. It's best if we just run for it."

I ran with the haste of someone whose life depended on it. Safety lay within those walls. I ran. The pain in my side intensified until it spread and I thought my heart would burst with the pain of it. When we finally reached the stone cottage walls breathing was agony, but I felt triumphant.

Safely inside I was heartened to see the *cailleach* and her friendly face. She ushered us in to the warm. "Hello mah dear, come in ahn' warm up bi' the fire. Ah've made sum fresh soup a*h*n' Ah've laid oot dr*h*y clothes that uist tae belong tae mah d*h*aughter.Theih shud fit, yuh're round about the same size. Y*he* kin wash a*h*n' change in the wee room thur if y*he* like."

I longed to be clean again, so overwhelmed at the thought, I barely managed to mumble a thank you, as she handed me a pile of freshly aired clothes. She added more peat to the embers, then fired up the glowing ashes with a few well-aimed turns of her poker. I couldn't resist, taking a seat by the fire, thankful of the heat, which began to warm my aching limbs. She looked at me a little sadly, taking in my wretched appearance. "Noh everyone on thi Island agrees wih auh thit goes on here. I'm sorry for you, lass."

I nodded, said thank you.

"Yhe've changed," she smiled, "Yhe sound auh proper."

"Changing my accent was an easy way to fit in over there. Others things weren't so simple," I said wistfully.

"A*h*n why would y*he* ever wish tae change? Y*he* are what y*he* are a*h*n awe'wies will be. Living wi' the Gift is no' easy, child. "

Twenty minutes later, I was washed dressed in the sombre garments she had given me. The *cailleach* had clearly loved her daughter. Her room was filled with childhood keepsakes, souvenirs of days that might otherwise have been forgotten, important memories. Seeing the tiny trinkets, I hated my mother more than ever. She had robbed me in so many ways. It would have been kinder had she let me go to another, who might have made my life as a child bearable.

Later I sat across from Cormac at the small table in the middle of the room. We gazed at each other, still unable to believe that we were in the same room together. He took my hand. "I'm sorry I didn't try to speak to you before you left. It was cruel. I just wanted to give you time to think things over," he began. "I thought you'd be as miserable as I was. When I got your letter I was hurt, but the more I read it the better I could read between the lines. I knew you were hiding something. And then I began to be afraid for you. Something, some sense was telling me that you had written it to protect me. Tell me if I'm wrong?"

"No you're not wrong. You shouldn't have come here, it's not safe, but I'm so glad you did, Cormac."

"How could I not follow you Ally? I love you. I just realised too late how much." He ran his fingers tenderly over my palm. " That's what I told Molly too. It wasn't that hard to sweet talk her into giving me your details. I told her I was so in love with you that I *had* to go after you. She thought it was very romantic."

I smiled, visualizing her expression.

"The first warning I had that the Islanders were a bit strange came from my landlady in Oban. She said the people on the Island were a strange lot and didn't welcome others, so I stayed put a few days to find out all I could about the place before I turned up. It was easy in the end. The Pastor was there on one of his jaunts to the mainland. There were several locals ready to tell me his whereabouts. I "befriended" him in a bar late one night, when he was a little the worse for wear."

The Pastor was tee-total. He forbade all the Islanders strong drink. What was going on?

"We hit it off straight away; I used my uni' connections to impress. He seemed taken with my credentials, so when I expressed my desire to study wild birds in their natural habitat, he invited me over to the Island for a few days. What a day I've had – he helped me catalogue my sheets. There's nothing I don't know about the bird population on the Island - cormorants, guillemots, kittiwakes on those cliff faces, in the fields, curlews, snipes and larks. Hell, I've even seen a falcon."

I laughed, trying to imagine Cormac as a birdwatcher."What possessed you to say that in the first place?"

"I had to come up with something."

As far as I was aware, the Pastor had never extended the hand of friendship in such a way before. But it seemed away from the Island he lived by other rules. Cormac's reception by the other Islanders had not been so warm.

"The Pastor kept me close, said not to mind them, said it was more suspicion that had ensured their survival than any innate hostility. I avoided talking about you until I saw what way the land lay. I had hoped, rather naively, to see you on my travels. Little things you had said in our time together told me how much you loved the Island; that you had been used to roaming freely on it. I thought that way the best way to find you. So with the Pastor's permission to explore the Island I began to hunt you down, for want of a better expression. On such a small place, I felt sure you'd run over my path sooner or later." His voice was far away, as if remembering his time getting to know the Island, feeling its power. "Days passed without me seeing you, and no one seemed to know anything about you when I made discreet inquiries. I stumbled by chance across this croft, and trusted the *cailleach* instinctively. She was the first one I spoke to of you. She knew you had come back home, and been hidden away, but she didn't know where you were. It tore me up, knowing you were locked up somewhere close by, yet I couldn't get to you." His eyes welled with emotion as he spoke, "I missed you so badly, Ally. All I wanted was to be with you again."

"I still can't believe you're here, on my Island. But I'm finished with it, Cormac. Being locked up like that by them…it changed me."

"So you're not angry with me for coming after you?"

"How could I be when I regretted sending that note every single hour of every day since I left?"

"In the end, finding you was so simple. Pretending to be such an avid bird watcher, they were used to me being up here on the hills. They didn't know I was searching for you, of course. When I saw their signal fires, I knew there was something going on, so I cut across the hills and was high above them in no time."

The *cailleach* interrupted him, placed steaming bowls of broth in front of us and we broke the bread she had made. It was the best food I had ever eaten. Sensing we needed to be alone together, she busied herself in the next room. We sat in front of the fire, basking in its embrace, conscious of a deeper understanding than we had ever shared before. Cormac slowly caressed my neck, running his slim fingers around the nape, till the skin tingled. At his touch, I came fully alive once more. Moving closer, he kissed me gently. Fearing almost to break the spell, I moved my body gently to encourage his passion. His hands slowly followed the curves of my body and found my breasts. My back arched a welcome.

He stopped and drew away. Immediately it was there again, the feeling of rejection. How could he steady himself so easily when my whole body was screaming for more?

I needed to ask what I should have asked so long ago. "Why did you never want to sleep with me? We had so many chances to be alone, but you never took them. Why?"

He ruffled his hair, his dark eyes pleading for understanding. "Stopping myself from taking you is the hardest thing I've ever had to do. I wanted us to be sure, to be married before we consummated our union. That way you would truly know I loved you for your mind and your fiery spirit, not just your physical body. You'll never know how hard it's been for me. You are a very sensual woman, Ally."

"But one day, you will make mad, passionate love to me, under the stars?"

He held my gaze. "We will be together the way we're supposed to be, that I promise you."

He had promised, and that was enough for me. "Then I suppose I can wait a little while longer." I wasn't stupid enough to let him kiss me again, not for the moment anyway. As I cleared the dishes off the table, I voiced the question that had been ringing in my head since my escape. "What happens now?"

"You stay here. They don't know I helped you escape. I'll go into the village, see if I can find out anything. And see if I can organise some way off this place."

And then I would leave this place for ever. Even now the Island haunted me. Especially now - I wanted to share it with him. He sensed my mood. "I spent so many hours scouring the Island I came to appreciate all you love about the place. I could spend hours telling you all I've seen and experienced. We'll have time for that later, once we're away and safe."

"It's so strange to think that when I was locked in that terrible place on the hillside, constantly thinking of you, believing you had forgotten me, that you were actually here on the Island." It was the cruellest part of my gift, not being able to sense anything about those close to me. It meant I had no way to protect them.

"Be careful, Cormac. I don't want anything bad to happen, not now."

"Don't worry. I think we can outsmart them without trying too hard. They wouldn't exactly qualify for MENSA, would they?"

I laughed, but still I was frightened to let him go. It took several minutes to persuade me it was for the best. "I have to go soon, Ally. It'll look suspicious to the Pastor if he hasn't seen me for a while."

When he was gone, I was convinced he'd be discovered. My greatest fear was being taken captive again. The *cailleach* tried her best to comfort me. It was only seeing her anxiety that I realised I was being selfish, inflicting my mood on her. She was risking her standing in the community to conceal me. Besides, I would need every ounce of positive energy I could summon if we were to get off that rock to freedom.

The hours passed so slowly, the clock ticking loudly on the mantle, keeping measure of each painful second. Not knowing if he was safe was agony. How long would Cormac be able to fool McGregor? I knew just how astute the Pastor was, knew what he was capable of. I had seen what he really was. I struggled to refine the vision I had had of him that day, the shape of his other form. Yet again my *sight* had deserted me. Unable to focus, I prayed for his safety.

He could well be held by those brutes we had joked about. I fretted. The walls closed in again as they had when I was held at my mother's. Where *was* he? I tried to distract myself. Thinking of Ally cheered me. But what were the odds I would ever see her again?

The *cailleach* made several attempts at conversation. After a while, she gave up, settling by the fire engrossed in her knitting. I grew accustomed to the gentle click clicking of the needles, as the colourful wool passed through her skilful fingers. The sound soothed me more than talking ever could. She looked so content, her fingers nimble at their craft. Every so often, she checked her stitches and moved the weight of the wool between the needles, distributing it more evenly. From time to time, she glanced my way and smiled. I smiled back, distractedly.

When would he return? Endless 'whys' and what ifs' floated through my mind in a constant procession. Until I saw his face once more, my mind could not be still. The light gradually dulled, the day heading towards early evening. Surely, he would come soon? The faintest whispering reached my ears. I turned towards the small window frame. Several *taibhsen,* unfamiliar to me, called to me on the wind. *"Theirig am falach, a Aluinn."* They were warning me to hide. Almost silent, no more than a whisper, it seemed their voices split, separated, and reformed within my senses. *"Bi air d'fhaicill."* Beware.

"You must hide me, quickly; I sense danger." Swiftly the old woman rose with an agility that belied her years and ushered me back into her daughter's room. Bending, she strained to lift the corner of a heavy wardrobe away from the wall. Behind it lay a small, concealed compartment. I squeezed into the recess, too frightened to wonder why she had gone to such trouble to prepare this tiny sanctuary. Footsteps approached until there was someone on the other side of the cottage door. Others followed.

I heard how she made her way slowly to the door, seeming far frailer now, a ploy, I realised. The door opened. Guttural voices filtered through but I was unable to discern their meaning. The voices grew louder. Footsteps approached.

Hide and seek, most children love it. The thought of outwitting another with some well sought out hiding place. But there was no fun in this game – the stress held me paralyzed in that tiny space. I was terrified I would sneeze or make some sound that would draw them to me. I prayed more intensely than I had ever prayed before that the threat would pass. I listened as the door handle of the wardrobe turned. If they pulled the room apart, I would be discovered. My heart beat so loudly, echoing in my ears and in my head until I wanted to scream. Beads of sweat gathered in my hairline, and in every crevice of my body. Now I knew what it meant to smell fear.

Drawers opened. The lovely keepsakes I had admired were thrown on the floor with no regard for the *cailleach's* feelings. I was ashamed to be the cause of her upset. She begged them to stop. "Please tell me what it is yur lhookin fur? Thurs nuthin here tae interest yhe. Please dinnae touch thaem, they're auh ah huv tae remind mih oh her!"

There was no compassion in the voice of the faceless, nameless aggressor. "Quiet old woman! Hav yeih anuther room?"

"Ah telt yeh aw'readih Ah huv ah small hut ahn that's auh! Yhe kin see Ah dinnae hae much. Yur wastin yur time!" Her defiant tone was undisguised; she had spirit for one so old. It was more than just my own life threatened by those people. The *cailleach's* bravery kept me calm now. Who was I to give her away?

But she was no threat to him. "If yur hidin her, yull be sorrih!"

Cunningly she changed tactics and began weeping. "Whur is there fur hur tae hide?" she sobbed. Most men hated nothing worse than a weeping woman.

"Thurs ... only two days tae go! Yhe dae understand what ahm talkin' about?"

There was a long drawn out silence. Her answer when it came was timid. "Ah hear yhe."

He left to join the others, saying, "All right auld woman. Jhist remember – yhe see any'hin', yhe tell meh."

They departed, having turned her small home upside down. I imagined other homes scattered across the Island had suffered the same fate. There had been no mention of Cormac. I was relieved, taking it as an omen that his cover had not yet been blown. I redoubled my prayers.

Long moments later she returned to release me from my prison. I thanked her for having risked her own safety, but she seemed more than pleased to have foiled them. Perhaps, I thought, she was trying in some way to make amends to her daughter who must have been chased away from the Island by their bigotry, just as I had. Much later, when the night was dark still and the fire smouldered in the hearth, I heard a low tapping at the window to the back of the cottage. I thought at first the *taibhsean* had returned to warn me again, but the *cailleach* appeared to recognise it as a signal. Immediately she went to the back door and pulled back the huge metal latch, which acted as a lock.

There stood Cormac, weary but very much alive.

"I'm sorry I've been so long. It's been a nightmare. I had to confuse them somehow about where I was, so I visited a few of the Islanders, giving them each a different story as to my whereabouts. More importantly, I found a few who are willing to help us. By tomorrow night we'll be off the Island."

"Tomorrow night? Why not tonight? They must know someone's shielding me, Cormac, the cailleach is in danger. "

"From what I heard there's more chance of them waiting for a report of a washed up body. They've combed the Island and come up empty-handed."

I was not so sure. I knew my mother well enough to be certain she left no stone unturned. Until she had some concrete evidence to the contrary, she would keep on searching. It was not her way to rely on the suppositions of others.

"There's no way she's given up on finding me. Maybe she's even put that rumour about hoping I'll do something foolish, slip up. They're just waiting for me to make my next move."

Cormac laughed. "I haven't met one of them bright enough to think out the box like that. You give them far too much credit!"

All the same, I had to be convinced he had not given us away. "You were careful making your way back here?"

His voice was calm and confident as ever. "Yes, trust me. I took the long route, so if anyone had been following me, I would've seen them. I even hid twice along the way, so they would've had to pass me. No one did, so stop fretting! Am I not to have a kiss after being away so long?"

I rushed forward into his arms, to the feeling of safety I had missed all day. He held me so tight, kissing the top of my head. He was cold and wet - but I could sense this man would give up his life to save mine. I had read of such a love, had thought it improbable. The reality was terrifying. There was loss of self, yet so much in return. I wished the old woman could somehow vanish. I ached to be alone with him. Cormac sensed my mood, teasing me with his dark eyes until I laughed at my own predicament.

"I was so worried about you," I whispered into his jacket lapels.

"I'm going to have to go again."

My sharp intake of breath must have been audible. "We can't afford to take chances now. I *need* to go back again. I only wanted you to know what's happening. I left Pastor McGregor drunk as a skunk – I'm afraid I had to sacrifice a bottle of single malt I had brought with me. He's mortal, which is just as well. He had started to ask me when I was leaving this place."

There was something in the way he said it that made me realise he felt at home on the Island too, was as much in love with its splendour as I was. I stared into his eyes, overjoyed at being reunited with him, even for a few moments, willing that no harm ever come to him.

He hugged me to him. "By this time tomorrow, we'll be off the Island. I've arranged a boat to take us back to the mainland. But I have to leave now, so I can be back before the Pastor wakes. Otherwise our cover is blown. Who would think to disbelieve the Pastor when he assures them I was with him the whole time?"

I was afraid, confused, but I sensed my selfishness would only add to the pressure he already felt. I was glad I had kept my thoughts to myself when I heard his next words. "What's one more day? After that, we can spend the rest of our lives together. Try and rest. We've neither of us had much sleep in the last while. I need to rest, who knows what's ahead of us when we leave? You should try to do the same."

"Have you seen my…. I mean have you seen her at all?"

He held me closer, understanding how hard it was for me to talk about her.

"Thankfully no, she seems to have gone underground. Even the Pastor seemed concerned with her whereabouts. God alone knows where she is. As long as it doesn't affect us, I've no wish to find out."

Reaching for him once more before he left, I kissed him as though it might be my last chance to ever to touch his lips. I was bereft when he moved away from me.

I couldn't help myself. "Do you love me, Cormac?"

He grew serious, solemn even and spoke calm heartfelt emotion. "How could I not love you, Ally? You're all I see, my every waking thought. If that's not love, I have no idea what it is."

I watched him leave, my heart aching. Sleep didn't come straight away, and when it did, it was filled with strange images. I was surprised I had slept at all, given the fear.

Chapter Fifteen

Twenty-four hours. I could hold out that long. My spirits lifted as I allowed myself to hope once more. Bored, I helped the *cailleach* with her chores, trying to express my gratitude. Later, sitting in the strong afternoon sunshine, I found her good company. She shared stories of her younger days, the way life had been back then. As I listened to the traditional tales, I felt a curiosity rising within me, a need to know if she herself had ever been involved in the rituals I had seen. Not wanting to offend the only person who had shown me any compassion in recent weeks, I kept my thoughts to myself. It was probably paranoia that wondered what other stories she could have shared with me. What good would it do, causing her pain just to settle my own curiosity?

But as she continued speaking, the feeling was there again. I was aware of her withholding things. At times she would begin a tale and then jump over details. The more I sensed her self-protection, the more aware I became of it. At times, she would be lost for long seconds. Coming out of her reverie, she visibly struggled to recollect her thoughts.

I felt for her. There were things over which I had had no control either. At least she had found the strength to stay and face her demons, instead of running away as I had.

She was far older than I – had been raised thinking it was the right way. Time and a sense of self had opened her eyes. I wondered why we two had survived the ordeal, been allowed to live outside their circle with our half memories. I suppose I was lost in my own thoughts, for when I began paying attention once more, she had reached her final story.

I sat up attentively. This was no tale she was telling. As she spoke all those strange images I had sensed, all the shadowy figures which had haunted my sleep formed a pattern, a sequence, took form. The tales I'd been told as a child – they were no stories. They were *actual events*, passed down through generations as mythical imaginings. As she spoke I could *see* the beasts down below the fertile volcanic soil of the Island, sensed their pleasure at their encasement within the heat, their disinterest in venturing further up towards the light.

What had changed? There had been a time of great scarcity, a need for new land. I sensed fear, rootlessness. The roaming had ended on the Island. I heard the settlers' hammers ringing as they built their homes. I sensed the sound vibrating down through the earth, waking the slumbering beasts below. Saw the sounds waking the beasts that lay dormant deep within the earth's core. As the old woman talked I could feel the great beasts' unrest, their balance changing. Awakened, they sensed the danger; the Island had cooled. Their earthen home was no longer the sanctuary it had been. Needing warmth they ventured up to the land of light, searching for survival. And there, on the surface, they saw strange creatures they had never seen before, heard their laughter. They listened with growing curiosity, becoming slowly aware of the existence man enjoyed. They saw the lightness of his spirit, despite his environment. He was happy. This knowing filled them with a jealous rage.

The monstrosity of their shape terrified the settlers, who ran screaming from them. And so they learned to use their hideousness to their advantage. They exploited man's weaknesses, his fears, understanding that he lived in terror of everything he couldn't understand. Terrifying and powerful, they were soon revered as gods. They grew aware of man's ignorance and superstition, watched the fools seek guidance from the seasons, water and fire. Their crude pre-Christian rituals formed the foundation of the New Rites, more deadly and more sinister than anything that had gone before. Years passed. The creatures became stronger, demanding sacrifice as offerings and sustenance, satisfying their bloodlust, and instilling terror in the people of the Island. Taking strength from the reverence man gave offered, they became prouder, stronger, ruthless, more cunning.

Few willingly searched out the Dark Island. Tales were told abroad of its dark secrets. Christianity won out on the mainland, but time forgot where the Dark Island was. Surrounded by water, isolated from other influences, the creatures appeared to thrive. But as the generations passed it became clear they were growing weaker. In going to the surface they had lost their ability to produce young. They found another way – shape changing, concealing themselves within human frame, exuding their wickedness through cruelty. But they could not prolong that existence, became desperate for heirs. And so they had turned to their worshippers, mating with them, trying to create a hybrid which would allow them to survive in some form, to mutate. They used young women as vessels of human flesh. But the vicious couplings were unsuccessful; the young were stillborn, with deformities too atrocious to look upon. For long years they tried, their frustration mounting as time ran out.

As I listened I understood McGregor was the most powerful amongst them, the leader others revered. His father and grandfather before him had been High Priest to these beasts. The rise in Christianity had been no threat. Outwardly they put paid to any 'pagan' attitudes. But behind closed doors the beliefs of the church became no more than entertainment on a cold winter's night. But the Pastor was different. He was not only linked to them as I had thought – he was *one* of them. I saw his joy as a pairing finally bore fruit. I saw how the beasts rejoiced at its arrival, an outwardly human child who would beget a race of protectors for them. Here the vision swam. I was unable to see the child's face, though I had a sense of it growing stronger into manhood. Ecstatic at their success, they had brought young women from further afield, strong young women destined to suffer their clumsy, brutal attempts at mating. Sensing danger, the Islanders insisted their young women be 'honoured' too.

A second child was born, a girl. The race was secure.

I had 'seen' all that was evil within the island. I understood it.

I had seen them as they truly were, a dying culture, which needed sustenance. I sensed their desperation, their vileness, trapped not just here on the Island but within the Seat at Edinburgh and at Berwick Law. Within their bowels lay others, dormant still.

The *cailleach* sat unaware of the revelations which had unfolded, her needles still moving in soothing rhythm.

Finally I understood. Understood the plague that rotted at the core of my Island. And I knew too that I would be the one to purge it of its scourge.

The old woman roused me from my thoughts. "A boat arrived in the bay ah few days ago. Many othurs huv come since. It wull beih the same as ever, an' then it wull be ovur fur another year."

Now I knew the truth. So I was no longer thinking of my own well-being. If I had disappeared, that meant that somewhere on the Island another innocent would die.

Silently I accepted the challenge. I had to save myself, but also prevent that life being lost. All my dreams were clear now, all those sightings, the rituals and the hooded figures. Those were not men within the jewel-encrusted robes I had seen, but creatures I needed to destroy.

I had to return to the Manse. It held the key to unlocking all the secrets buried within my subconscious.

I smiled, grateful to the *cailleach* who had inadvertently awoken my subconscious. I had the chance now to save that child's life, but more than that. I had the chance to free the Island from oppression and fear. In doing so, I might save myself.

Chapter Sixteen

If I had been impatient for Cormac's return before the waiting seemed interminable now. I had no intention of sharing with him all my sight had shown me, but I would have to tell him enough to convince him. He would refuse to put see me in danger. I understood his fear, but how do you say no to your own destiny?

When he finally arrived, he looked relieved. "Everything's ready. The boat sits at anchor in the South Bay. We need to get there quickly. Then we can be gone before anyone notices. "

His urge to protect me was clear, yet my own need to remain was far stronger.

"I'm sorry, Cormac. I can't leave." I stared straight into his eyes. He needed to know I would not be turned away from this decision. My instinct to protect him made me hold back, but I told him what he needed to know.

"So you see, I can't run away, knowing that someone faces what I have seen for them. And soon."

"But why do we have to go to the Manse? There have been so many making the journey up there today. It looked to me as if they were preparing a festival of sorts. They were carrying flowers, corn... emblems of fertility."

I felt the bile rise to my stomach. Of course that was how it would appear to Cormac, an innocent festival, a curiosity, a mingling of old and new beliefs. Memory took me back until I was that small child standing behind a gravestone once more. The symbols they carried today they had carried then. As I grew older I had become aware of their origins, pagan Celtic images, but traced upside down. "Don't ask me to explain, Cormac, I'm just convinced that they are holding a girl up there. They intend to sacrifice her. I can't let that happen."

"So what do you plan to do?"

"Breach their defences. I just don't know how."

It was as though a light had gone off in his head. "I think my time observing those bloody cormorants has just paid off."

He looked at me, his handsome features serious. "We still have to go to the boat, Ally, but I promise on my life, I'm not taking you off the Island just yet. Do you trust me?"

"With my life," I said and meant it.

We made our farewells swiftly to the old woman. There was no time to waste. Every second was precious. Staying close to the trees that lined the gravelled road we made our way from the small croft around the perimeter of the surrounding fields. There was no one to hinder us. Their proceedings had obviously revved up a gear. They had better things to concern themselves with than to continue their search for me. Knowing I had no way off the Island, they had decided I could wait.

A small fishing boat lay within the shadows of the cliffs. Sailing boats lay at anchor in the bay, bobbing on the water in great numbers. Every year the same surge of humanity came to an Island that was otherwise shunned. This year, it seemed they had come in greater numbers than ever - or had I simply forgotten?

We waited until the last of them had come ashore. As the torch lit procession made its way up the hill from the bay, we made our way carefully to the south side, staying in the shadows, praying no one would see us. When we finally reached our boat Cormac called to the men on board. Within seconds, they had laid a wooden plank across to us. I was suddenly seized with dread. That feeling of fear and revulsion I had had back in the cottage was a hundred times stronger now than it had been. But what could be wrong?

If Cormac had lied to trick me into leaving the Island, I would be powerless to prevent it. I stopped midway across. "You're not taking me away from here, Cormac? I would never forgive you, even if you thought you were doing it for my sake."

He held out a hand to encourage me onwards. I refused to move. The wood was swaying under my feet. He walked back out towards me and held me steady as he walked me into the boat. "Relax, Ally I have a plan. It's a bit foolhardy but it's the only one we have, so just stay calm. I'll explain it once we're out of the bay."

I went forward to the bow, eager to be doing something useful, but there was no task for me. All the men – men I didn't recognise - were quietly going after their own work. I stood looking across the tranquil waters of the bay. My ears, after so much silence were sensitised. The engine was louder than I had thought – what if someone heard it? The very sea seemed loud and defiant.

We stayed close to the shoreline, tucking ourselves in under the cliff sides where possible, to lessen the chances of being observed from the hills. As we approached the menacing North face of the Island, we began slowly to head out to sea. I panicked. "You *promised* me, Cormac. How could you lie to me?"

"I haven't lied to you. We need to go out just a little further to turn the boat around to point directly towards the North cliff. There's a cave deep within the rock face. It's well hidden but I reckon we can reach it with the high tide. I found it the other day when I was exploring. As soon as I realised how determined you were to go through with this ridiculous plan of yours I knew this was the solution."

To my mind, it was madness. "Are you serious, Cormac? It looks like we're sailing straight into the face of the cliff. I can't see any opening there, it's solid."

His calmness didn't alleviate my tension. "Not quite. There's a small gap at the bottom of the cliff face, but it only really shows when you're almost up against it, when the water level's slightly higher like now. Don't worry Ally, I know it's there. If we can take the boat through that channel, the cave I'm thinking of should be directly in front of us. Once we land, the men will take the boat back to the bay and wait for us there."

"But how do you know you'll be able to make it through the channel?" The water level was very variable, depending on the weather and wind direction. More worrying still were the rocks and jagged cliff edges which would undoubtedly shatter the boat if we were to run aground.

"I don't, so you'll have to trust me, won't you?" He smiled to reassure me. If it were humanly possible, I knew he would get us through. The men followed his instructions without question. I had no idea he was so knowledgeable about boats. What else about this man did I not know?

Nothing ever prepares you for the strength of the sea as it does battle with something it would destroy. I hadn't seen this primordial struggle at such close quarters for many years. The sky cast broody shadows low and menacing over the jagged edges of the rock face. We were at the elements' mercy. Crossing through the channel was terrifying. Fear exploded within my soul as the monstrous North face suddenly towered above us. The unrelenting wind whistled around my head like a banshee, paining my ears just as those *taibhsean* did.

The nesting cormorants were immediately alert. The stench of their guano made me retch as our fishing boat wove back and forth. It seemed to go on forever, the small boat against the watery chasm and the vastness of stone. Forced downstairs by the pungent smell, I felt trapped but I knew my nausea would increase if I went back above decks. The men on the upper deck fought for control, struggling for just the right angle as the narrow passage drew nearer. The waters rose furiously around the edges of the boat.

Unable to bear being below decks a second longer, I came up from the cabin to be hit by a backlash of salty water. I had sense to keep my mouth well shut as I held tightly to the metal railing around the protective hub of the stairwell. Cormac was up in the bow, shouting to the man at the wheel. My heart was filled with gratitude. There were things I didn't understand about him, but if we survived this night, I was determined to change that.

It seemed he had achieved his goal. The water became less frenzied. We had breached the channel. With relief I made out the cave he had described up ahead. Its opening led into the hillside, almost hidden from view, and unseen from the grassland above. The ledge in front of it that had been marked by the cormorants.

I had never heard the cave mentioned. Who would be foolhardy enough to dare such a channel to seek it out? Once through the entrance it was relatively easy to steer up the channel. Within no time, the boat sat alongside and Cormac and I were lowered onto the ledge. We had no time to watch the boat's retreat. The skipper must have been paid handsomely to risk the channel twice. Navigating it had been largely down to Cormac's skills. If they failed to make it out... The thought hung heavy. How would we escape then?

As we clambered down to the cave's entrance, I was glad to have made it that far. I scraped the skin off my hands as I lowered myself down from the filthy ledge, knowing the pain was nothing in comparison to what awaited whoever they had chosen in my place.

The cave went back almost thirty metres before Cormac found what he was looking for. At the far side of the cave, almost completely hidden by a huge rock, stone flagged steps spiralled downwards. Cautiously we began our descent, and my level of unease rose sharply. It was clear that route had either recently been used or would be used soon. Torches hung at uneven intervals in metal baskets lighting the way. But there was no guard, no one protecting the tunnel. Did they feel so secure, so sure they were safe? Cormac was beside me, yet strangely, he brought me little comfort. I knew he would protect me if obstacles arose. But it was my fate to end the Pastor's reign of tyranny. I refused to entertain any thought of failure.

The air in the passage was musty. As we lost height, my ears throbbed as if they were about to pop. I swallowed hard, trying to ignore the sensation, glancing at Cormac. He was rubbing his own ears in an effort to rid himself of the discomfort. Sounds muffled and low, travelled towards us. We would soon be at their base. We reached the bottom of the winding stairway and stood within its shadows, unsure what to do, and unwilling to leave the relative safety of our hiding place. But we had to make a move. Time was running out. From the sounds in the distance, I knew that the celebrations hadn't yet begun. There was still a little time before the sacrifice began.

Chapter 17

I gazed out over the open ground, taking in the silhouette of the Manse from our side angle; the moon lit it all too well. We would have difficulty in approaching unseen. Scanning to the right I saw the small chapel through which we could enter the main building. It completely blocked our view of the secluded garden, walled on every side. That was where the crowds had gathered. There was a tremendous well of sound from behind it as the crowd's anticipation grew. My awareness of them heightened my fear. As we peered out from behind that cold, stone wall, then slowly crept forward, I was aware of my fear deepening. I breathed deeply, forcing myself to focus.

A figure, a man, appeared and began to check the area around the manse. We were still too far away to be noticed but lay flat rather than chance discovery. I held Cormac's hand tightly, hearing my own heartbeat as the man made his rounds and moved on. I forced myself to relax , to calm my breathing. I wasn't feeling brave, in fact I wanted to run. But I knew I would not.

Directly ahead stood the chapel. Built into its sides were small recesses. We ran to the first one, hardly daring to believe we had made it. The chapel was just as I had remembered it all these years. It was the old burial chamber of the McGregors. The graves outside the chapel were overgrown and in disrepair. I found that strange. Why take such care upholding their supposed heritage, but neglect where it had all begun? Or was this just another symbol of their disrespect for all life?

Faint voices floated on the wind from the far side of the house. Cormac put a warning finger to his lips. He needn't have worried. I had a strong compulsion to go into the Manse itself. What I needed lay within those walls.

It was past the time for fear. Our route was mapped out in my psyche. All those dreams and images, confused through time and place, led me now to this place. My senses once awoken never failed me. I had been guided to this moment.

Cormac seemed happy to follow my lead, as though he understood my sixth sense. Perhaps he thought I knew exactly what awaited us within those old stone walls. As I walked towards the house, I realised much of my fear had abated. I was doing that which had been decided for me.

As we approached through the narrow walkway with its high, ornate iron the wall offered protection from the elements, leading away from the dilapidated chapel towards the side entrance to the Manse. We had almost reached it when the door opened. There was nowhere for us to hide.

It was though I had been taken back in time. I struggled to breathe as a large procession of hooded figures, as dark and foreboding as I had remembered them, poured out of the manse. They passed within feet of us. If they had even glanced to the side, they would have seen us. Their hoods restricted their sight, causing them to look straight ahead. What sort of people were they that concealed their identities? Their fear must be greater than any I had experienced. They found strength in their numbers, but their courage would soon diminish if they were left on their own.

We stood silent until the last figure had passed, then waited long enough to be sure no other would follow. It was exactly the same scene as I had witnessed all those years before, unchanged, never ending. Suddenly my seer's sight burst into life. I saw their victim, hazy yet, a girl's frame being led out into the heart of the throng. So they *had* chosen another, it was true. There she stood, the one they had chosen to sacrifice.

I found myself filled with new courage. This was why I was here.

The image faded within my mind as my sight closed once more. As we began to walk towards the doorway, Cormac began whispering to me. I barely listened. He was a stranger here - I saw his need as a man to protect me, but I would not allow him to deter me from my path – even though it was out of love for me. I understood my goal, knew how close I was. My whole life had built towards this night.

It was likely there would be few of them left inside. I saw no reason not to use the front entrance. We made our way boldly through the huge, ornate door. The original owner had plainly spared no expense. As I passed the threshold, I sensed someone had built that house out of love. At one time, there had been happiness there.

A passageway led into a small scullery, where servants had once sat, duties over. Another door led into a huge kitchen. I almost expected a huge pot of boiling water to be cooking human remains, stripping the meat from the bones. Instead it lay covered in dust. The sensation of the Pastor's presence was stronger than ever now I was in his domain.I shivered with outrage. Part of my fear was not knowing his whereabouts. Strange, he had made no further effort to see me since my arrival on the Island though he had haunted my dreams. I understood his aging now – he was greatly weakened. But though his body craved the blood from this ritual, though he was not at his full powers, he was still the beast I feared most.

I sensed without doubt that he feared me just as much as I feared him. I had tossed and turned the night before, looking for a sliver of hope. So it was that I discovered the connection; a memory seemingly insignificant, yet the crux of his weakness. At one time he had allowed me access to his Achilles' heel. I had buried the memory so deep that it had been the last to surface.

When the old Pastor had still lived he had taken me on a grand tour of the manse, sure I would be interested in all the great things preserved there. I pretended for his sake to pay attention, for my mother would be vexed if I upset him. At first it had been hard not to yawn as he told me stories and histories I had heard so many times before. The first thing to stir my interest was a huge wall hanging full of the strangest images I had ever seen. The old Pastor went to great lengths to explaining the tapestry, its detailed colouring, its details drawn from a heavily bound book which stood on a podium in the corner. Mesmerised by any book, I reached forward. Strangely the old man stayed my hand.

Annoyed, I ran ahead of him into the next room, a room far grander than the last. I was almost upon the long altar before I knew it. It was covered by a long velvet cloth. At its centre lay another book, far bigger and more elaborate than the first. Its worn leather caught the light streaming through the windows, and I placed my palm opened wide on the heavy hide. Instantly my mind was assaulted with images, the Island as the first settlers had discovered it, symbols from their ceremonies, their meanings. And then came faces, the pastor's family line, traced back through the centuries, his ancestors, cruel and heartless, ravaging other islands, pillaging, killing, only to settle here. When the images had hurtled back to the first of the McGregor line there was no misreading them. From the first they had been evil, possessed with a longing to abuse and destroy others. The line moved forward again until it stopped where a fissure had been breached into Otherworldliness. My seer's sight really awakened then. I saw clearly how it was the McGregor line that had supplied sacrifices for the beast's sustenance, satisfied their blood lust with their cunning. I saw how they had travelled far and wide to find victims, often amongst the dispossessed, young women living on the edge of society.

I had not heard the old Pastor come in, but instinctively drew back from the book as soon as I had sensed him behind me. For all his outward kindness, I knew now the people he came from, the spirit of his line. How he must work to control it. It must have been like a living thing within him. I had not feared the old man then, but rather felt pity for him, understanding the schism within him, the abhorrence he felt for his own kind.

He passed me, moving up onto the platform, leaning down to kiss the leather covering of the book. "You are deeply honoured Alluin, for few have looked upon this treasure. You must never speak of it, child." His warning was unnecessary - it terrified me to know that it existed at all. The old man gazed at the manuscript with rapture and in that second my seer's awareness told me that this book was their strength and their weakness all rolled into one. Whatever maintained these people, whatever allowed safe passage between the beasts and their protectors, whatever allowed them to cross that divide and enter this world was *here*, within its pages. His son had not withstood the unrelenting demands of his lineage so well – in him the yearning for cruelty was deeper, stronger, limitless… And now it endangered the whole Island.

We had to find that manuscript.

Daringly I walked into the main hall. I had seen it only once before but it had been enough. It hung there just as I remembered it, a magnificent, epic tapestry, unseen for so many years, but still strangely familiar. It had dulled, the intricate colours heavily faded in parts. The finer strands had lost their bold contrast, so that certain sections appeared to disappear into the background, becoming fragments of the greater whole. Yet many of the images on the coarse material were very real to me. I had an urge to *dissolve* into them, to lose myself in the detailed imagery. As I stared at it, I realised if I looked a certain way, shapes began to appear in it. The shapes swam, and then appeared with total clarity. And there was a familiarity about the grotesque creatures which emerged, clearly depicted on the tapestry if you had the sight of a seer. They were engaged in perfectly ordinary activities, enjoying simple pleasures, relaxing beside the river, eating from large baskets, or picking fruit. I had no abhorrence of them at all. Almost reverently, I approached it, this huge symbolic representation of the Island's past. I touched the cloth, felt the richness of it, brushing my fingertips one way then the other over the thickly interwoven threads that had withstood the test of time. In my disbelieving mind's eye the entire tapestry moved, and somehow came alive.

It was no longer a depiction of fables, designed to disturb the imagination of young children. It was much more than that. I connected somehow to all the individual creatures that were staring back at me. I stood still, my fingers frozen in time as they began to welcome me. Their large limbed bodies gathered round, beckoning me to them. I stared aghast, disbelieving, unable to tear myself away from the image.

It was as if the very boundaries of the tapestry no longer existed. The lines between realities grew hazy. I was no longer looking at a historic relic. I was there on the river beside them all and they were calling to me. They used not my given name. Instead they called me *"Breecha"* chanting the name repeatedly.

My head was swimming in confusion as I bent down. Still merged within the great icon I placed my hands in the icy water, then pulled them out, watching the water drip away. The sensation of wetness remained as the beasts knelt before me. That huge throng should have terrified me, yet all I experienced was calmness, a feeling of something restored.

Suddenly the chanting stopped, the image dissolved. I stood once more in the Manse. A coldness had crept over my soul and I pulled my hand from the surface of the tapestry as though I had been burned. What burned me more was the awareness of *why* I had returned. I had been holding my breath. It was the need for air that had drawn me back.

Struggling to steady my breathing, I sensed Cormac behind me.

As I turned to look at him, unsure quite what to do next, my body still reeling from the experience, he took my hand and led me away. His warm touch gave me the reassurance I needed. Swallowing hard I stepped back out through the doorway to the main hall. We stood under a grand staircase. A huge balcony ran in a perfect circle above. It was exquisitely hand crafted, an ornate design following its entire route in silver and metal. Its maker would have been wounded by its current state of neglect, the dull metal unable to capture the light that illuminated the hall. The entire house was in a state of disrepair. It was an empty shell, I realised, an illusion, its true purpose to instil fear, in order to protect their wickedness

I was struck by the intense silence. So many passages; the Manse was a tardis, a maze of confusion. As hard as I had visualised that great leather-bound book of secrets I had no idea where it would be found. It had to be upstairs, for there was no room downstairs grander than the tapestry room. The worry playing at the back of my mind was more insistent now. What if our search was futile? What if we didn't find the manuscripts?

I brushed the fears aside. I had come too far to be put off now. A young woman's life hung in the balance. As we reached the top of the stairs, I was more relieved than ever that Cormac was with me. I had been so desperate to get inside the house and find the manuscripts, I hadn't given a thought to what would happen if we met any resistance. What an absurd assumption that they would be unguarded.

Cormac saw them first. Boys rather than men, they stood in a small group not ten paces from us. One shout from them would alert the Pastor to our presence. Strangely, when they saw us, they hesitated, as if unsure how to react. Their eyes were somehow anxious. I held back, unwilling to make the first move. Cormac stunned me then, uttering words I had never heard before. Not words as I knew them, but a chanting. Within seconds the sound had lulled them to sleep, yet they stood upright like before, their eyes tight shut, as though frozen in time and place.

My mind couldn't fathom it. "What…what have you done to them?"

"Hypnotism. I learned it as part of my psychology major. Listen, Ally, I don't know how long this will hold them, but if I've done it right, they won't remember us being here at all."

I was relieved to have found a route past the beasts, but perturbed too. What else about him did I still have to discover?

For now I'd just be thankful he possessed the skills he did.

We hurried round the circular top floor. The door they had been guarding was small, insubstantial. Compared to the splendour of the manse, it seemed lacking in the grandeur and extravagance of the Manse. It didn't look in the least like the door to a treasury I had been expecting. In fact it was the last place I would have thought to look. As I turned the handle I realised there was a threadbare curtain hanging behind the opening. When I pulled it back it revealed yet another stairway.

As I climbed the tiny staircase I was suddenly seized with a sensation not unlike vertigo. The steps were built tightly together, the angle so steep I was almost crawling before I reached the top. Trying hard not to choke on the dust that had gathered there over decades, I almost screamed as a huge spider ran across my hand. On the tight landing, two doors faced directly onto each other. I glanced at Cormac. He pulled a face. The decision was entirely mine to make.

I picked the one to my right. Already sure it would be locked tight, I pushed and met the expected resistance.

"Looks like we'll have to pick the lock."

Cormac had other ideas. Before I had a chance to say, "Be careful" he had pushed forcefully against the old panels. With one dry crack, the door swung open.

Beyond it lay a large circular room, with a beamed ceiling. We were in the very roof of the Manse. Fussy Victorian wallpaper was repeated in busy patterns along the walls, drawing the room inwards and encasing us in a flowery hell. There was little furniture. Save for the great wooden chests all around its perimeter, beautiful mahogany kists, intricately carved. I stared at them, hearing the growing chants outside. The sound drew me to a small paned window. Wiping away its film of dust I peered through the cracked glass. It gave me a view down the entire length of the garden and onto everything beyond. The whole area was illuminated now by the full moon. I could make out the tiny fishing boats within the harbour, and the scatterings of small crofts. My eyes returned to the scene directly below me. There were so many gathered there now, great throngs of worshipers in long robes, all turned to face a raised platform at the end. So many of them. The whole Island must be there, to welcome their friends and take part in the bloody sacrifice.

My old fears returned. How were we supposed to overcome so many of them? How could we rescue her? We'd have to work fast. The proceedings were still low key. But they would liven up soon. I hoped for that girl's sake that we found the sacred writings before they came for them. Without them, there would be no ceremony.

There was a low table under the small window. A heavy burgundy bound book lay on it, modern in design, discordant with the overall appearance of the room. My curiosity was peaked. Perhaps there would be some clue here? I opened it warily, desperate to find some evidence that could be used against them if need be. Something to make sense of all the madness that surrounded me.

A vast collage was laid bare as I turned the pages. There within its gaudy frame was the sickening evidence of every person who had suffered at their hands. A scrapbook of death, it was filled cover to cover, haphazardly mounted, a confusion of clippings and newspaper cut outs of missing teenagers, mysterious disappearances, strange occurrences and other seemingly unrelated events. Their faces stared up at me from the pages of the book, questioning.

I was diverted by the sound of Cormac trying to prise open one of the chests. It wouldn't budge. We should have thought to bring some tool with us. I found myself moving my hand to my hair, scorning the idea even as I had it. Pulling out a grip, I straightened it and moved over to Cormac. He looked at me as though I had lost it as I placed it in the keyhole and began to move it back and forth. Nothing. I tried again. Just when I was about to give up, I heard an unmistakeable click.

Between us, we lifted the huge lid. There before us were garments of clothing, mismatched and of differing sizes. With horror I recognised some of them from the scrapbook – how freakish that these scraps of clothing had been kept when their owners were long since disposed of. Anger built inside me. Why did they keep them? And then I remembered how as a child, when I had outgrown my clothes, new ones would miraculously appear. My blood ran cold. Revulsion filled me, so overpowering I wanted to scream. Cormac looked at me, uncomprehendingly, frustrated by our lack of success. "Should we open the next one?"

They could all be filled with the possessions of their victims. The thought was almost too much to bear. On the other hand, the next one we opened could contain the manuscript we so desperately needed. Or we could be in the wrong room entirely. "We have to decide. Do we keep on looking here or try elsewhere?"

He shrugged. "It's odd, leaving all these chests here that serve no purpose? Maybe it's to confuse anyone who gets this far."

I closed my eyes, summoning my senses which seemed most meagre now when I needed them most. Still I tried. "I have a strong feeling about this room."

"Well, we'd better get a move on. Things are livening up down there. They've started chanting again. Believe me, it'll get a lot worse before this night is over. Let's try the rest. But you'll have to give me another hairgrip. This one is wrecked."

I took another Kirby from my mane. A long section of hair fell over my face. I tucked it quickly behind my ear, then straightened the metal. We soon got into a rhythm. Each chest provided more personal items, showing how their sickness had reigned through several decades of fashion changes as young woman reinvented themselves, changing their appearance so as to differ from older generations. One chest contained nothing but underwear. The saddest was filled with sentimental keepsakes, jewellery, many inscribed *with love*, sad and poignant mementos. When ten of the twelve were lying open, we stopped a moment, sickened by what we had found. Still no manuscripts.

We stared at each other. Only two chests remained. Outside their chanting had grown louder and more fervent. We turned to the eleventh chest. As Cormac placed the metal grip inside the keyhole, he smiled encouragingly, and then listened for the release of the catch inside. We prepared ourselves for more sickness or worse emptiness but our fear turned to ecstatic relief.

On top of ceremonial robes superior to those I had recognised earlier lay two leather bound books. The bindings were ancient and worn, sprayed with blood. The leather had absorbed it into its intricate patterning. The robes too bore the stains of bloodshed. Their owners, cloaked within them had surely carried out those sacrifices.

We placed the manuscripts side by side on the rough flooring and opened their covering. Tattered and worn, they held paper unlike any I had ever seen. There was a strength, a thickness to it which gave no yield. As I touched it I was filled once again with the deep abhorrence I had felt as a child when I had touched it. Like with the tapestry it was as though its evil had transferred its sickness to the cloth, for it lived and breathed, had a life all of its own. The stench invaded my nostrils. Death lingered there, stale decay. I let go of the book abruptly, my face streaked with tears.

The pages were written by hand, elaborately decorated with gold leaf. Neither of us able to decipher the words, but my heart knew our search was over.

*

"We wait until just the right moment". My tone allowed no room for discussion. Cormac accepted without question. I was aware as he agreed that he had no idea what awaited us, or the horror of the proceedings we were about to witness. Nevertheless, he sensed the change, a transformation strongly enough to make this strong man follow my lead.

We sat cross-legged on the floor, in silence. I had sensed my purpose in coming there, but the details had been concealed. Now the shroud around my mind had been lifted. And with its removal came an absolute sureness of what we had to do. I didn't fret for the girl. Nothing would happen until the time was right. The outcome was beyond my control. All I had to provide was the courage to go through with it. I was more determined than ever to revenge those who had perished. If necessary, I would die trying.

Cormac grew restless, walking back and forth to the window, my calmness beyond his comprehension. What he hoped to see out there I didn't know - he wasn't capable of recognising the moment. I understood its crude elements, knew it wasn't yet time. *Not yet,* the *taibhsean* told me.

Cormac was growing nervous. Being told I was relying on spirits wouldn't help him understand. "Look, Ally, I've gone along with everything you've said so far, but why wait now? Why are we sitting up here, when that girl's down there?"

"Please just trust me, Cormac," I pleaded. "It won't be much longer, I promise. Conserve your energy, as I am doing."

He knew then I would not be moved and returned to sit beside me. I smiled as he took my hand. Its warmth calmed my weary heart, as much as his words. He reached up to stroke my hair with his other hand. "When I saw you for the very first time, you stood out to me. I thought it was because of your hair, that it made you somehow different. But being here, on this Island, has made me realise that I could have met you anywhere in the world, and I would have felt the same. I can't begin to put into words how I feel about you, Ally. More than anything, I'm terrified that you'll never understand how much I loved you if we should fail. I've cheated you greatly."

Cormac's expression was so sombre, my heart went out to him. How could he doubt that what he had given me had been enough?

"Knowing you love me is all I need, Cormac."

"I do love you Ally, but it's more than that. When I realised you'd left Edinburgh I was devastated, but then some strange *force* pulled me in this direction. Do you see? I had no choice but to come and protect you. The only thing scaring me is I might let you down."

"Cormac, please, don't torture yourself…"

He pulled me close, silencing me. "Did you hear that?"

I shook my head, straining to pick up any sounds. And then I heard…what *was* it? A low sound, like murmuring, only not a natural sound. It had no voice, more a drone. Whatever it was, it was moving towards us.

Then came tapping. Not gentle, like fingertips, but heavy, as though something were being hit hard onto the steep staircase outside. Slowly, very slowly the sound rose, towards us. Soon whatever was making that sound would be on the other side of the door.

I suddenly remembered Lorna's experience in Edinburgh. She had described a sound just like that, and now I connected the sound with the tales I heard often, but never really believed, not until now. The girl we had seen would be only the first in a long line of victims. Their sick rituals would go on for days until their thirst was quenched.

In the air, they gave no sign of their weakness. But now, almost spent, they were unable to fly. They were diminished, these vile creatures, at their lowest ebb, starved of their sick supplies. Their movements were exaggerated, slow. They were deteriorating, desperate for their feast to begin. Only the terrible fear of their blind followers allowed them to rule without fear of overrule.

I finally understood my dream. The Old Pastor hadn't died. He had been slain by his own son. The cycle had to be broken. These beasts had to be wiped out, and with them, the Pastor, their protector. He had no heir. With his death the line would be eradicated.

McGregor had always feared me. I knew that now. Just as I had known from my earliest childhood to fear him. It was something felt inside, an instinct I hardly understood. And now I knew why. *I* had threatened *him*.

This time there would be no gravestone to hide behind.

My eyes were drawn to the door. I stared at the handle, paralysed. Slowly it turned. As the door moved, the fear subsided. I pictured the girl's face, then the faded photographs in the scrapbook. Whatever I did now would determine whether or not she became one of them.

The door moved further. A small line of light invaded the room, growing steadily wider. I stood tall, ready for whatever it took. A low, gurgling noise reached my ears as a form took shape within the doorway. Not quite an animal, it walked on two legs, swaying slightly on claws hugely out of proportion. Its lower limbs were as thin as sticks. The body retained its human form, but the arms were no longer visible, lost somehow within the torso. I knew then that the thing was not human. Not even Nature could produce such hideous malformations.

Cormac had moved to the back of the door, as a tall winged creature, its birdlike-claw effortlessly gripping the floor, allowed its form to grow within the room.

It saw me. I stood, frozen to the spot as it prepared to attack. I was powerless to move. It was as though my mind had developed a paralysis I could not overcome.

Cormac threw himself at the beast, undaunted and powerful, his muscles taut as he attacked the evil that was preying on my soul. It was as though he had broken a spell between us. My head cleared as he grappled it from behind, using his fists, clubbing it repeatedly. It fell to the ground with a tremendous thud, then struggled to rise again. In its fury I could see the man that lay within it, the thin veil of deception removed.

Cormac frightened me then. His second attack was even more frenzied than the first. He felled the beast with one final, heavy blow, rendering it lifeless. My seer's view dimmed, scattered by the ease with which he had ended the creature's life. The only emotion he had shown had been elation.

All that remained on the floor were the remains of a mortal man who had fought him with superhuman strength. Cormac sat back on his heels, breathing heavily, wiping droplets of blood from his face. For a moment, I didn't recognise him.

I felt strangely beholden to him too. Was it because I had expected this victory to be not his but mine? I placed the thought in the darkest recesses of my mind. There was too much to be done now. As we looked around for a hiding place for the body, the empty chests still lay open. We sealed the lid and took the precaution of locking it, just in case.

The tapping had begun again outside, growing steadily louder. I knew this time what to expect and that I must not hold back. It was unfair to expect Cormac to fight alone. As the second creature approached, Cormac was ready and I no longer hung back. My sight had shown me all that lay contained within those creatures. He was only one man and besides, I wished it to be over.

As the door opened, I found a strength I never knew I possessed. Even as I struck the first blows, I wondered who I was attacking, for change was upon him. One of the Islanders I had grown up amongst had leant their own being to that thing. The knowledge of it made my own sin less. The creature was still readily recognisable, its beak covering the now clearly human face. In seconds, I would recognise my attacker. Deep repressed anger grew in me and I slashed at it mercilessly as it mutated into a human.

Those beautiful robes were soon splattered by blood, crimson sprays staining the fantastically embroidered detail as grotesque as the deformity they covered. The robes were too short to cover their true shape. I realised they must take part in the rituals in human form. If only the Islanders could see them as they really were, as I saw them.

I had been sure I would turn away, not wanting to know, but some need made me look again. I was hardly surprised to see a face I recognised, Stuart McDonald, who had terrorised Sarah so needlessly. As we heaved his body into a second trunk, I realised that it made sense, the metamorphosis.

Time passed. We waited. No others came.

They had clearly come to fetch the manuscripts necessary for the ritual. Unless they appeared soon, the others would become restless. I made my way over to the second chest. There was a need in me to see once more the beast that lay within the man. I secretly hoped that perhaps, even in death, perhaps it had changed. Perhaps if I laid my hand on its cold body I would understand…

I unlocked the lid and lifted the heavily ornate lid upwards.

Cormac was quickly by my side. I assumed he wanted to help me, but he slammed the chest shut.

"Why did you do that? I only wanted to look again… to make sure. I don't want anymore surprises once I get down there!"

"They're dead, what's the point looking again? We haven't got time Ally, remember the girl. I don't even know yet what you plan to do."

He was right. "I'm sorry Cormac. This is what we have to do…"

He listened intently, and when I was done nodded grimly.

The scene below us was set.

All we had to do was act out the roles I remembered seeing, directly before the ritual mating. If we could keep our nerve.

Chapter Eighteen

I realised now that it had been my fate to witness those terrible scenes as a child. Without intimate knowledge of their rituals, I could not act now. The sight of the two figures that had stood either side of the child was burned into my sub consciousness. I knew exactly what was required of us and how we could get within reach of their intended victim. I only prayed we could reach her without anyone realising. Otherwise, there would be three deaths instead of one.

Inside my costume, with its great linen-like hood, I was perspiring. The crowd fell silent, as two hooded figures appeared, carrying the great book wrapped in a velvet cloth. As we passed through the crowd, heads low, I barely made out the incantation. I concentrated on the ground underfoot, conscious of odours of varying strengths, pungent body scents, and the smell of incense. The crowd parted to allow us through.

Woodland had been painstakingly cleared. The clearing shone in the moonlight, beams of light pouring down in silvery shafts, creating a churchlike effect in the trees. The altar stone gleamed. How many lives had been lost on it?

This was not a thanksgiving feast for the rejuvenation of life. It was intended to cut life short. The sense of excitement was palpable as we made our way slowly towards the altar. I dared not look around, yet I was desperate to catch a glimpse of their sacrifice. Would it be a local child, someone I recognised? Or someone lured to the Island against her will?

Figures either side blocked our view, yet I was deeply aware of her, sensed her pain and fear. It grabbed at me. My seer's sight saw her soul crying out in utter hopelessness. Her terrible death would be a mere precursor to what was to follow.

There was no such emotion in the others on the altar. They were fervent, ready to enjoy all the pleasures of the flesh as soon as their victim lay lifeless. At the altar, the crowd parted again, left and right. We passed through, slowly. Unhurriedly we climbed the steps and took up our positions, standing either side of the girl whose head remained covered. She too stood perfectly still, either drugged or in a hypnotic state.

The large crowd closed in once more. Now it could begin. Excitement accelerated through them. They began chanting again, slowly, rhythmically, waiting for us to begin. I understood the ritual. I had seen it performed before. I knew what I had to do.

I stalled, knowing I was playing a dangerous game.

They grew restless. I could not hold them back much longer.

I glanced towards Cormac, briefly, from under my heavy covering of cloth, so as not to give myself away. Though I couldn't see his face, I could feel his tension. I steadied him with my thoughts, reassuring him all was well. The crowd grew impatient. Thirsty for blood, their chanting increased, until it grew frenzied. One amongst them, hungrier or braver than the rest, spoke out.

"Give us the girl! What are you waiting for?"

Once more, I looked towards Cormac. This time he understood and reached under his heavy robe, holding up the book they wanted. I could see the embroidered emblems on the cloth we had wrapped it in. They had no merit, based on falsehoods, misconceptions designed to confuse and enslave them all to the will of those beings. How ironic that those very emblems in which they stored so much faith were being used to confuse them. Now their very own symbols of power would defy what should have been confronted long ago.

It was only as I removed my hood that they understood what was happening. There were gasps of horror and fury.

I spoke first, unafraid. "What you intend to do here this night is murder. And it's not for the first time."

Hissing, the crowd moved towards us.

I stared boldly into each face that defied me. I feared no one. Not the McGregors, nor the McDonalds nor all those other families who had lived out their days on the Island, generation after generation. The same families who went about their days tending their sheep, growing their crops, ploughing their fields were here, waiting for the lifeblood of this young woman. In the crowd I could see other faces, strangely familiar, though I couldn't recall the time or the place. No matter. I had more urgent matters at hand.

I saw fear on their faces. But also frustration – they had chosen a girl to die. As the angry mob approached us, their guilt made them more distorted. I had discovered their secret. If I were to tell nothing would remain as it was. I stood between them and the way things had always been. I was intent on destroying their ways, just as they were intent on destroying the girl.

My own anger rose. They were no better than savages. This way of life they had chosen had no merit. Their rules had been set down centuries beforehand, the same codes that set the beasts above them. What of human compassion? What of truthfulness? In me, in my threat to them, they sought vengeance for their own failings.

The crowd moved towards me as one. I continued to speak, unaffected by their show of strength.

"It's over. From this night on, it's over."

Cormac's nerve couldn't hold a moment longer. "Look to the house!" he screamed.

The mass swung around in the direction of the great Manse. There was a surge of noise, almost a shrill screech, as their sight synchronised. Small bursts of smoke, pearly grey, escaped through the broken panes of the attic's window. They stood, momentarily frozen. The fire seemed to gather momentum all of its own. Cracks appeared in the walls, emitting blasts of smoke, in white and grey. The fire gathered strength, until the red flame burning within was clearly visible, desperate to consume everything in its wake.

Some screamed their desperation. Others ran towards the Manse unsure of what they should or could do. But any effort would be futile. The fire had taken hold it. It would not be prevented from destroying the structure. A small number began pressing in our direction. "The writings - give them to us."

I opened the leather pages, showing them to be empty, except for the filthy scrapbook and some folded garments. "Do you think we would risk any of them actually surviving? Those writings have enabled those vile creatures to be kept alive for centuries. They have not always existed amongst you – you can live without them again."

The remaining crowd panicked and ran screaming, as though their very lives depended on whatever they could salvage. It was too late.

Flames billowed out of the windows as shattering glass exploded out of the framework.

In the confusion, Cormac and I made our escape. Untying the girl, we lead her awkwardly from the platform, only to be stopped in our tracks. Not all the hooded figures had run. There stood McGregor, flanked on either side by a henchman. His expression was taut and unflinching. My courage fast diminished. The man personified my fear – and here he was, defying me to defy him. For a second all those old fears were restored.

But it only took one glance towards the still shrouded victim, unmoving and docile, to convince me otherwise.

McGregor was their leader, whose hold on the Island had to be destroyed, if its people were to have any chance. I saw behind his façade, the evil and debauchery lurking there. A kaleidoscope of faces, lives lost and ruined, whirled through my mind far stronger, more forcefully than ever before. Despite the weakness of the others I was sure now that he was at his strongest, revelling in his own wickedness and thriving on stealing of yet another soul.

"So you think you destroy us by burning our books, you foolish child? How good of you to give yourself up this way, so that you can take your rightful place among us."

What was he talking about? Without the words in their sacred doctrines, they would not have the ability to restore themselves to their human forms. Was this a ploy, playing for time until his acolytes returned?

"Don't try to fool me, Pastor. It's over. Those Islanders were blind fools who needed rules to control them. Without the manuscript they've been set free. How else will you hold your rituals, say your incantations? One day they'll thank me."

"Do you really believe that, Aluinn? There is one thing you haven't considered. Why did your mother go to the trouble of bringing you back here?"

I had no interest in his sick theories. "It makes little difference now, Pastor. I have thwarted your plan, that's enough."

"On the contrary, dear Aluinn, you have fulfilled my plans. It was never my intention to sacrifice you. You're far too important to me for such a swift death. You see, you were always meant to be *mine*. I was promised you many years ago. You are my inheritance."

A wave of revulsion washed over me. I would rather have no life than a life at the side of this man. McGregor had turned to Cormac. "I see, Aluinn, that you have met my house guest. And, it's clear that you two have formed an attachment to each other. A sly move on your part, Cormac. I would have thought better of you than to behave in such an underhand manner."

"You won't have her, McGregor. She's mine." His confidence angered McGregor greatly.

"You've hardly proven yourself worthy, boy. You've behaved more like a fool than a gentleman."

"That depends very much on what you would expect of a gentleman. I protected Ally, when no other would."

The Pastor raised his voice. "Ah, but then she does not know you as I do."

I was confused. These two knew each other far better than their short acquaintance would suggest.

"Nothing you say will turn her against me." His cheeks were dark red, his eyes shining in the torchlight.

"We shall see, my boy, and very soon."

My mind was still reeling. The Pastor laughed, that mocking laugh I had always hated. It triggered my awakening.

"How could you and I ever be together? My love for Cormac burns as deep as my hatred burns for you and all you stand for."

"It seems we have no choice then. Cormac and I will fight for you, in time honoured fashion. You, Aluinn will be the prize."

The thought of losing Cormac at the hands of this man was more than I could endure. Part of me, deep within understood the beast within that man. I had seen it often enough in my dreams – father and son fighting for what was right. Cormac was no match for the McGregor. I had seen all that he was.

I watched helplessly as they began a ritual, a dual for my affections, as men have done over women since the dawning of time. I was terrified. My sight failed me entirely. All I could do for Cormac now was pray.

There they stood for the longest time each studied the other. For the Pastor's hard set expression, cruelly lined, and one I had been vexed to look upon, almost seemed arrogant of the outcome before it had indeed occurred. Cormac's in contrast was set determinedly as though unafraid of the man Though it looked to others like a fight between men of flesh and blood, I knew what was concealed within him. The *fitheach*, the great raven overshadowed the man. As I watched in horror it came alive again, solidifying and stretching beyond the boundaries of what was and what was not, until I could no longer separate them in my mind's eye.

Cormac was changing subtly too. There was a mingling of images within his flesh, like a child's toy, displaying hidden elements. I saw him clearly, as he was, but then his torso would ripple under McGregor's hand and I saw the shadow of a malicious beast, his own anger and determination beneath the surface. Others looking on would have seen two men locked in combat. Only I saw the truth of their souls.

Eventually I could no longer see the Pastor at all. The image beneath grew too powerful for my senses. Before me stood the tumultuous anger of the raven beast. I did not have the power to control such malevolence. I sensed the evil lurking in his heart. Every image my eyes captured showed a different facet of his metamorphosis, a glimmer of what lay buried within him. His hand moved in a skilful sweep, but when he pulled it back to attack again the skin's leathery texture was mottled, repugnant, non-human.

I turned away, repelled. As I turned back, my seer's *sight* was still deeply aware. Two or three others had gathered. I was conscious of them, felt them long to change too. Within their concealed form, I saw them as they were. They gained in height, their faces sharpening into protruding beaks. I sensed their anxiety. Far less dominant than the Pastor, they were weaker. Without those manuscripts, their rituals, they were vulnerable, so weakened they would be forced to accept the outcome of the fight. No one had the strength to intervene.

The two men grappled with each other, changing holds, manoeuvring each other round to get a better grip. For long minutes they wrestled, neither man gaining the upper hand. Then McGregor feigned left, pulling Cormac down to him and striking a blow into his face. Cormac pulled back his elbow, returning the rage with a fist to the Pastor's chest, knocking the wind from him. The two began rolling on the earth, each struggling for supremacy. Cormac rained blows on his opponent, who returned them with a speed that belied his years. I felt myself grow more fearful as the Pastor found his feet and rose again, edging back a few paces, winning strength before he went on the attack once more.

But before the fight could properly begin again, the Pastor stopped abruptly, holding onto his chest as though in agony. He shouted out, "No, it's too soon!" then fell to his knees, writhing in agony. His body had twisted into the foetal position and he moaned as he squirmed in the mud.

I cared nothing for his pain. We had to get out of there as quickly as possible. I moved towards the girl, intent on removing her shroud, to see how badly her responses were affected.

Cormac shouted to me to come to him.

I was angry, turning my head over my shoulder to tell him to run. The Pastor was in my line of vision.

He metamorphosed before our very eyes. There are no words to describe the vileness.

"Please Cormac, we have to destroy it now!" I shouted, afraid for our safety. Cormac stood rooted to the spot. Unafraid, almost, he looked down at the thing that had once been McGregor, but would soon be something much more sinister.

"He won't give up. You must destroy that thing he has become. Do you honestly think he'll let us leave, if it lives still?" Though he understood my motive, he seemed appalled at my lack of compassion. Cormac moved hesitantly towards the hideous mound that lay there like a chrysalis. It pulsated and writhed. There was nothing left to distinguish it as the Pastor.

"It's at its weakest now, Ally. I'll destroy it." I saw him wipe away a tear with his forearm. Much as I hated McGregor and all he stood for, I took no satisfaction in sanctioning his death or witnessing Cormac's distress. I had no wish to see it suffer, but my own release would only come through his death. Unless he was killed the entire Island would continue to lie in fear.

Cormac paused and looked around him, as though he was searching for something. He picked up a large piece of wood and, without a second's hesitation, rained down more blows upon the grotesque shape, which writhed in its anguish. I was repulsed, abhorred the cruelty inflicted on it, but knew there was no other way. As the blows continued, I prayed for it to be over. Finally, the form went rigid. It ceased pulsating and began shrivelling into an empty shell as the bloodied pulp within escaped into the sodden ground.

I looked away, horrified, but knowing that Cormac's deed had freed me.

The girl moaned behind us. I went to her, my heart full of compassion, and moved behind her to where the shroud was knotted from behind. It was wrapped so tightly I was surprised she had been able to breathe. As I turned her around, and lowered the hood, for a second I thought my mind had finally, irretrievably turned.

For there stood Lorna.

When I looked into her beautiful face, it might have been that of a stranger. There was no connection. Perhaps more than anything, this vengeful act, this attempt to sacrifice someone I loved, alleviated any doubts I had had. Her mind was somewhere far off. I could only pray that in time it would return. I fell on her neck, sobbing, uncaring that she didn't know who I was.

Cormac put his arms around us both. "They must have searched her out, taken her when the time was right. Perhaps she was meant as a bargaining tool, to make you comply with their wishes."

"All the time I was in isolation, they had her too They can't have had her drugged all this time, Cormac?" I shivered as I hugged her once more.

All those long drawn out days of my isolation, I had taken solace in the thought Lorna was safe and well, unaware of my plight. Yet she had been amongst them all along, had suffered even more than I, for she had no understanding of their motives or their beliefs. No one had cared whether she lived or died. Her own family were not likely to go looking for her. Her face would have become one of those that looked out from that terrible scrapbook. Still sobbing, I looked into her face once more. She looked utterly lost.

I prayed they hadn't broken her spirit. The Lorna of old would never have given into anything without a fight. Her eyes were vacant, unfocussed.I had seen that look often enough in Edinburgh, recognised the tiny pupils, the drug induced catatonia. But I had never seen anyone so far gone. This was no longer a mere high. What the hell had they given her?

She was zombiefied, unable to move. Whatever they had forced her to take had immobilized her system. It was only the shell that stood before me. But inside, inside, I sensed Lorna screaming for release.

I would never forgive them.

We worked to remove Lorna's restraints, which had bound her to the spot. We dragged her with us away from the scene, retracing our route back to the burial chamber, aware of eyes following us. They had grown weak without their leader. None challenged us. Unsure of their position they waited. As for me, I thanked whatever had protected me so far for his staying with me.

We were making for the beach, praying the boat would be there to meet us. Between us, somehow, we managed to keep Lorna moving. Stumbling, cursing, we managed to make our way back down through the labyrinth that had brought us there and out the cave mouth. All that remained was to make our way back along the coastline towards the Bay. But up ahead was a large gathering. They held their torches high, illuminating the cliff face. Their torches were unnecessary in the first light. Perhaps they drew strength from them. All those identities hidden beneath their heavy robes. Under the hood were faces I had known since birth. No doubt they were intent on retribution for the fire, for it still burnt high in the early morning sky. All that lavish craftsmanship, all those secrets curling into the sky in the spirals of silver smoke. No matter what the outcome of this confrontation, their traditions were lost. The focus for their worship – lost. Their leader – gone.

The sea roared far below. Real terror gripped my soul. They could overpower us and send us hurtling to our deaths, with no one to know what had befallen us. Instead, as we approached they parted into two lines. They respected our power. The realisation filled me with disgust. Confusion ran amok within my mind. My vision of this Island would never be the same. I fought my own bewilderment, pushing it to the furthest recesses of my mind. If the boat was waiting as arranged, it would take us back to reality.

They followed behind, as though they waited for some sign. How mindless. Like the sheep they tended they followed us, not knowing what else to do. The road down to the bay was slow and tortuous as we half pushed, half-dragged Lorna, who had begun to waken and resist, along the shingle beach. Still they followed us, down past the harbour and along the sea wall, rounding the corner to the South Bay a few dozen paces behind us. Exhausted, we arrived at the Bay, and sat on the hard sand close to the water's edge.

I could have wept. Cormac's boat wasn't among the craft.

I looked behind me. The crowd had stopped, following a semi-circle behind us. In the growing light I could make out some of the faces. As I looked more intently, it was apparent why I had feared those people at Berwick Law. Gazing back at me were those same faces I had run away from, leaving Cormac to explain my disappearance. Even then my instinct had known they were followers of the *fithich*, come now to the Island for feast and revelry.

From behind me huge birds flew high into the early morning air, their caws loud as they lowered their flight path before flying out to sea. My instincts heightened. These were raven men, reverting back to their true forms, having decided to leave the Island. No doubt they would be grieved for, but not by me. Who knew what atrocities they had been party to? I stared after them, unafraid, as they rose higher and higher, until their gross frames appeared no more menacing than small cormorants.

As the light grew, I looked at Lorna properly for the first time. Physically thinner than I had ever seen her, her skin was drawn tightly over her frail body, a clear sign of dehydration. Beside me Cormac was subdued. Emotions ran through my confused thoughts, though like him I was silent. What was there to say? We had both seen enough to occupy our minds forever. Even if my seer's *sight* had worked around him, I would never have intruded on Cormac's reflections. We both needed to process what had happened in our own way. And so we sat on the shingle beach, gazing out towards the sea, so calm, under the morning light. It was almost as if we were under a spell. It would be wrong to break it; it would be cut short soon enough when the boat arrived, if it arrived. Behind us the remaining crowds began to drift away.

We waited, three sorry-looking figures, huddled together in the soft dew of morning. But still, in the background those others remained, watching, waiting, my mind too tired to fathom their continued encroachment.

Lorna still had no perception of where she was. I was relieved she was showing signs of recovery and that she sensed the greatest danger had passed. There was life in her eyes as the effects of the drugs began to wear off. I refused to imagine how I would feel if she never made a full recovery. Her mind could be lost forever in the trauma she had been forced to endure.

In the distance, a small boat appeared on the horizon. Was our ordeal over? Cormac smiled at me then. I sensed briefly that he was as anxious to be gone from the Island as I was. There were no words needed. All we wanted was to be far away from those shores. I would miss the Island. I belonged there, not amongst them but at one with nature. But I would have to find that serenity elsewhere.

The hatred and distrust, the bigotry and misconceptions – how had I ever survived for so long? With the sighting of the boat, the remaining Islanders behind us vanished, slipping away into the mists, almost as though they had never been. My *Darna sealladh* was hardly aware of their leaving. Instead, it was confused, and the confusion grew as the boat came nearer. I sighed. What did it matter? Our ordeal was almost over. Only the truth remained, that the Islanders had enjoyed their practises, had craved more, had thirsted for crueller deeds. They had justified their acts in their own hearts so long, that no one cared for the truth any longer. No one but me.

The fishing boat slowed down, manoeuvred through the mouth of the harbour wall. We watched and waited, eager to be gone. As the boat approached, I grew excited. Cormac showed none of the joy I would have expected. I wondered at his lack of enthusiasm. Now the boat had drawn close enough for the figures aboard to sharpen into focus no longer blurred from sight.

I willed the craft to speed up, my impatience growing by the second. I scanned the boat with grateful eyes, panning absentmindedly over the small cabin I had retreated to when seasickness overcame me. It might have been a trick of the light or perhaps tiredness catching up with me. I was almost sure I had seen my mother's face in the small porthole.

How could that be?

I had presumed her up there at the Manse with the others, one of the hooded figures afraid to identify themselves. How had she managed to find the boat that was to be our escape? How had she beaten us to it?

My own imagination, always wild, had been placed under such tremendous stress I couldn't trust my eyes, or trust my thoughts any longer. The very idea of seeing her again brought forth so many conflicting emotions. But it was no trick. My mother was staring straight back at me.

My confusion gave way to terror.

Had I survived everything to be beaten now? By the woman who had kept me down all my childhood? It was as if she had the power of life or death over me.

I was so dumbstruck, I couldn't even make a sign to warn Cormac that I had seen her. How had she been able to win over the men he had made contract with? Or had the crew been part of the huge conspiracy, the never ending deceit? Had they merely allowed Cormac to be lulled into the belief that there was a way out for us? Was there ever a time when they had been unaware of our movements?

But if that was the case, why had they then allowed us up to the Manse?

Unless…they had wanted the Pastor gone?

I had thought their fear of him was so ingrained that they could not survive without his insight. Did *she* mean to take over, now that he was dead? Some strange reasoning, some instinct, told me not to alert the others. Perhaps, I had already given up inside? Whatever the reason, I stood still, unable to move, as though everything was happening around me, yet I had no part in it. Uninvolved, disconnected. Even oddly relieved.

Was she not my biggest foe? Why was I afraid to voice my thoughts to Cormac? I couldn't even look at him at that moment. All I could do was watch the approaching boat.

The men disembarked first. Their faces, stern when they had risked their lives to bring us across the channel, looked far more solemn now for they were her followers. Of that there was no doubt. They seemed to look past me.

I waited for Cormac's reaction. None came.

Behind me, Lorna muttered her first coherent words. "Where am I?"

Her timing could not have been worse. I hadn't the strength to comfort or soothe her. My own world was upside down. My mother had me in her power again. She had won.

Lorna had started crying. I found I could not go to her. "Quiet Lorna, hush, please!" I prayed she recognised my voice and understood. She made no response, but wept quietly. Possibly, in her weak condition, it was all her energy allowed.

I continued to watch the boat. She would be stepping over the side at any moment. I wanted to be the first to greet her. She owed me some sort of explanation, regardless of everything else. I had to understand.

This ending – this was not the way it should be. The Island was my birthright. I had always sensed it. Why then had I needed to fight so hard to be free of it? Without any sense of wrongdoing on my part, I had been rejected. Why had they never accepted me as I was?

In the few seconds it took to process the thoughts she was there. She stood directly in front of me, looking past me, showing her strength.

Chapter Nineteen

I stood silent, waiting for her to speak. She would expect me to rant, so I continued my silence, refusing to give her satisfaction. If I were to die, it would be on my own terms.

No one moved. Still she said nothing.

Even Cormac and Lorna behind me remained silent. I couldn't understand Cormac's reaction. I had good reason to be still, but why was he so quiet? Why was he making no effort to defend me? He stayed silent as the woman I was ashamed to call mother approached. I played a waiting game, determined not to be controlled, no matter what the cost.

Finally, her eyes turned towards me. "So, Aluinn, y*he*'ve learnt the truth. But thurs still other truths kept hidden fih y*he*. Yhe chose badly when yhe chose this man."

I stood stunned by her words.

"Dih y*he* think Ah was never young once? Ah loved once, just a*hs* strongly as y*he* love him."

She appeared distant; as though reliving another time, before life had changed her. "He was the only one f*hur* me. Ah was carryin' his bairn when he went up against them. *H*is ain sister had bin taken just like the others. She was y*hur* mother, Aluinn. When she died it broke his heart."

I had taken a step backwards, feelings forming and dissolving, belief and disbelief. She grabbed my wrist, pulling me towards her, her hot skin like a vice around my cold flesh. "She came tae me f*hur* help, freely. Her family had shunned her. When ah lost ma ain bairn ah pretended hers was mine. Ah tried so hard tae keep y*he* awa' f*hih* others, so y*hid* be safe fih harm!" This woman who had barely broken words with me all my childhood was talking now as if her very life depended on it.

My thoughts were reeling. She had been *protecting* me? "Thi *cailleach* up at the cottage wis the one that brought yhur friend tae the Island. Yhur ain grandmother. Yet she chose Cormac against y*he*."

So the bedroom at the cottage with all the souvenirs of a lost child…was my *mother's?* And what did she mean, she chose Cormac against *me?*

Cormac turned to me, a strange, fearful expression on his face. "Ally, there's something you need to know," he whispered, pushing his hair from his face. "I should have told you from the start but there was never the right moment. Time just got away from me and then it was too late for honesty, without you doubting all we had ever been to each other."

I was afraid of the answer. "What is it Cormac, what are you not telling me?"

Struggling with his emotions, he took a deep breath. "Simply this. McGregor – he was my father, Ally."

My mind was reeling – not in disbelief, for I knew instantly that he was speaking the truth, but in horror.

"Before you say anything, I knew of your loathing for him, even before we met. I knew if I told you before you trusted me that you would hate me for it. I was waiting for my moment, to help you realize it could still be ok between us…But your hatred of him, of the Islanders, your refusal to discuss things or confide in me…you never gave me a chance."

"What about those people in North Berwick – you said they were your parents!"

"My mother and adopted father – McGregor's best friend. They raised me as their own son. He's a surgeon, a very skilled man. If he hadn't delivered me by caesarean, one month ahead of my due date, I doubt very much whether I would have a mother at all. It was decided I should be reared on the mainland. My father never had the courage to tell his own father about me. He said he would have been shunned. Some things are sacred - the mating should only have been carried out under supervision…"

My mind ran in confusion. His words made no sense. Mating? McGregor? Suddenly the Pastor was standing there once more, summoned by my sight. I searched his face, looking for something that would connect the thing I knew to exist at his core with Cormac. Try as I might I couldn't, wouldn't join the two. They refused to fuse within my mind, remaining as separate as love to hate, dark to light.

All those belongings in those chests, all those innocents slaughtered. No one but McGregor was responsible for those losses. But if Cormac were his son? If he had been raised among those evil people at the Law? What did that make *him*?

My mother was fighting to make herself heard. "We met the boat outside the harbour. If he had taken y*h*e and Lorna out tae sea – if he had tried tae take y*h*e both then, what wid have happened? Y*h*e couldnae huv destroyed him, no *bi*h yursell! Bih thih time *he* arrived back in Edinburgh, he w*h*ud begin again, gatherin' followers, beginnin' auh over again!"

She gazed behind me. I instantly knew all she would say and the hurt I felt increased to a new height. "He's his father's son, lass."

It had to be a ploy. She was terrified I would report her to the authorities. She was lying to protect her own skin.

"I don't believe you! Why would you stand here and lie, tell me you're not my mother?"

Callum cut in quickly, I had not noted his presence amongst the crowd til then.

"She tells thi truth Aluinn, jist listen, don't fight it. Y*h*e noh it makes sense Ah can see thi recognition in yur eyes, for they belie yur hardheartedness. Yur noh like them, y*h*e nevur wur. That's why wih protect'd y*h*e sae long an' hard."

Slowly Calum's words registered, far off, as though pieces misplaced long ago fell into focus, cleared and formed. It seemed I had been deceived on a far grander scale all along. I found myself staring at the jagged scar still so vivid across his face, the scar which had never been truly explained.

"How did you get your scar, Calum?"

"McGregor did it tae me, as a child. It'll take less time tae heal than the hurts you've had, Aluinn." I looked again and saw the marks made by a talon's sharpness. Calum had been lucky to survive the attack. I looked to my mother for confirmation of my suspicions. If Calum were not one of them, and if he and my mother...the word stuck in my throat... if they were allies, then that meant...

She sat down on a nearby rock, looking wearier than I had ever seen her.

"Yur muther came tae me as soon as she realised she wis carryin'. Durin' thih m*h*atin' dance, she'd bin taken bih one oh them. Her ain kin were happy tae lit it happen. But we acted as though my dead child was hers, for as much as she hated them, she couldnae find it in herself tae hate yhe, g*h*rowin' inside her. She stayed wi me until she had yhe. She was goin' tae smuggle yeh awa'. But things went wrong, she wisnae strong enough…there was nothing ah could do an' she died, like aue thi rest. But ah pulled y*h*e oot. Barely breathin' y*h*e wur. Ah hud made ah promise tae her afore she died, tae look efter yhe." She was sobbing now, her shoulders moving soundlessly. "Aue thae othur bairns thit died, Ah never took thur lives. Thih didnae survive thur muther's belly. Only twa ever lived through those unholy unions. A*h*'m sorrih tae say lass, …one wis yhe. Ah'm only thankful that y*h*e have the seer's gift, that protected y*h*e more than ah ever could."

She looked at me, red-eyed. A choking silence devoured me. I stared at her, uncomprehending. "Tae show ma real feelings f*h*ur y*h*e would have spelt yur doom, for it would have been even harder f*h*ur y*h*e tae leave the Island if y*h*e loved me as I loved y*h*e." Her eyes begged me to understand. "Whin y*h*e left Ah hid ma joy. Yhe whur safe at last. Bit they went after y*h*e, tae bring y*h*e back f*h*ur thi Pastor! Tae make ah new line oh them, strongur thin afore! Ah couldnae lit it happen. That's why I locked y*h*e up. I hoped tae keep y*h*e safe til after the festival but ah never knew, he," she pointed back towards Cormac disdainfully, "would come for y*h*e."

I hardly believed what I heard. I had striven all my life for a glance, a gesture that showed she cared, a little kindness. Now she was telling me she had withheld it for fear of keeping me there?

The anger still burned for the lonely child I had been. I attacked her with words rather than physical blows. "Why should I believe you? What if these are lies to get me to stay?"

She refused to argue, just tilted her head sadly, looking at him. "Tell her, lad."

A terrible apprehension, a foreboding overpowered me. For the longest time it had seemed Cormac had remained silent. I sensed his silence, turning around slowly, willing him to give me the sign I had been waiting for, to pour a torrent of abuse on her head. But I knew he would not.

Cormac stood perfectly still. He had changed slightly. There were subtle undertones I picked out. The longer I stared, the stronger they became, coming into focus as my sight sharpened. My own senses had been blocked and the Pastor was dead. There was no blame to be laid elsewhere, nowhere to hide from the truth that grew more transparent with every second.

In front of my eyes he was turning. Slowly his face became covered in huge-pus filled pockets that reached outwards and upwards, till the skin fell from his bones, revealing all manner of vein and tissue. The bones revealed grew longer as they shape changed. For with my seer's sight cleared I saw Cormac as he was - no different from the Pastor, though younger, more virile. How could I have loved such a man who held such darkness within him? In my mind I saw the full extent of his evil, even as his feet curled upwards, extended and bent inwards, as his back arched dramatically, the shoulder blades bursting through the skin already torn. There was no noise, just a silence so profound it seemed alive. The others, including my mother, stood mesmerised unable to tear their eyes away from the monstrosity.

I stood with them in silence, trying to associate this horror before me with Cormac, knowing that I would never again be able to see him as anything other than in that gross form. Even if he were to change back… how could I ever…with the awareness of what he had become, could become, at any time?

I had been wrong. My mother's look had been meant, not for me, but for the being that was changing behind me, as I stood there, ignorant of his betrayal. I had almost joined with it through love.

Within minutes, all growth stopped. It stood absolutely still, but as I strained my eyes, I picked out tiny feathers still growing to cover the flesh that lay bare to the elements. Were the others seeing him as I was? They stood, trance-like, staring. Suddenly my mother stepped forward and urged the crowd that had gathered.

"This is our chance. We must kill it now afore it changes!"

I turned around fully to face her; my heart screaming that she was wrong, but knowing she spoke the truth. I had to accept that Cormac was no more. The thing that had taken his place, was devoid of the man I loved. It smelt of evil. With the Pastor gone, this was the last bridge with the past.

Part of him wanted it – I could see that as I looked into his eyes. I had witnessed him destroy his own father as well as others of their kind. He had known their weaknesses, used it to his advantage. That was why he had been able to kill so easily. I clung to the sense that he had protected me, was protecting me still with his own death.

He had wished me to live. He had wanted to put an end to his father's reign, to the evil on the Island. The only mistake Cormac had made was believing he could belong in my world.

I forced myself once more to look upon him.

The repulsive changeling stood concealed within a huge cocoon of its own making, remaking and rearranging itself, preserving itself...

Seeing what had happened the crowd had turned back, crowding around us on the pebbled beach. Again my mother pleaded with them. "Listen tae me. If y*he* want tae huv a chance at a normal life y*he* must destroy it before it hus a chance tae mate again. Rip it apart. It hus nae power fhur now."

I watched transfixed as those who had clung to the old beliefs banded with those who sought freedom, as they finally joined as one, moving forward, gathering round the ever changing chrysalis. It was beginning to break free....

My mother reacted ahead of the rest. They appeared to stall, afraid to venture nearer. But she ripped forcefully at the shell. Fired on by her, they followed suit.

That old longing returned in them. They would have their blood. The frenzy of the attack sickened my soul as they formed a tight knit circle and began to pull, cutting and ripping apart anything they connected with. The changeling had been almost complete. It experienced great pain. Its howling shrieks echoed all around the bay, terrifying, bloodcurdling cries of sheer terror, as the creature inside realised it was dying.

Gradually the cries diminished. Slithers lay in tatters on the damp sand. The part that was left, attempted to crawl away. In vain for one amongst them decided to end it humanely, aiming a boulder at the jellied mass. For a split second, I saw Cormac as he really was, his body wounded and broken. Yet strangely, he smiled at me as though glad it was over. I sensed his love for me then, so complete I cried out for them to stop. But with one blow the sight was gone forever, the remains lying flat on the grainy sand of the bay, waiting to be swept out on the returning tide, to be broken up far out at sea. There was no remnant left of the man I had loved.

My mother came and spoke softly for I knew her words to be true then, no more torment could she give, than all I experienced in that moment, "It's done we're rid oh thim."

She patted my shoulder gently before she said, "Stay here, think hard afore yhe leave us."

The crowd slowly dispersed, leaving Lorna and I alone.

We stood, bound together by this experience in a way that would never diminish. Outwardly, I remained silent. Inside I was screaming my pain and disbelief.

He was gone.

I would never really know how he had seen our future. Had it all been a lie? Had he never felt the emotions he shared with me? Or were his words of love a deliberate ploy? Was it true he had meant to conceive one of them by me? Or was that why he had never taken me to his bed, to stop that happening? Had he been protecting me then?

The truth was although I would never know, I preferred to believe that his love for me had kept me safe, not a sick lust as his father's was but a genuine love filled with goodness. Grief-stricken, unable to turn off my feelings for him, I knew only that I could chose bitterness and regret or remember things as I had believed they had been. Nothing, no wishful thinking or stark reality would alleviate the horror of his death throes.

Lorna's touch on my arm jolted me back to the present.

"Where are we Ally?"

Her voice was frightened, her skin pale. Yet her eyes had life in them again. She made no mention of her ordeal. I prayed she had no memories of it. Cupping her face gently in my palms, I soothed her. "It's okay, Lorna, we're home on the Island. I'm going to find a way off for us."

Lorna seemed to have only a vague idea of her surroundings, yet my reply satisfied her. She stayed silent as the woman I had called mother approached, her manner giving nothing away. I had no idea of her intentions towards us, whether she would let us go, or if she would fear the risk was too great. Once again, I played a waiting game.

Her tone was gentle. "Ah understand lass, y*he*'ll need time tae come tae terms wi' whit's happened. Ah've somethin' thit wull help yur grief. Ah letter fih yur mother, thit she wrote afore she died. After y*he*'ve rested Ah'll gie it tae y*he*. Now the danger's passed, Ah hope y*he* can accept ah acted out oh love. "

I could barely look at her still. In my confusion, I still felt a terrible betrayal.

"Look a*ht* yur friend. She's in nae fit state tae travel. She needs a place tae recover. Stay put a few days, dinnae go rushin' awae. Stay, please, an' try an' find thi peace y*he* need. Come home when yur ready."

I watched her go, sensing for the first time her own need for healing.

Had she really been my saviour all those sad, miserable years?

All those time I had been so sure she was against me, had she actually been on my side? She had more or less said she loved me. Could it be true? What of the letter? Could I leave the Island without knowing what my own mother had written all those years before?

I needed to know. What had she written to me, the child she had wanted so desperately, she was prepared to risk her life to bring me into the world? A pattern of death had been set in force by whatever creatures had first used the women on the Island. As for me, it would be no sacrifice to go without a child – who knew what I could unleash on those around me by such selfishness?

Chapter Twenty

Several hours later, we still sat side by side on the harbour wall gazing out to sea. Although we had spoken little, it was clear that the Lorna of old was gone, replaced by a frail creature beside me. I vowed to protect her from that day on.

Rain began to fall, rushed by the wind, working together toying with anything that crossed their path. I sensed, for myself, that the danger had passed. But there was still so much I didn't understand. Was it true that I had not just misunderstood my life, but that I had not had the information I would have needed to understand it? Her offer to show me the letter, this proof, that alone had brought peace. Perhaps there was no more need to fight or argue. Perhaps we had been doing that for far too many years already.

There was no more need for pretence, for acting out scenes to cover up the lies she had woven. Thinking back over all the years of fighting and rebellion, I realised the gift she had given me. She had forced me to become a survivor. Perhaps too she would feel I had suffered enough. She too had lost the one she had loved above all else. All those times she had warned me not to follow those processions that twisted and wound around the Island and always inevitably ended at the Manse. She had been protecting me. For all my mother's seemingly hard exterior her rules forbade me those things I should have been protected from. A barrier had formed between us as she shut her emotions off from me.

What more could she do to me?

I had sat there long enough to work through in my head what could have happened between Cormac and I. If I had not balked at the first hurdle. My introduction to his parents had been my first inkling that something was wrong. I had been meant to settle in Cormac's 'parents' house, marry from there, unaware that one day I would give birth to a new, stronger dynasty than the one which lay dying on the Island.

No wonder they had taken Lorna. They must have been terribly angered, by my putting paid to all their plans. It gave me great satisfaction, knowing I had thwarted their schemes.

We remained there for quite some time, long enough for the rain to stop.

We watched the tide go out and I looked towards the sky. Radiant shafts of colour, prominent yellow and blue hues shone out against a backdrop of water-laden clouds cutting through the sky from one end to another, placed there by an unseen hand, a rainbow perfectly formed, keeping covenant with the earth.

I was hopeful for my own future. Life would go on. Rising, I took Lorna's arm and led her to what had been my home.

No matter the contents of that letter, I could never forget the terrible things that had happened there. But I could move on, safe in the knowledge that she couldn't hurt me anymore. From then on, my life would be my own to live. Facing it without a child to comfort me, was a small price to pay for the future that lay ahead.

I missed Cormac so badly, I knew instinctively that no one would ever take his place. I had and I always would love him, not the thing he had become, but the man he had been.

The sun shone as I approached the house, supporting Lorna along the narrow lane around the harbour, down the small winding dirt path. I had considered it my prison all those years before. I seemed to be looking at it all again for the very first time.

The Island was a beautiful place. It was my heritage. I smiled for the first time in many days, as I entered my childhood home once more.

She kept her promise. The letter was waiting for me.

My dearest child

I don't even know if you're a boy or a girl but you are my child. I love you already with all my heart & soul. I am as ready for your birth as I can be. I'll never hold you in my arms or see your sweet face. The thought that keeps me going is the belief that you'll live a long and happy life.

I was so afraid when I knew you were growing beneath my heart, but I never found it in me to hate you. How could I ever harm a blameless child? When my family disowned me, I took shelter in the kindness of the woman I pray you'll call mother.

I pray you'll be as strong and determined as she. I pray you'll find a way off the Island, that good souls will help you. And I pray that you grow into a fine man or woman, someone I'd be proud of.

My fate is set. I can feel my body grow weak. But I will give you this gift, child, the gift of life. Make the most of it, live it well for me.

Mhari McDonald, 31 March 1961

She had written it the day before I had been born. I had thought ill of my protectress all my life. She had allowed me to live, nurtured and protected me when others would question her motives if she were to show me affection. They had all sensed my disgust at all that reigned within the Island and as much as they feared and revered it, I had fought against and ridiculed all that was and that was why they feared me more so. She had deliberately made our home a sad place, knowing I would never want to return to it.

Now I had my answers – why it had hurt so badly, why I had needed her approval. I had sensed her love for me and could not explain why she would hide it.

We talked for hours, and when I went to bed that night I was more complete than I had ever been at any time before - in history, mind and body. I had moved forward to a place where I could face whatever adversities arose. No longer doubting, no longer afraid. I was free.

Lorna was weaker than even I had thought. She needed a long period of recuperation. So weakened she couldn't travel. I tended her night and day, caring for her when she vomited out the drugs and the weakness in her system. During those days, I got to know the woman who had cared for my physical, if not my emotional needs all those lost, sorry years. There was no secret between us any longer. We found it easy to talk freely.

I came to understand how she had saved the life of dozens of Island women over the years. Many had been too far gone when they came to her. Those she had been unable to save. All those needy young women…she had been a friend to them. When they passed she had felt sorrow, and anger at her powerlessness to prevent the loss of those young lives. Many times, she told me, she had been tempted to take her own life, hurl herself from the cliff top and end her own suffering. But then, who would have helped the women who needed her?

The creatures had been afraid to harm the woman who had raised the only female born to them on the Island. For the old Pastor had always known the truth of my birth. How pleased had the Pastor been, when only three weeks later, a male had been born and survived, his own heir. Only by the rights of passage, that female should have been his, not his firstborn's mate. All the time I had grown up isolated on the Island, Cormac had been sampling the very best life had to offer, being feted as a prince, hidden away from the old Pastor in secret, acquiring all the skills he would need when he matured to manhood. He had been raised by the Pastors loyal friends, who instigated a following for those creatures, far away from the Island on the mainland, hoping one day their kind would rise again.

They had almost succeeded. All the wealth they possessed gathered over the centuries by their families, would have fallen to Cormac. It frightened me to know that there were others out there prepared to believe and follow such wickedness still. She warned me never again to trust strangers, to think constantly of my own protection, at least, until I could no longer bear a child. For without I, there could never be another generation, my seer's sight protected me, warned me against their existence, if another existed, that ethereal world would hold me safe, until my body no longer breathed. For love had blinded me to Cormac's true stance but never again would I be fooled. Then, perhaps, I would be safe…

Our days together were peaceful. We enjoyed each other's company. There was no anger. The resentments I had harboured simply ebbed away into nothingness. I was saddened greatly therefore when the *bean nighe* appeared for the briefest moment, whilst we enjoyed the summer sunshine out in the South Bay. There was no one present but my mother and Lorna. I thought it cruel of fate to try to claim her so soon after we were reconciled. I had only begun to understand and appreciate all she had done for me. I was determined not to allow my foresight to weigh down our life together, for whatever time my mother had left. The irony was clear at least to me, that the reason I had returned to the Island with Calum was actually true.

I looked defiantly out at the *bean nighe*, standing quite still, my arms around Lorna and my mother, drawing them into the circle, our bodies formed so naturally. We laughed, soaking up the love of that moment and the sun's warmth.

Inwardly though, I moved quickly towards the *taibhse*. It seemed cocooned, wrapped tight in a mist like vapour, yet not cold, as I had feared it would be. There was a brightness and lightness to her form, I had not expected to discover. We intertwined in spirit. I remained unafraid.

"I feared too long that which I had no need to fear. It would anger me if my mother, who has given her life to helping these people, should die any other way than peacefully, in her bed." There came no reply, yet I sensed my words, accepted, a truce formed.

Once again, I stood by the water's edge, the warm sand encircling my toes, the waves allowing them to protrude the surface of the sand before burying them once more. I looked back towards the *bean nighe*, then at the others, unaware of her presence. And then she disappeared.

*

I had a recurring nightmare, one that haunted my days as well as my nights. I saw a shadow in the lamplight behind me and as I turned, caught sight of a figure. I knew it to be a woman by her swollen stomach, but never saw her face, for the image blurred and distorted. I awoke puzzled, longing for the image to leave me, understanding somehow its message. There would be no half measures.

Time passed. We remained on the Island together, Lorna and I. The experience had deepened our relationship. She couldn't remember everything that took place, but sometimes I noticed a strange look pass over her, as though a shroud had closed over her mind. At those times, I sensed she was in some far off place, where no one could ever reach her. Then, just as easily, she returned.

I had noticed changes to her character. She no longer liked the brightness of morning. She often slept by day and spent nights, wide-awake. I assumed it was her way of handling what had taken place. We shared perfect days. I wanted Lorna to see my Island through my eyes. Although she could never see the *taibhsean* I lived with constantly, she sensed enough to understand what the place meant to me, now that there were no more secrets.

Four months later, I discovered she had hidden a terrible secret of her own. I awoke startled during the night, positive I heard voices. In the small croft we shared, few movements went unnoticed. Convinced Lorna was in trouble, I hurried quickly from one room to another but there was no sign of her. The only place left to look was the bathroom.

I opened the door forcefully. At first, my eyes refused to acknowledge what they saw. Lorna lay there on the cold tiles. Her face pained, her legs drawn upwards. Sweat saturated her thin nightshirt. She had pulled up the huge fisherman's sweater she had favoured all those months. It was only then I understood why. She had used it to conceal her swollen belly. The child she had hidden was about to be delivered.

Lorna screamed, earth shattering sounds. I hurried to her, trying to soothe her. I wanted to tell her everything would be all right, but I knew in my heart it would not.

"Not you, Lorna, not you!" I sobbed, placing my arms protectively around her shivering body. Another contraction wracked her slender frame. She screamed again. There was nothing I could do to end her suffering. My healing powers could not prevent the inevitable. I cried tears of frustration, as I watched her fight against something she had no control over.

As the pain subsided, I asked the question whose answer I feared.

"Lorna, I need to know. Who did this to you?"

Her eyes misted over, less from the pain, and more from the awful truth she had concealed. She spoke so quietly, I had to strain to hear her. "I'm sorry, Ally, I never meant it to happen. I knew it would break your heart. That was why I couldn't tell you."

My mind acknowledged her words, but my heart refused to accept them. "What do you mean, break my heart? "

The painful realisation hit, the dawning of their betrayal. She had lain with my Cormac. The pain of it washed over me just as another contraction swept over Lorna. My face drained, the strength departed my limbs. As I weakened, I reached out to steady myself on the cold floor.

"Please, Ally, don't leave me…"

Despite my anguish, I knew I would not leave her there lying all alone. She had suffered more than I ever had, and was suffering still. Now she lay, wracked with guilt and shame, across my body, terrified of what I would say or do. How could I be angry? I had loved them both deeply, in different ways. Lorna had become the family I never had. Cormac, the love I had never had. When I looked at Lorna's swollen belly all I saw was new life.

My life, for a part of Cormac lived on in Lorna's child. I would not turn my back on her, any more than I could have refused to be with him. The past and present had become entangled. I still had love to give. I would live my life as my mother had done, protecting this child when no one else would.

I pictured Cormac's face then, so clear in my memory still. I saw him alive, full of life. He smiled his smile, his eyes sought mine, even as a memory. It was an unbreakable love, one which death would never sever. My heart lifted at the very thought of his eyes still on me.

I already loved his child within Lorna's womb. How could I not? I brushed Lorna's saturated hair from her brow, cradling her upturned face. "It doesn't matter, Lorna, what went before…All that matters is the child."

She smiled her relief, as another excruciating wave of pain surged through her. I held her until it had ebbed, lying to give her comfort. "We'll be okay, you'll see."

"It was always you he spoke of. He never cared for me, it was always you…" Lorna's words trailed away, as another, more violent surge caused her back to arch. I called for my mother then. She needed more help than I could ever give.

There was no surprise on my mother's face as she knelt down beside us.

So had she known? What did it matter? Lorna's breathing was erratic. My mother's concerned expression was enough to allow her access to meet the urgent demands of Lorna's body.

"I'm not going anywhere, Lorna, but my mother will help you deliver your child. I promise it'll be okay, you'll see," I said, as I once more clasped her hand in mine. I stayed, gave physical support and tried to calm her emotions. And in the back of my mind the truth that surrounded this unborn child.

I finally understood why all those young girls had cried out in fear and pain. There had been no wrongdoing on my mother's part. She merely tried to help them survive a birth their own bodies were not intended to withstand. The act of joining two entirely different species, each fighting against the other at birth, meant she suffered inner torments. I focused all my attention on Lorna, trying to ease her suffering. Through the hours that followed, I whispered comfort to her, throughout the long labour and the arrival of her child. I held her hand throughout the delivery.

I held it long after it had grown cold.

My mother understood my need to cling to my friend just a little while longer. She left me alone to grieve.

I hoped in some way Lorna was aware of my sorrow at her passing.

"Oh Lorna, I'm so very sorry. I never wanted to hurt anyone, least of all you. I only ever wanted a friend, someone to understand me," I whispered, picking up her body and holding her close. She still watched from above. Comforted by her presence I heard the words, "Part of us is with you still."

I looked at her face, so serene and free of pain, so unlike the one that had endured that terrible pain. I covered it gently with a sheet.

My mother sat huddled over the small bundle cradled in her arms. I approached silently and looked down over her shoulder at the small child lying there.

Outwardly, there was nothing sinister about the child, yet we both knew the truth.

The child was more like me than Lorna. We were the same, we shared the same order. In a strange way, it gave me comfort.

Lorna had given me the greatest gift, yet along with it a greater responsibility. I could not now foresee the difficulties that would arise as he grew to manhood, but I would never withhold his origins from him. I only hoped that if I raised him in full knowledge of his inheritance he would never turn to their ways. I hoped Lorna was looking down at me and smiling. In the hereafter, I prayed I would be able to thank her for this gift of Cormac's son.

I took the child from the woman I no longer hated, held him close. We bonded instantly. Goodness had the upper hand. But if I ever sensed that he no longer heeded me, I would have no alternative but to end his life. I had to have faith that the good in his mother, and the good in me would prevail. I had to try, or all her suffering was in vain.

She had been worth so much more than that.

That small infant no more deserved to die than I had. We were kindred spirits, so I named him Cormac, in memory of my lost love.

The way was clear now. I would stay on the Island and raise Cormac as my own. There was no gain in worrying about the future. For now it was a blank canvas. I looked forward to it being filled with precious memories.

Chapter Twenty-One

The unsightly cast iron pipes littered the slopes all the way down to the hydro station. A small compact unit it would supply the Island with much needed power. In turn, it would keep the Island self-sufficient. For life to flourish on the Island, for my son to have a home where he was safe, the people had to prosper.

The Pastor had used the Island's resources for his own selfish interests. The Islanders had revered him, never questioning him. There had been so many layers of fear, so deeply interwoven. Now the guilt could begin to lift. Each man was as guilty as the next, each family a part of the shame. Ties of reconciliation, of reparation were being made. The Island was becoming the extended family it had been once before, the bonds were growing stronger now that suspicion had no more place amongst them. For who would cast the first stone?

Meetings had been held, the past discussed. The Pastor's role was not overplayed – he had manipulated them, but no one sought to divest himself of his part.

Every man put his hand up, admitted his blind ignorance, his willingness to be led. And that was the root of their fear again. Which of them was fit to lead the community?

In the end, Pastor McGregor decided. He had been so certain of his plan he had signed the deeds of the Island over to me, as his legal partner. I was to be protector of the Island for as long as I lived. The next boats, which came to the Island at night, would not be so warmly welcomed as before. They would need to find a new leader, a new successor.

We had nothing more to hide. But I wished to keep it free from the changes that would inevitably come if we didn't take steps to protect the Island. We would do as we had always done, use the mainland to our advantage without drawing undue attention our way. For the first time we were all truly, free from the fear.

Not all things had departed the Island. The *taibhsean* remained.

I had almost reached my destination. I had braved the journey to the shrine I had made for them both. It had seemed natural to place them side by side. I had erected two headstones, hewn from the Island's rock, to stand for eternity. It was an empty grave for Cormac, but Lorna's small frame lay there beneath the ground.

I had wanted them commemorated out on the loch that filled the dam. On the small island within my Island. As a child, I had always wished to go there but there had been no way across. Pastor McGregor's intricate plans had specified a steel bridge, narrow but sturdy enough to withhold the strongest storms. I grabbed the thick rope strung between the metal supports, the only divide between the walker and the dark water to each side. It was time to pay my respects.

I took the first faltering steps, afraid some strange force would pull me under. As if to justify my fear, a low branch swung out towards me from a tree, which sat half within the water. It appeared to come alive, reached out to grab me, but I stared hard through the water that blurred my view and stung my senses. As the icy water pelted my already soaked face, I saw that the tree had detached itself from its roots. The water still lapped around its base, but it lay, inert. As soon as I placed one foot on the island the sky brightened. Silence surrounded me.

Late autumn was upon the trees. Tall and majestic their colouring mottled with golden brown, the leaves were giving way to the elements, covering the forest floor. A few evergreens' stood tall, their branches thick with leafy covering.

I stood alone, my thoughts heavy, my mood sombre. I approached their final resting place, trying hard to console myself. The *Connall* must have approached silently, for I was unaware of his presence. I sat and broke heather sprigs between my fingers, as I tried to make sense of all that had gone before.

I lifted my eyes in desperation. And there he sat, my long lost friend. "*Connall*, I thought I'd never see you again?"

He placed his huge hand on top of my own. "The pain in yur heart wus maire thun Ah coud endure taeh seeh yeh suffer Aluinn. Ah came taeh console yeh. Ah'm here taeh listen if yeh want meh taeh."

Finally, I voiced the words. Only he could understand my torment.

"I was so happy Connall, happy to be free, to love someone. I would have willingly have died for him Connall, yet I let them kill him. "

He regarded me seriously, "Powerful emotions fur one saeh young, Aluinn."

I stood up, allowed the air to circle my body. "I don't feel young any longer *Connall*. I have lived a lifetime in such a short space of time." I paced around the tiny brook. "He's with me still, it'll never die."

The *Connall* looked sad. "Ah knew Cormac wud find yhe, but Ah had naeh clue how it wud end. Ah thought yeh wud fight. Ah never considered thit yeh wud fauh in luv. There wis naeh wihe taeh predict it. Luv finds ah wihe."

"Connall, would you do something for me?"

"Just ask it."

"Would you stay and protect the little one; I need to know he will never be alone on the Island. If I knew, you would be there to watch over him when I could not it would make my life bearable."

"Ah wull Aluinn. Ah wudhuve even if yeh hud neverah asked it. He wull be special, Aluinn, just like yeh were taeh meh."

Tears sprung to my eyes. For a moment I thought Cormac was moving towards me over the walkway, but my heart knew it to be an illusion. Someone was approaching, though I could not clearly define the features.

It was a man, his strong build plain to see. Eventually he reached the shore and I understood all.

Calum stood a short distance from me.

"Your mother told me I'd find you here. How are you Aluinn?"

"I'm no better or worse than you'd expect."

"I'm sorry, Aluinn. Cormac found me, convinced me to take you to him. He said if I didn't help him, my sister would be next."

We stared outwards across the Loch, the waters calmed. The Island lived and breathed with life. I surrendered to the overwhelming awareness of my life fulfilled with peace. I smiled as I looked into the kind eyes I remembered from my childhood.

As the tears fell freely, I held his hand to my cheek.

"Calum, would you stay here with me awhile?"

He encircled my body within his strong arms. I drew comfort from the warmth of his spirit. He answered me in a voice that gave comfort. *"Gu brath, a Aluinn, gu brath."* A whispered promise of forever.

Epilogue

Cormac thrived, a healthy fourteen month old, with startling dark brown eyes in a chubby face. He was my life. As he grew so did my faith that I could teach him right from wrong. As the months passed, my awareness heightened. Time unlocked senses I had kept buried, because my son shared those gifts.

I had been right to keep him. Who could raise him better than I? I understood him, his strengths, his weaknesses, his gifts. Understood too how to use them for good. If he grew to love me as I loved him, I needn't fear for him, though he would one day grow into a man far stronger than I. I could still protect him, in a way I had never been protected. In my awareness of what he was capable of, there was hope.

There had to be a purpose to all that had happened. If I taught him well he would grow to understand. He had Lorna's love of life, her ready love. And Cormac, my love lost, I saw reflected every day in his eyes.

It will never happen again. I am glad it is over. But I will never forget.

Out somewhere in the world, I fear there may be another Island like my own. That they have created one like myself, or another, much like Cormac, vulnerable, as we were.

I have vowed to keep him safe. It will be many years before he reaches manhood. He will be a fine man, with Lorna's ready laugh and Cormac's handsome features. Death is never the conqueror.

P. A. Ramsay